The Governor's Man

JACQUIE ROGERS

First published in 2021 by Sharpe Books.

For Peter,
cheerleader and first reader.

CONTENTS

life is warfare, and a visit to a strange land...
Marcus Aurelius, *Meditations*

Prologue

AD 224
Roman Britannia

The bitter day was dying. In the settling dusk, the messenger boy swaying on his stumbling horse could no longer make out the milestones set into the verges of the road. He was as tired as his mare, but forced himself to stay upright, searching in the easterly gloom for the pale limestone gateway of Cunetio. How many more days until he reached Londinium? He tried to remember what the clerk had told him, but all he could think of was thawing his numb feet at a tavern fire.

The mare shied. The boy grasped the reins, pressing his feet reassuringly against her flanks. She was usually responsive to his signals, but now she stopped, refusing to walk further. He stroked her neck, murmuring into her ear. Still she would not budge. He dismounted to lead her on foot. There was a rustle to one side. He had time to wonder if an owl was swooping nearby when a sword struck him, taking his head off in a single blow.

Two men had been waiting in hiding. The taller, dressed in a fine cloak dyed an expensive bright blue, signalled to his companion to retrieve their horses while he crouched down to look at the detached head. He slid the boy's mouth open, placed something on the boy's tongue, and gently pushed the jaws shut.

'No idea who that is.'

'Did you expect to know him?'

The tall man shrugged. The other man, dark face twisted in the fading light, handed him the reins of a handsome roan, and picked up the head to launch it spinning into the trees. The taller man moved to a hawthorn tree on the verge. Then both remounted, the slighter with economy, the taller with practised grace. The fine wool of the tall man's cloak slid easily over his shoulders as he pulled the roan's head round. They set off west, leaving the headless trunk soaking blood into the gravel.

The boy's horse nudged the sprawling body, shivering at the raw smell of death.

Chapter One

Rome, two months earlier

Two mud-spattered riders, one an officer in his early thirties, the other a young slave, dismounted at the gates of the Castra Peregrina, headquarters of the Roman secret service. Frumentarius Quintus Valerius handed his reins to his shivering groom.

'Get the horses stabled, Gnaeus; I'm going home first. I'll be back later to report to the Commander.'

Quintus shrugged off his own fatigue. He did not notice his slave's ashen face as the man took the plodding animals around to the stables.

Quintus walked across the city, up the Quirinal to his family home. The Valerii had lived here time out of mind. It was a venerable old house, the embodiment of their status as an ancient Roman family, but today the house seemed unusually quiet as Quintus banged on the front door. His elderly steward Silenus opened promptly, bowing with a look of surprise on his face.

'Sir, welcome home! We didn't know when to expect you, that is the mistress didn't …' The man trailed off, as Quintus looked past him into a deserted atrium. Completely empty of furniture, lamps, not even a household slave in sight. It was dark and cold in the room. At this time of day there ought at least to be someone lighting the oil lamps and candles.

A door opened.

'Brother!' A young woman, petite and dark-haired, dashed across to him, crocus-yellow *palla* trailing.

'Lucilla!'

She flung her arms around him. 'Come into the salon. The hypocaust isn't lit but Silenus brought in braziers.'

He allowed her to drag him into a large dimly-lit room, where Lucilla's husband, tall and quiet, was waiting.

2

'Justin? Why are you here? Is my mother with you?' Quintus glanced round, dreading the mournful chill that trailed his mother into any gathering. And where was his wife, Calpurnia? It was unlike her to miss the chance to act the Roman society matron.

'No, just we two. I heard from the Castra you were expected. We wanted to be here to welcome you back,' said his brother-in-law, standing to grasp his arm in greeting.

Justin and Quintus had both joined the Praetorian Guard at sixteen. They became firm friends. A couple of years later they were joined by Quintus's younger brother, Flavius Valerius, and the three of them had been posted as junior officers in the army of Emperor Septimius Severus to serve in his Caledonian campaigns. When Quintus returned from Britannia after months of injury, he found his sister hero-worshipping the quiet young Praetorian. His mother made Lucilla and Justin wait years; she had hoped for a more prestigious match for her only daughter than a career army officer from Etruria, without patrons or suitable connections. But in the end the despised Justin became a relief to the dowager when the family lost almost everything; he was welcome then to take Lucilla away to his modest estate.

Lucilla was fidgeting round the room.

'My dear, we must tell him,' said her husband calmly.

'Tell me what? What's going on?' Quintus brushed down his uniform and sat on one of the two remaining couches in the room.

Lucilla also sat, taking his hand and stroking it. She was the only person in the world he would accept this intimacy from.

'Calpurnia …' her voice trailed off. Quintus stiffened. He should have guessed that this had something to do with his wife. Justin lifted a heavy scroll of papyrus off a small bronze side-table, and handed the papers over to Quintus in silence. Quintus unrolled the paper in the pool of light from a nearby candelabra, and squinted to make out the official words.

Divortium …remancipatio… retentio dotis …

The document was signed by seven witnesses, as the law of divorce required. His wife had kept the part of her dowry allowed to a divorcing adultress. At the end was appended a

3

vicious little note in Calpurnia's own hand: *I'm keeping the baby. It's not yours, of course. When it's born it will be the legitimate heir of my new husband. You never wanted children anyway, did you? I don't think you ever really wanted a wife.*

Perhaps he hadn't, not after Britannia. The marriage to Calpurnia was his mother's project, a pathetic attempt to shore up the family's status after his father and brother died.

Lucilla was watching him, worry in her eyes. 'Say something, Quintus.'

'There's nothing to say. I suppose she took the household slaves and the rest of the furniture with her?'

Lucilla nodded. 'Not Silenus - we have offered him a home with us.'

The steward edged into the room.

'Sir...'

Quintus smiled tightly at the old man, and forced himself to look round the room a final time.

'Sell the house, Justin. Please. Send the proceeds to Mother. Tell her I hope it's some compensation for having such a disappointing son.'

He stood up and left through the darkening atrium. Soft steps rushed after him. He twisted round, catching his sister up into his arms. She was crying.

'It doesn't matter, Lucilla. It's the right thing for all of us.'

'But where will you go, Quintus?'

He gave a short unhappy laugh. 'Wherever the Emperor decides I am needed.'

She touched his face.

'I'm so sorry, Quintus. About Calpurnia, the baby, your home. I wish we could go back to how things used to be.'

'That was another world, before I went to war in Britannia -- before Father and Flavius were lost.'

Justin broke the silence as he came into the room and took his wife's hand.

Lucilla said, 'One day, my dearest Quintus, you will discover you still have a heart, and find you can let people back into your life. Till that happens, you'll always have a home with Justin and me. Don't forget us.' She turned to Justin.

Quintus left the house quietly before he had to look at their faces again.

The Castra gateway guards saluted as Quintus passed under the imposing marble portico and headed straight to the Principia. His mind was on his most recent mission: Palaestina, again. Dust, zealots, and the constant rumble of uprisings. That province was never truly secure. On this trip Quintus had been hard put to choose which sect was the more troublesome, the Jews or the Christians. He expected he and his *stator* Gnaeus would be posted back east again after their upcoming leave.

The commandant raised his eyes from his paperwork as Quintus entered the room. An administrator sat at a small table to one side making notes of the meeting.

'Sit, Frumentarius Valerius. I'll keep this brief.'

Quintus sat, grateful for brevity. They were on professional rather than cordial terms, the commandant of the Frumentariate and his most experienced investigator. Quintus expected nothing more; it derived from the miasma of scandal enveloping his family since his father had been driven out of the Senate. He got on with his missions without question, did his duty, went where he was sent.

The commandant picked up a paper.

'The Governor in Tyre has sent in his praises, Quintus Valerius. Job well done, as always. So I'll ask you again if you will reconsider my standing offer of promotion. Your career would benefit, and you could spend more time at home…'

More time bearing his mother's reproaches at his lack of will to climb the slippery political pole to restore the family's fortunes? More opportunity to regret the end of his barren marriage, the loss of the old house on the Quirinal? More chance to listen to the well-meaning platitudes of his father's ancient friends and experience the downright avoidance of his former Praetorian colleagues?

He shuddered. The commandant's mouth twitched.

'No? Well, just submit your final report in the next few days and then take some leave.'

The commandant paused. Quintus looked up to find his

superior looking not unkindly at him. It seemed he would say more, had there been the slightest invitation. Quintus waited, and the moment passed.

'Report back next month. The Saturnalia holiday will keep us quiet for a while; I'll consider your next mission in January.'

Quintus saluted, and turned to leave.

'Oh, Quintus Valerius…'

'Sir?'

'Pack cold weather clothes.'

'Germania, sir?'

That might make an interesting break from the routine run of assignments; it had been long since Quintus had been to the German *limes* or seen the Rhenus.

'You'll be briefed later. I'll just say you've been paid the compliment of being requested by name. Enjoy your leave, Frumentarius.'

There it was again - a look almost of sympathy flashing across the commandant's face. Quintus shrugged mentally, not caring. He called into the Duty Office to sign Gnaeus onto leave, and then walked blindly back to the sad shuttered house on the Quirinal to collect his few belongings.

Chapter Two

Britannia

Quintus steadied the portable cabin desk with his knees as the naval packet from Gesiacorum lurched into the choppy estuary of the Tamesis. The scars on his right thigh itched; he ignored the irritation. The storm was easing, and the waves abated as the ship manoeuvred in from the open sea. He could hear the reverberating drumbeat on the deck keeping the sailors to a smart rowing pace.

Nearly there.

He spread out his commandant's orders. It seemed that the Imperial Procurator in Rome was unhappy. When a mission came from the Imperial Procurator, it meant money was involved. The head of Rome's financial administration was currently uneasy that the Emperor's income from British mines had nose-dived: specifically, the dwindling silver extracted from the lead ore of the vast Vebriacum mines in south-west Britannia. Quintus read on.

You are to be attached for the period of this mission to the staff of the Provincial Governor in Londinium, Gaius Trebonius, and are directed to undertake his orders as you would the Emperor's. You will, of course, also report by Imperial messenger service direct to the Commander at Castra Peregrina.

Gaius Trebonius. A name he knew well. Gaius had been his superior in the British Legion 11 Augusta, when Quintus had been attached as liaison to the Augusta from the Praetorian Guard. The Praetorian, with brand-new Centurion Quintus Valerius, was among the troops brought to Britannia by Septimius Severus to wage his Caledonian wars.

So many years ago. Quintus tried to picture the youngster he had been then. Proud of being appointed to the Emperor's bodyguard; full of his first service outside Italy. Happy to make a new friend in the Second Augusta, the burly young Tribune

7

Gaius Trebonius. What a heedless puppy he had been back then!

His old comrade's name meant much more than that. It had been Gaius Trebonius, a skilled soldier, who had thrust his gladius up under the breastbone of a painted Pictish warrior during that hideous skirmish in the northern bogs, stopping the Caledonian dead. He who had pulled a poisoned spear out of Quintus's thigh, and bound his own scarf rough and tight over the deep gash. Gaius had saved his life. And he was the only person who knew the whole truth of that dreadful day.

After that had come Eboracum and the long process of healing.

He dragged himself back out of the long tunnel of memory. Great Mithras! Why had he come back here, to this cold, dreary, backward place? He should have requested an alternative mission, asked to be sent somewhere - anywhere - else. He stood, stretched and took two long deep breaths, concentrating on letting the air trickle slowly out of his lungs. It was a trick he had learned in the east, a useful one.

He was here because it was his duty to the Emperor. Because for thirteen years he had owed Gaius his life, and been unable to repay the debt. He wouldn't think about the rest: the forced marches into mist and mountains north of the old Wall; the bitter hit-and-run fighting; his crippling wound; the agonising withdrawal from Caledonia. Then long days in hospital fighting a maze of nightmares and hallucinations brought on by the poison on the Pictish spear; then the girl in Eboracum. Most of all, he wanted to forget her: the girl, her bright eager face...

Inevitably he stared blindly at the cabin walls, twisting the bronze ring with its little engraved owl on his fourth finger, seeing only the girl: her animated young face with its dusting of freckles turned to his, her loose fair hair lifted by the summer breeze as they stood on Eboracum's walls, looking out across the grey-stoned northern city.

He shook his head and sat back down at the desk and his papers.

*Let's see...*the mining estate at Vebriacum in the Mendip Hills was let to a businessman who extracted the minerals, mostly lead, and sent an agreed amount back to Rome. He retained the rest as profit. It could be a very lucrative business, and these mines had been a valuable source of income to the Imperial Estate since Britannia was first added to the Empire.

The lessee was a Claudius Bulbo. Interesting cognomen, Bulbo. Quintus wondered fleetingly which part of his anatomy deserved to be called "swollen". Bulbo had already been written to by Aradius Rufinus, the Provincial Procurator in Londinium, responsible for the financial affairs of the southern British province. But apparently Rome was not satisfied with Bulbo's answer that the silver lodes were depleted. Never one to let go a source of income, the Imperial Procurator had called in Quintus to look into the matter.

This was his mission in Britannia: to help Gaius Trebonius, and to satisfy the Imperial Procurator. *Keep those two aims foremost in your mind, let the rest go.*

The rowers slowed as Quintus stepped out onto the deck. The northern sky glowered grey-white. It was a cold damp day, which did not surprise Quintus. He had not forgotten the deceptive British climate. The warm clothes hadn't been for Germania after all. But Britannia was even darker, and with such an unpredictable climate it was probably the worst possible assignment this early in spring. He picked his way along the deck, bypassing the ship's broken mast.

'Sir, we'll shortly be docking. A safe crossing after all, thanks to Neptune!'

Quintus frowned at the shipmaster, just then remembering Gnaeus. The poor man was lying sweating and white-faced in a cot below the foredeck, one leg badly broken when the mast broke and dropped the mainsail during their storm-blighted voyage.

'About my *stator* below - get him carried onto the dockside, would you, and I will arrange for the doctors at the army hospital to take care of him.'

The Gaulish captain looked relieved. 'Thank you sir, I wasn't sure if you would need me to make the arrangements myself.'

Quintus turned away, his mind passing onto the difficulty of getting another groom. Gnaeus had been at his side for many years, since shortly after Quintus had been transferred to the Castra Peregrina from the Praetorian Guard. They had suited each other: the quiet slave and his withdrawn master. It occurred now to Quintus that Gnaeus' competence in travel arrangements would be hard to replace. The Gods only knew what kind of assistant would be available here in Britannia.

The naval packet threaded its way through an increasing throng of cargo ships docked beside the wharfs on the north bank. New walls encircled the sprawling city, pale stone and red rag-tile towering above the muddy foreshore. Had he noticed the budding foundations as the departing galley had lifted oars to carry him back to Rome, long ago? He couldn't remember.

Once the unfortunate Gnaeus had been borne away in a hospital cart, Quintus walked west along the revetted riverbank to the Governor's Palace. Two guards snapped to attention at the sight of his *hasta*, the miniature lance badge on his shoulder sash. He was clearly expected. The guards handed him over to the Governor's major domo, who bowed and led the way through several large chambers, all with surprisingly good mosaics. At the back of the villa he was shown into a smaller room, where a broad man stood up to greet him. He was wearing two fine white woollen tunics over each other and red leather boots, despite the warmth from the heated floor.

'Quintus Valerius, Brother!'

'Governor.' Quintus bowed slightly.

'Nonsense, Quintus,' said Gaius Trebonius, stepping out from behind his desk. 'Let's greet properly as old friends should. You've not forgotten Caledonia, eh?' Quintus tried to relax as Trebonius clapped him on the back.

'Gaius Trebonius, it's good to see you. Congratulations on your promotion.'

His comrade's rise in less than fifteen years from legionary tribune to Governor of a province was impressive. It spoke volumes for Trebonius's quick-thinking political ability that he had continued to prosper in these times of shifting allegiances.

Trebonius shook his head, smiling. He motioned to Quintus to join him in worn leather camp seats near a brazier. The

Governor poured wine for them both.

'Safe journey? And the leg?'

'Both fair enough, thank you sir.' He wasn't in the mood for chitchat, even with an old friend.

The Governor nodded, and took a swallow from his beaker. He fixed Quintus with a direct look, reminiscent of the younger officer briefing his raw new subaltern.

'I never wrote, but I was sorry to hear about your father. Your family…they prosper, I hope?'

Quintus felt his face harden. The wounds were old but still surprisingly raw. It had been too much to hope that Trebonius had not heard about his father's disgrace and fall from the Senate. Quintus didn't know who had engineered the accusations, but he would find out — one day.

'My mother and sister are well enough, thank you, sir. I was able to make adequate provision for them. My sister is married now to a dear friend of mine, and my mother lives with them.'

Trebonius nodded, then returned to business.

'What did they tell you in Rome about this mission, Quintus?'

'I understand it involves suspected loss of income to the Imperial estate from a mine in south-west Britannia. Hence Rome sending me to be attached to your staff during whatever investigation you deem best.'

The Governor frowned and picked up his beaker again. He seemed to study the depths of his wine before continuing.

'Well, it is my great good fortune to have your service. I need the best for this job, and Rome sent you, thank the Gods. Let me be straight with you, Quintus. The income from the Vebriacum mines has dropped to almost nothing in the past year or so. The current lessee, Claudius Bulbo, has petitioned my colleague the Provincial Procurator Rufinus for a reduction in rent, claiming the silver content is now so low the cost of extraction is not worthwhile. Bulbo has a reputation as a competent man of business. He ran some sort of large enterprise in southern Gaul before moving to Britannia a few years ago. On the face of it I have no reason not to believe him. The silver in a lead mine *can* give out after many years of extraction. But we need to know for sure. Other mine lessees have tried to defraud the Emperor in the past.'

Trebonius looked uncomfortable. 'And there is another reason I asked for you in particular, old comrade. There have been one or two reports in recent months, unsubstantiated but still worrying, about a resurgence of Druidism among the Durotriges.'

Quintus cocked his head, puzzled.

'Ah, you won't know. One of the larger native tribes of the southwest. Their territory covers the Summer Country and south to the coast, including the hills where Vebriacum is sited. They were among the last to be subdued by Vespasian at the time of the conquest, and a difficult job he had of it.'

Quintus thought this an understatement. He remembered reading of that famed campaign, including the massacre of the defending natives at the Fort of the Maiden.

Trebonius continued, 'We've had little or no trouble there for many years, but all the same I'd prefer not to have to worry about a Druid uprising so close to the mines. As Imperial business, it's a sensitive matter. I need an experienced and incorruptible officer to get to the bottom of this. I need you, Quintus, to be my Governor's Man, reporting directly to me.'

Quintus wondered about the politics in this province. Normally matters of local policing would be dealt with by the Governor. But anything touching on provincial income, whether loss of taxes, fraud or rebellion, became a matter for Procurator Rufinus too. All too often, in Quintus' experience, the military and fiscal heads of a province's government were rivals in power. Plus Trebonius knew very well that Imperial Investigators sent by the Castra in Rome remained the Emperor's men first and foremost. He decided not to mention that.

Quintus glanced at his friend. 'And the Procurator…?'

The Governor's eyes flicked away. 'Aradius Rufinus is an effective official. His background in Rome is…influential.'

Ambitious, with friends in high places, Quintus translated. He understood now why Trebonius seemed twitchy, and why an officer as experienced as Quintus had been summoned from Rome to deal with the matter.

'Very well, sir. A tactful but top priority investigation, then.'

The Governor looked relieved. His shoulders relaxed as he stood. 'I knew you would understand, my old friend. There's not much more I can tell you. I'll give you an authorising message for the garrison commander at Aquae Sulis in case you need support, but it's up to you how you proceed. I suggest you go quickly. Even in this chilly province, native tempers can heat to boiling point once the right flame is set. And the Vebriacum question must not be left long.'

Quintus also stood, briskly. 'Of course, sir,' he said, back onto a formal footing with the Governor now he had his brief. 'There is just one small matter to sort out before I leave Londinium.' He told the Governor about Gnaeus. 'With your permission, I'll requisition horses, supplies and a replacement aide immediately.'

'Of course. Authorisation for your travel costs and expenses will come as usual from the Procurator's office in Southwark.' Trebonius paused; competing expressions chased each other across his broad face. ' You might do well to seek a replacement assistant at the Londinium garrison. The commander there has authority to assign military staff to me on request, and he is a personal friend of mine. He'll sort out a suitable man. Best to keep the more sensitive details of your investigations to yourself, Quintus. There is a bad smell about all this.'

Quintus respected his old commander's instincts, and waited for more.

'Sir?'

Trebonius held his gaze. 'Just…be discreet, Quintus. Travel carefully. And report only to me.'

Chapter Three

The cell door slammed open, metal lock clanging against brick wall in a hideous cacophony. Tiro jolted awake, his head skewered by light and noise.

'Off your arse, you drunken skiver!'

Two guards dragged Tiro out of the dark cell. He worked hard on putting one foot ahead of another, head exploding as he marched along the corridor of the Londinium Guard headquarters to the tribune's office.

The tribune was reading a letter tablet, pale wax glowing white in the waning light of a branch of candles. A stranger—dark, wiry and alert-looking—stood next to the tribune's desk. There was a miniature lance-head on his leather baldric, the *hasta* of a detached officer on Imperial business. The man looked at Tiro, grey eyes giving nothing away.

Frumentarius. So, an Imperial agent. A policeman, or a spy, or both. What is he doing here?

Tiro felt clumsy, a provincial yokel next to this refined figure. He thoroughly disliked the foreigner at first sight. The tribune glanced down again at the wax tablet, then up at the stranger.

'Centurion Valerius, this is Optio Tiro. Ah...*ex-optio*, of course. Tiro, I have orders from the Governor to release you.'

The tribune opened a desk drawer, letting out a faint lingering odour of cedarwood. Tiro remembered to salute, late and sloppy, but the tribune did not look up. He pulled out a rolled-up document from the drawer.

'Your discharge from the Londinium garrison.'

He held the paper out, but Tiro could not take it. His head was thudding violently again, and his hands were trembling. 'Sir, please... I know I was drunk on duty, sir. It won't happen again. I beg you—'

'Take it, you fool. The terms of your release. And be grateful you weren't flogged in front of the whole cohort as well.'

'I can't read, sir,' Tiro said, shame forcing a rough edge in his voice. The tribune frowned.

'An *optio* who can't read? Maybe the *frumentarius* will remedy that lack. Well, here it is, plain enough. You are hereby detached from the Londinium cohort, and assigned to accompany Frumentarius Quintus Valerius as *stator* on his travels in Britannia. Quintus Valerius has been sent by the Rome authorities and in addition holds commission directly from our Governor.

'This is an undeserved second chance for you, Tiro. I will suspend reporting your dismissal, for now. Assuming you serve the *frumentarius* to his complete satisfaction, you will be re-admitted to the Londinium Guard at your former rank on your return. Fail in this duty by the slightest degree, and your discharge from the army will take immediate effect. Without pension. Understood?'

The tribune looked at Tiro for the first time, and Tiro felt anger and shame tussling within him. His voice was raw as he answered, but he managed to look steadily through his superior officer at the back wall.

'Understood, sir.' He wondered if the shame of being parcelled off as a servant was worse than being locked up in barracks for dereliction of duty. He looked at the *frumentarius*, wondering what mission they were to undertake.

'Best I can do, we're short of good men,' the tribune was saying. 'I hope he'll do the job you need.' His expression implied doubt.

The stranger looked long at Tiro, who felt his own gaze dropping.

Damned if this Italian is going to look down his nose at me like that. Who does he think he is? He'll soon find out that the Britannia Superior pancratium champion, bearer of a phalera award for conspicuous gallantry, is not someone to sneer at. Then Tiro remembered that they'd taken away his treasured silver *phalera* too, stripped from his breastplate in front of the cohort before he was marched away to prison. His hangover headache redoubled.

The *frumentarius* waited till they were out of the tribune's office and around a corner. Then he turned sharply, nearly stepping on Tiro's feet. His face was still impassive, but the officer's breath hissed between his teeth as he leaned in close, his voice harsh and one hand bunched into the neck of Tiro's tunic.

'Right, you barbarian vermin, listen! The only reason I don't reject you out of hand for this assignment is because the Governor himself chose you. The Gods only know why. He must have a damn good reason I don't yet understand.' The brown hand grasping Tiro's tunic twisted and lifted suddenly, and Tiro was slammed against the wall behind. The Italian was stronger than he looked. Quintus pushed his face right into Tiro's, so close the breath was hot in his nostrils. 'One foot wrong — just one — and you're back here in gaol, with the key thrown away.' His eyes, hard as flint, bored into Tiro's. 'Do we understand each other?'

Tiro croaked,' Yessir!' and slumped as the *frumentarius* dropped him. He tried to catch his breath, recover some dignity. Quintus Valerius stalked away, leaving Tiro to scramble after him.

His headache didn't lessen as they headed south from the fort, but the brisk pace Quintus set caused new waves of nausea to compete with it. Tiro had rarely felt more miserable, not even when his parents died in their fire-swept Londinium slum, leaving him homeless and starving at sixteen. He was a proud Londoner who loved his buzzing city, but boys need food. Back then he had no trade to earn his keep. The Roman army opened its arms to Tiro, and very quickly the men of his auxiliary cohort became the only family he needed. He was naturally quick and tough, a born fighter and happy to pile into any danger. He wasn't a bad soldier. He had made Optio by the time he was in his early twenties.

What good was all that sweat, discipline and work now? All thrown away for the sake of a night drinking to the pretty eyes of a tavern slut when I should have been on duty. No warrant officer rank now, no bravery award, no mates, no snug garrison quarters. Just a new boss, and long cold miles to travel without the good company that makes life bearable.

16

The moment of returned pride fled as quickly as a girl's virtue in a garrison *vicus*. As they crossed the long wooden bridge to Southwark, Tiro looked down at the rough waters of the river and half-wished he had the courage to jump.

'Wait here,' Quintus said, as they were stopped by the guards outside the vast Procurator's Palace on the south bank. Tiro shivered as gusts of cold air forced their way through his tunic. Along with his pride and rank he'd lost his uniform, and now wore shabby homespun clothes like any other city pleb. What wouldn't he give for a nice thick *birrus*, a good bit of British wool to keep the early spring wind at bay?

The *frumentarius* was saluted smartly and escorted inside the courtyard, past a large bathhouse range and gardens and into the imposing building where Aradius Rufinus, the Provincial Procurator of Britannia Superior, held sway. Tiro didn't envy Quintus Valerius. Word in the fort was that while Governor Gaius Trebonius was a good stick and straight as they come, the same could not be said for the Procurator. A crafty customer, they said. But then all men in charge of money were crafty, in Tiro's experience of quartermasters and supply officers.

A steady stream of people came and went from the palace, none paying any attention to Tiro. He amused himself guessing their business with the Procurator:

The clutch of overfed traders in second-hand togas? He reckoned they had been lunching with the Procurator, proposing sure things that just needed the right tax break to come off with a nice little earner guaranteed for the Provincial coffers.

The drab older woman with a pretty red-eyed daughter in gold earrings and a low-cut *tunica*? She was looking for an introduction to a suitable marriage partner, youth for money. The older woman came out alone a few minutes later.

The well-dressed man on a prancing roan, and his companion with a drooping right eye? The first had a fine blue cloak flung back over his shoulders, and clattered out under the arched gateway in style. His companion was mounted on a rather less showy nag. The first man paused, and a passerby in frowsy clothes stepped off the pavement and made his way over to them, exchanging a few words before the horsemen moved on.

The cohort of tired auxiliaries trudging through the gateway? They'd been seconded from their rathole fort, and would soon be posted somewhere muddy upcountry to ensure the flow of taxes from reluctant farmers.

The wait lengthened as the faltering afternoon dimmed. Tiro lost feeling in his hands, then his feet. The guards began to cast amused looks at him. A third guard came out of the palace and soon they were all three laughing. Tiro straightened up, took a few turns up and down. Marching to keep warm was all. The third man laughed even louder, and held up his middle finger. Tiro caught the words "Governor's Man", with emphasis on the word "Governor". The three guards lit a brazier and hunched over it. Tiro's skin crawled. He did not like this group huddling together. It was no way to behave on guard duty. He bristled, stuck out his chest, and set off to give them a few choice words. Let's just see how they handled themselves, three onto one or not. Some people called it street fighting, but Tiro, twice all-comers Provincial Champion of the mixed martial art *pancratium*, knew better.

He nearly barged into Quintus, who was coming back through the gateway leading two saddled and laden horses. Glory be to Mars and Jupiter, there was a *birrus* strapped to the back of the horse Quintus handed to him.

'On our way, Tiro.' Tiro's arm was grasped hard, and he was steered hard about away from the guards, back towards the river. They crossed on foot, the bridge being too busy with traffic to mount the horses.

'Sir,' Tiro began. Should he tell the *frumentarius* about the insolent grouping around the brazier? But Quintus ignored him, keeping up such a scorching pace that Tiro soon regained feeling in his extremities. His lingering hangover blew away with the brisk north wind biting his face. *So what if the Procurator's men were ignorant gossips? Nah, keep your thoughts to yourself, my lad.*

He was hungry now, and looked longingly at the hot snacks set out for sale on fast-food counters along the city streets. Quintus seemed oblivious. They didn't pause till they had left the city through the west gate, mounting their horses at last where the tombstones of the cemetery cropped up through thick grass along the road.

They rode steadily west. The weather held cool and turned damper, successive waves of thin rain blowing into their faces. The road seemed endless to Tiro, despite his years of slogging around the province with the army. It wasn't the same without your mates. This close-mouthed *frumentarius* was no kind of officer in Tiro's books. No company to lead, no salutes or smart uniform, no burnished weapons on show. Not even any barked commands. Just the occasional low-voiced order to break the long periods of silence as they trotted the horses through Pontes towards Calleva Atrebatum. Drizzle turned to longer showers, and then hardened into a steady rain.

Quintus was a competent horseman, but seemed to have no intention of pushing their mounts hard to reach their unknown destination. Tiro was no slouch on a horse after a decade as a mounted auxiliary rider, and couldn't understand why they weren't using the posting stations. With a wave of the boss's lance-head badge they could have been speeding along, with frequent changes of horse all to the tune of snappy salutes. Why the secrecy? He didn't even know where they were heading, or why.

'The road west beyond Calleva, and on to the Summer Country,' was all Quintus said when Tiro asked. Summer Country? That was a good joke, Tiro thought, scratching the itchy wool of his sodden cloak and twitching it up to cover his civilian clothes. Maybe the Investigator just wasn't very good at his job. That's probably why he'd been posted from Rome— exile for upsetting someone, no doubt.

By Jupiter Best and Greatest, couldn't they just get the job done quickly? The sooner they arrived at this wretched place in the west, the sooner Tiro could be back home in the comfort of his fort, drinking with his mates in the Londinium wineshops. All the same, there was something forbidding about the wiry officer that made Tiro hesitant about open challenge. Quintus said little, and despite the modest pace he was setting, everything he did was spare and direct. The Briton settled back into his soggy *birrus*, and resigned himself to a slow muddy journey.

Tiro was already regretting this assignment instead of the quicker, more painful punishment for being drunk on duty.

Chapter Four

Julia Aureliana glanced around the whitewashed ward of the Aquae Sulis hospital, smoothing down the plain *stola* she wore for clinic work. She smiled at a plump nervous woman standing deferentially by her father's bedside. Julia picked up the hand of the old pilgrim drowsing in his narrow cot.

Good. The erratic pulse had started to slow and deepen since he'd taken Julia's mixture, a few powdered foxglove leaves stirred into rainwater with a little cinnamon to smooth out the bitter taste. Julia checked that the old man's feet were raised on a pillow, and smiled again at his worried daughter.

'Your father will be fine. He just needs another day or so of rest here before you take him to the Goddess's sacred spring. I'll give you some more medicine for him. And don't let him walk too far, or bathe in the very hottest waters. He should take it easier at his age.'

The woman looked relieved, murmuring her thanks. An orderly lingering nearby said quietly, 'Lady Julia, the *medicus* wishes to speak to you. In the third cubicle.'

'Ah, Lady Julia. I would value your opinion.'

The garrison surgeon, Anicius Piso, straightened from examining a young man as Julia entered the side-room.

Piso ran this little clinic and hospital for soldiers, pilgrims and holidaymakers who needed medical attention while visiting the busy spa town. He was nominally attached to the small Aquae Sulis garrison across the river, which policed the famous Temple of Sulis Minerva. In the years since a younger, less-assured Julia had come to his clinic begging to work in exchange for his surgical teaching, he had quickly moved to a wry acceptance of her skill. He discovered that the tall, reserved girl had been taught medicine by a respected Greek physician, a freedman who was tutor to the girl's distinguished family in the Summer Country. Julia later let drop that she had also trained in Eboracum.

Then there was the tuition she did not admit to. She had been apprenticed to wise-women herbalists, inheritors of the Druid tradition. He didn't ask, and she didn't tell. He knew her to be a devout worshipper of the powerful goddess, Sulis Minerva, knowing more about medicine and herbal healing than he did. That was all that mattered to Piso, a pragmatist. He was grateful to have Julia's expertise in his hospital.

Julia looked carefully at the injury. The young man's right leg had been crushed. A race between town youths, involving three horses and a heavily-laden wagon all entering the north city gate together as the young men thrashed their horses into the spa resort. Inevitably there had been a dreadful smash. Two days ago Julia had held the sedated patient steady while Anicius operated to remove splinters of bone and set the fracture. The leg now lay straight and correct. Anicius had cleansed the area on the shin where bone had broken the skin, and the wound was neatly sutured. But the injury had got inflamed and puffy. She leaned over, sniffing for infection. The patient was slipping in and out of consciousness, moving restlessly. His face was slick with sweat and his skin felt hot to the touch. She was not hopeful they could avoid amputating the shattered leg. *Lady Minerva, give me your wisdom, I beg. How can I best help this young man?* She touched her gold necklet, adjusting it in place round her neck, considering.

'I think …' she paused, turning over in her mind various options. 'First, I would suggest more poppy to keep him sedated and less likely to move and undo your fine surgery.'

The bustling little doctor turned red with pleasure.

'Would you agree his constitution and age make it possible to keep the poppy treatment going for some time yet?' At his nod, she continued. 'I'd like to wash the wound again with tincture of hellenium. Fresh bandages, and the splint back in place, of course. Then when he wakes, perhaps the orderly could give him a drink I will mix up for him: rosemary for the swelling, and horsetail to fight the infection? Yes, it's vital to get that swelling down and allow his blood to circulate, to cleanse and heal the break.'

'Rosemary,' she muttered to herself, moving away to the little pharmacy where she prepared and stored her medicines. She had forgotten Anicius already. He smiled, signalling to the orderly to have fresh bandages ready as soon as Julia had cleansed the wound. There was no need to linger; Julia would summon help if she needed it.

'Mistress? Mistress! Lady Julia!'

Julia looked out of her dispensing room, frowning. There was no mistaking that rising tone. It seemed that Britta was here, and determined to attract her attention. Please the Goddess, she would show the deference expected in public by a servant addressing a noble lady. She so rarely did so at home, after all. Julia put down her pestle and went quickly to meet her housekeeper by the ward entrance, where Britta was blocking the attempts of a ward orderly to carry urine jars out to the latrine.

Julia sighed, her mind still more than half on her patient. Britta had that look on her face, the look that combined impatience at her mistress's choice of occupation with the certainty of her own priorities. Britta came from a family of free tenant farmers who had lived on the Aurelianus estate for time out of mind. Her brother Morcant worked Home Farm, and managed the large Bo Gwelt estate for Julia's brother, Magistrate Marcus Aurelianus. Britta herself had come a long way from the shy little russet-haired playmate and maid-servant Julia's parents employed when they were both young girls. These days Julia's plain-speaking friend was more of an unofficial confidante than ordinary housekeeper.

And not to be denied when she had that stubborn look on her face.

'Mistress, I beg a word in private.'

The words were conciliatory; the tone was not.

'Sorry, Britta. I'm all ears.'

'Well, Mistress, someone's come you've been wanting to see for a long time.' Britta paused, full of importance.

'Yes?'

'It's Miss Aurelia.' A hesitation. 'Arrived at the house just now, on her own horse.'

23

Julia's mind switched fully to what Britta was saying. She wasn't expecting a visit from her niece. Aurelia was only thirteen, and never travelled this far from home alone on the public roads. Not without her father writing to Julia first to let her know she was coming, and sending a family escort. Aurelia was a more than competent rider — of course she was, being of the Durotriges of the Summer Country. But she was also a noble from the leading family in the area, gently born and bred. She should be travelling in a litter or wagon, with attendants, and luggage…

'Luggage?'

'Just saddle bags. But Rufus is with her. I'm sure he could return to Bo Gwelt to fetch more of her baggage, my lady. It must be an impulse visit, she's so fond of you…'

Julia snorted. It was strange that Aurelia, whom she loved more than the girl probably suspected or needed to know, would ride so far with only a groom. Even stranger that Marcus, or Aurelia's stepmother, the correct and thinly-elegant Claudia, would allow such a thing.

Julia administered her patient's medicine, and told Piso apologetically that she had to leave for the day. After pouring a libation to the Goddess at one of the altars in the Sacred Spring complex, she left with Britta. The two women walked the short distance east along the river bank to Julia's home.

They arrived to find the pretty stone townhouse in uproar. Julia's distracted servants were gathered round in the atrium, all vying for the attention of a slip of a girl, a flash of dark wavy hair and quicksilver movement.

'Senovara, how wonderful! I'm starving!' The smiling cook was offering Aurelia a platter of fresh honey cakes, while Julia's personal maid was shaking out Aurelia's fine lilac mantle. Julia's head groom was disputing with Rufus about whose job it was to hand down the young mistress's saddle bags.

Aurelia caught sight of Julia and Britta, and flung herself at her aunt.

'Dearest Aunt Julia!'

Julia caught Aurelia's hands, and held them a moment, while

Britta signalled to the dishevelled household her disapproval of the scene. The atrium fell silent as it emptied.

'What a pleasure this is, Aurelia,' said Julia evenly. 'By all means come into the salon, and tell me why your delightful company so unexpectedly comes our way.' Britta accompanied them, and swung the wooden door shut behind them. The two Aureliana women sat down on a long sofa. Julia looked quietly at her niece.

Aurelia bridled a little.

'Oh, well, if you're going to be cross, Aunt…'

'I am not cross, my dear. Just surprised, and rather puzzled. Why didn't I know you were coming? Did your father's message go astray?'

Aurelia flicked the dark hair away from her face, and cupped her pointed little chin in both palms, turning her head to survey the room. Her eyes darted around as if admiring the familiar wallpaintings of songbirds framed by red and gold panels for the first time.

Julia tried again. 'Aurelia? Of course, you are always welcome in my house, but…' Julia paused to let the young girl speak. After a moment or two, Aurelia jumped up, avoiding her aunt's gaze.

'It's just - just been such ages since I saw you. And you know how much I love to visit Aquae Sulis, and …'

This was news to Julia, who understood Aurelia to prefer the soft green hills and marshes of her own lands, and to be much too keen a horsewoman to ever wish for town walls and pavements. She remained silent. Aurelia looked at her, and flushed.

'Well, I did really wish to see you, and Britta, too.' This was said with feeling, and Julia realised the girl was on the brink of tears.

'Nevertheless, dear child, for you to arrive without forewarning and on horseback is unusual.'

Aurelia held her chin up a fraction, and the brimming tears fought with stubborn pride. Julia knew that look, having seen it in her bronze mirror many times during her own girlhood.

'My dear, I wish you will tell me what is the matter.' She

glanced at Britta, standing calmly in front of the door. 'Do you want Britta to leave?'

'Oh, no!' Aurelia flung herself up and into Britta's comfortable embrace. 'Dearest Britta is my best friend, after you, Aunt. And darling Father. ' She paused to blow her nose on a scrap of linen twisted out of her robe. 'I had to come. I had to get away from that woman! And even …from Father.'

Ah, yes. Julia understood. Now that Aurelia was moving towards womanhood, her headstrong personality was bound to clash with the cold, perfectly-mannered Claudia.

'Aurelia, it will make your father very unhappy if you quarrel with your stepmother. She only means what is best for you, I am sure.'

The girl stared at Julia, hot tears falling down her face.

'Means the best for me? By marrying me off to that scheming nephew of hers, that bullying wretch, that cruel monster —that Lucius!'

Julia was astonished and couldn't find words for a long moment. Britta's eyebrows shot up, and she took herself out of the room, closing the door gently behind her.

Aurelia fell into Julia's arms, weeping openly. 'Please, Julia, let me stay with you. Don't make me go back home.'

The girl sobbed while Julia held her close, grim-faced. Marriage at thirteen was not unheard of among the British upper classes. But Julia knew it wasn't right for Aurelia. And to Lucius Claudius, of all young men? He would break Aurelia's heart and crush her spirit.

Once she had calmed the girl and got her settled in the guest room, Julia called Britta back. Britta fully understood the special relationship she had with her niece, and knew the hopes Julia had for Aurelia's future. These did not include a premature marriage to a young man like Lucius.

Julia had several times met Lucius and his father, the fat businessman Claudius Bulbo. Most often since Bulbo's sister Claudia, a sophisticated widow from Gaul who moved like a cat and looked like a goddess, had married Marcus. Julia reflected on how quickly the lonely Marcus had been enticed away from his books and into a second marriage. Then she thought again of her soft-spoken cultured brother, left bereft with his baby daughter when her gentle sister-in-law had died a decade ago. It was understandable that he should want company, a hostess to welcome the guests and supporters a Magistrate inevitably attracts. And a mother to help bring up his little girl as the heiress to a large, prosperous estate.

'Aurelia can't stay here more than a night or two, I'm afraid. It looks like things are not right at Bo Gwelt. No point in writing to Marcus. I'll have to go myself, and it's only proper that I take Aurelia with me. I'll send Rufus straight back to Bo Gwelt with a quick note, put their minds at rest till we can get there. I need to talk to Anicius Piso and leave some directions for the orderlies at the clinic first.' Her brow wrinkled. 'I hate to bother Marcus when he's not well, but it can't be helped now. Actually I'd like to see how he's doing. I'll try to persuade him to let Aurelia come back to visit us for a few weeks. With his official approval this time, and enough luggage to clothe the girl.'

Britta nodded in agreement.

Chapter Five

The rain was easing on their third day of travel as Quintus and Tiro entered Calleva Atrebatum, passing a cluster of round temples near the east gate. Weak gleams of sunlight shone fitfully onto puddles. Tiro squinted round. A reasonable enough town, but nothing like Londinium. Tiro's forebears came from Kent, but his family long ago cast in their lot with the bustling new city on Tamesis. Within a generation they had forgotten they had ever lived anywhere else. Londinium was surely the greatest city in the Roman world, and Tiro couldn't wait to get back.

Home for tonight was a large white-washed *mansio,* with a range of stables off to one side. The building was substantial and clearly busy. Water dripped slowly off the thatched eaves. *No bathhouse, seemingly. You can bloody stick the countryside.* He was disgusted.

'Stop day-dreaming, Tiro. Take these horses round to the stables. I'll see to our rooms.' Quintus swung down off his horse and pushed his way past a party of civil servants arguing with a serving man over their accommodation. Tiro was tired and bad-tempered. He didn't need reminding by anyone how to look after horses. He led the mounts into the muddy stableyard, his mind working on ways to make it clear to his new boss who was in charge of this trip. *Who does he think he is? This is still my parish, even this far from Londinium. I'll show him.*

Quintus found the innkeeper dashing around with a tray of wine and beakers, shouting at his staff. It was dinner-time, and it took some effort to secure them a single small chamber. Quintus expected they would sleep little that night; the *mansio* was full of guests.

'Take this cloak and dry it,' he said sharply to the serving girl who brought wine up to their room. 'And bring a brazier to warm this freezing box.' She looked astonished, and said she didn't know as how her master would feel about that, not being in the way of warming the bedchambers beyond the winter months.

'It *is* still bloody winter. Just get a brazier.' She blinked and hurried away. Quintus saw with resignation that the second bed was a mere truckle rolled under the main bed.

He thought back to his briefing in Londinium. Claudius Bulbo apparently lived in a pretentious house in Iscalis, a small town at the foot of a striking gorge where the river Axe broadened out enough for a small river port. From there lead ingots from Vebriacum were transported to the coast for onward shipment around the Empire. Key to uncovering any fraud would be finding out whether and how silver was expropriated and then sold on. Getting proof might be tricky. A lot of money was at stake, and Quintus well from his years of investigative police work that money is frequently the cause of trouble.

Quintus stretched his arms out above his head, feeling his spine stiff from the wet journey. He lay down on the bed, muddy boots and all, and closed his eyes for a moment. He and Tiro would need to step carefully…

His nose wrinkled at the thought of Tiro. Where in Hades was that provincial layabout? He should have been back from stabling the horses by now. Then he noticed that the noise below had subsided and complete dark had fallen outside. How long had he been lying here dozing?

Strapping on his dagger, Quintus hurried downstairs and outside. The path to the stables was muddy and rutted, but Quintus was light on his feet. His knife was ready in his right hand. A lamp shone above the stable doors. Shifting clouds revealed glimpses of the waxing moon. He listened for a moment outside the stable door. All was silent. He entered cautiously. It was dark inside. His horses had been turned out into loose boxes and whickered gently at his approach, but there was no-one else there. Then he heard a soft dragging sound, outside. He went quickly out of the stable to investigate, but once away from the lamplight he tripped and almost fell. He reached down to feel a heavy *birrus* like the one Tiro had. The dragging sound stilled. It was sheer good fortune that Quintus looked up just as the moon was briefly unveiled, casting a fleeting gleam onto the edge of an uplifted dagger barely a pace away. Quintus leapt aside, thrusting his own knife hard. He had no idea which way his assailant was facing, but he did recognise the satisfying sensation of his knife sliding deep between ribs. There was a grunt, a thud, as something jarred against his leg and landed heavily on his foot. It was a body. He crouched down to find a widening pool of hot sticky blood, and the gurgle of a final breath.

It seemed he had killed someone. But had the dead man already found Tiro?

Quintus unhooked the stable lamp and brought it back to light the scene. Two bodies: Tiro, his face a mask of blood; and a stranger, skinny, dirty and dressed like a sewer rat. He heard a groan and a British curse in the unmistakable accents of Londinium. Quintus leaned over the swearing Tiro, checking him for wounds.

'Bastard got me while I was settling the horses. Must have slugged me over the head with something. Where is he?' Tiro tried to peer around, blood dripping into his eyes from a wide shallow cut across his brow.

'Right here, and dead now,' said Quintus.

'Blimey, boss, that was quick work.'

'At any rate you're alive and not much hurt.'

'Apart from a bloody great hole in my head.'

'Just a cut. You'll live,' Quintus said, pulling Tiro to his feet. Tiro paused to look at the dead man. 'Seen you before, somewhere…Gods, my head! Sometime, somewhere—*where* have I seen you, you bastard?' It seemed recollection wasn't coming just yet, so Quintus supported his bleeding *stator* back into the inn.

The innkeeper was horrified. He armed his barmen with cudgels and sent them outside to retrieve the body and check the area for more brigands.

'We keep a good company here, sir,' he assured Quintus, looking worried. 'We never have trouble, apart from the odd drunken dustup, not mostly anyway. Was anything stolen from your man?'

Quintus shook his head. He was keen to keep the incident as

30

quiet as possible. He did not believe for a second that the attack was a coincidence, and anyway the innkeeper wouldn't want word to get around that his guests were being attacked.

'Nothing missing,' he assured the unhappy man. 'But I'd like you to come out and take a look at the body. You might recognise him.'

Quintus wasn't holding out much hope. Potential witnesses were frequently as blind as a forum beggar. But the Calleva mansio-keeper was observant, making it his job to remember his customers. He looked closely at the corpse, clothes now blood-stained over the filth of long wear, narrow face frozen in a death snarl.

'Yes ... I have seen him, sometime recent. Let me think—'

'He was here along of two other fellows just last week, Master.'

The stable-boy, none too bright but keen, had loitered to hear the gossip and now broke in. 'I see'd them all, three of them drinking together. Him and two others.'

'What did the other two look like?' asked Quintus.

'Dunno, sir, it was too dark-like. Just one tall, the other smaller.'

'Did you hear their conversation?'

'No, sir, and wouldn't do no good if I did,' the boy said simply. 'They spoke foreign.'

'Foreign?'

'Yep. Like that one, all foreign.' The boy pointed at Tiro, who laughed despite the pain in his face at this description of his Londinium accent. Actually it was Quintus with his clipped Roman speech who was the real foreigner. 'But I remember 'em fine,' the boy went on. 'The tall man had a fancy roan horse. What a beauty that horse was!'

'If it helps, I can report the incident to the Aquae Sulis garrison for you,' Quintus told the innkeeper. 'We're awaited by the commander there on another matter and expect to see him within a couple of days.'

The innkeeper expressed his gratitude. He bustled away once his wife had arrived to salve Tiro's bruise and bind up the cut with a clean cloth. She gave as her opinion that stitches wouldn't be needed. Quintus accepted the offer of a free meal and a flask of decent wine to be brought up to their chamber. Tiro, who enjoyed bars and company, began to grumble until Quintus said, 'Best we keep to ourselves. Until we know who attacked you and why, we watch our step.' Tiro agreed, and shut up. Quintus said no more; he apparently wasn't ready to share his thinking. *Still the close-mouthed toff,* thought Tiro. He reckoned one of them needed to do some working out. About this attack, its purpose, who had known they were on the road. He tried to recall all the people he had seen coming and going at Southwark. *Dodgy place, Southwark. Merciful Juno, my head hurts!*

They turned in as soon as they had eaten. Tiro woke once in the night, disturbed by the *frumentarius* thrashing around and groaning in a dream. Tiro was glad Quintus had put his gladius out of reach under the bed. By dawn they were away again, heading out through the western gateway of Calleva for the crossroads, where they would turn south-west towards the sacred spa of Aquae Sulis.

Two days later, having spent the night at a more salubrious *mansio* in the prosperous town of Cunetio, they stopped to eat on the way to the small settlement of Verlucio. Tiro found the meal tasty: a picnic lunch of local ewe's milk cheese and bannocks, with a handful of hazel nuts. No competition for the greasy hot food he often bought from street takeaway stalls in Londinium. But still, not bad for country grub. The rain had stopped and the day was brightening; the air felt cold nonetheless. Tiro persuaded his silent boss to let him light a small fire, but the firewood to be found by the road-side was damp and smouldered reluctantly.

Tiro thought back before the attack at Calleva.

'Sir, I was wondering about a couple of blokes in Londinium — '

Quintus raised his waterskin to drink, then paused, turning his head sharply.

' Can you hear army horses, Tiro?'

Tiro could do better than that; he had sharp vision. He looked

32

west, shading his eyes from the thin shafts of southerly light.

'A patrol, sir. Perhaps a dozen cavalry?'

Quintus nodded, and Tiro guessed lunch was over. He kicked dirt over the smouldering logs, gathered up their packs, and unhobbled the horses. A party of horseman approached at a canter, kicking up spurts of muddy water. In the lead was a young red-headed centurion, who waved his troop to a stop, dismounted, and saluted Quintus.

'Frumentarius Quintus Valerius?'

'You are?'

'Centurion Marcellus Crispus, commanding the spa garrison at Aquae Sulis, sir. We had word you were on the road. We have a serious crime to report, sir.'

Tiro watched with satisfaction as surprise turned to concern on the face of the Imperial Investigator. It was a fleeting look until the calm face of Roman authority returned.

So, this trip is getting more interesting by the day. The night attack at Calleva and now this.

'Quite a coincidence, Centurion. We were on our way to report a crime to you. You have saved us the trip to Aquae Sulis.'

'Sorry, sir,' the young redhead said. 'I'll need to escort you there in any event. A murder victim was found a couple of days ago near here, and is now in the morgue at the Temple clinic.'

'I'm unsure why this concerns me. Surely something you local troops can handle?'

The young officer flushed.

'Well, sir, it's not that straightforward. The body was found on the road between Aquae Sulis and Cunetio. A dead dispatch rider, perhaps attached to one of the Imperial waystations. There've been a few muggings on the main roads recently, but this is different. The body was discovered by a local farmer driving stock early to market, maybe the first passer-by that morning. As I say, the body was found, and reported to me.'

The young man seemed to run out of words.

'Well?'

'Well, sir …'

'Spit it out, man. I'm on important Imperial business. Surely

33

the death of a courier can be dealt with in the normal way, reported to Londinium with whatever investigation you would do for a mugging that's gone wrong?'

Tiro recognised the note of impatience in his boss's voice. He pitied the centurion. But the young officer surprised him, drawing himself up and taking an even breath before replying.

'Sir, apart from an empty dispatch bag, the body is *all* that was retrieved. No head was found. The victim had been decapitated.'

Tiro looked round at the riders, and spat sideways for luck. They all seemed uncomfortable. One or two were shifting in their saddles, anxious to get away from even the image of such a death. He could hardly blame them.

A beheading? And the head taken away? Tiro was a city boy, through and through, but even he had heard tales of the long-ago when Rome first came to Britannia. Stories of the Druids, those powerful religious leaders who could turn men berserk, making them deal dreadful death to any enemy. Including Roman soldiers.

He looked at Quintus, waiting for the haughty Italian to dress down the young centurion. To Tiro's surprise, Quintus seemed to take stock carefully.

'No head, you say? I have served in Britannia previously, Centurion, and I remember during the Caledonian campaign headless bodies sometimes turning up. A mark of the regard the Caledonians had for their enemies, I seem to recall?'

The centurion responded with relief. 'Right, sir. And the British warriors of these parts also followed that practice once, long ago, believing the head is where the soul resides. To separate a dead enemy's head from his body as a trophy was a great honour.'

'Long ago? No recent reports of Druids in action round here?'

'Oh no, sir. I haven't heard of that happening for many years. In fact, never in my lifetime. To kill a civilian that way and take his head in peacetime is unprecedented.'

'Maybe a relic of ancient superstition, then. Or perhaps someone disguising the identity of their victim. Impossible to tell which.' The investigator seemed to ponder. Tiro was

34

intrigued. Their dull mission to chase down missing Imperial silver was turning into something darker and more interesting. *How do you like the real Britannia, Imperial Investigator? Not just a muddy backwater, eh?*

There was a note of impatience in Quintus's movements as he remounted. The *frumentarius* flicked the reins to turn his horse's head.

'I am on an urgent mission, but as there may be an aspect of provincial security to this death, I will have to find the time to investigate. If the body was found near here, it might be useful to search the vicinity. Lead on, Centurion Crispus.'

Chapter Six

The trooper left to guard the scene saluted as they drew up. A large puddle of blood was clearly visible, a thick sticky mass coagulated on the road.

'Rained here overnight?'

'Yes sir, not heavily.'

'Right. Centurion, spread your men out to check the verges on either side for anything that shouldn't be there.'

Crispus raised an eyebrow in inquiry. 'Sir?'

'Anything like a head!'

Quintus turned away abruptly, calling Tiro.

'I want you to go further into the woods on this side, a spear-cast from the road. I'll search the other side. Take one of the centurion's men with you. Spread out, move carefully, check the undergrowth. It's not just the head we want. Find me anything that connects this murder with something else. We need to get this investigation out of the way quickly.'

The woods away from the road's verge were utterly silent as Tiro cast to and fro. He kept the trooper behind him, not trusting the rural clod to avoid trampling evidence. In his capacity as *optio* of a century of the Governor's Guard in Londinium Tiro had had occasion to conduct investigations from time to time. He'd led military details to help the City Vigiles find missing people, tracked down contraband, and generally ridden the streets of criminals and thugs. The city, with its day and night din, was his natural environment. But as well as good eyesight, he had a sharp eye for detail, allied with a strong sense of things that didn't belong. A sense that had saved his life and limbs many times on the mean streets of Londinium.

Nothing.

Tiro extended his search, moving carefully on into the darkening woods. There was a single sound: the call of a solitary bird, making a "dit, dot" sound. If Tiro had been a country boy, he would have recognised the song of the chiffchaff. What he did recognise — immediately — was the smell of rot. The stink of old filth, a sign of blocked cesspits and dead dogs. He was used to narrow alleys smelling of piss, rubbish, and violence, of dark corners where the sewage system had backed up. He was used to every kind of foulness, and he could smell that rot right here.

After that it wasn't that hard to spot the head. It wasn't even hidden, just lying among bushes as if someone had tossed it away. Tiro had a strong stomach, coming from years of living in flea-ridden dosshouses before he signed up with the army. And some latrine-cleaning since. He crouched down to pick up the sightless head, cradling it carefully. A young face, pale and fair-haired, with an expression of trepidation lingering on it. *Poor sod, you never knew what hit you.* Very young, perhaps only fourteen. Too young even for the army postal service. Maybe a private courier?

The clots of the great gaping wound had long since solidified, but he could see that it was a clean cut. The neck vertebrae had been sliced superbly. A single stroke, with a sharp sword blade. Could hardly be any other kind of weapon. He pictured a long leaf-shaped iron sword, like those once carried into battle by the old warriors. The sort used by Boudica's boys to wreak revenge nearly two centuries ago.

He sighed, holding the boy's head in his arms.

'Sir – found anything?' It was the rural clod.

'Yes.' He stood slowly, reluctant to reveal the dead boy to public repulsion. He shrugged off his *birrus* and wrapped the head in it, shivering as the chill afternoon breeze filtered through his tunic. Something white and fluttering caught his gaze. A strip of coarse white cloth, tethered on a long black spike of hawthorn. With a telling blood-brown smudge at one end, where the fabric was torn.

The troop clattered over the Abona bridge towards Sulis Minerva's temple in Aquae Sulis. It was dusk, getting cold now, and the flambeaux lighting the way for wealthy tourists and pilgrims were wavering and flaring in the breeze. At the entrance to the sacred precinct Marcellus Crispus dismounted and dismissed his troop to their headquarters, taking with them Quintus and Tiro's tired horses. Tiro's horse had thrown a hipposandal and gone lame.

The centurion led them into the hospital adjoining the temple. The courtyard building surrounded a herb garden, and included a small room that served as a morgue. Tiro was still carrying the bloody head, his arms quivering with the effort. Quintus made no effort to help him.

They were greeted at the morgue door by the army doctor. He wasted no time in introductions, merely holding out his arms to take the head before leading them inside.

'Lady Julia!' he called.

A tall slim woman emerged from a side cubicle. She was wearing a white *stola* over a homespun tunic. Her fair hair was tied up in a cloth on her head. Quintus guessed her to be a cleaner or some sort of orderly. Then he looked again, wondering.

'Ah,' said the doctor, 'I'm glad you're still here, my lady. I'm sorry to delay your leaving, but could you help me with this?'

The woman moved forward quickly, and without hesitation and to the amazement of the three soldiers, unwrapped the bloody head.

'Anicius, you've found him.'

'No credit to me. It was our friend Marcellus here, and his, er … colleagues.'

Crispus saluted, saying quickly, 'Surgeon Piso, may I introduce Frumentarius Quintus Valerius, and his assistant, Tiro?'

And to Quintus, 'Sir, the Lady Julia Aureliana. She dispenses medicines, and assists Anicius Piso here at the clinic of the Goddess.'

The woman turned sharply to look at the two strangers. Her movement felt disturbingly familiar to Quintus. She gazed at them in silence. A moment more, and her attention was back on the head. Looking at her fair oval face, he felt an unwelcome tug of old memory. Surely not, though —it couldn't be her, this far south?

The doctor pulled back a cloth covering a body on a nearby

pallet, and gently placed the head where it had been joined in life. Young, headless: it didn't take a genius to realise this was the reassembly of the murdered messenger boy.

'Your thoughts, my lady?'

Quintus jumped a little. He hadn't misheard the first time; judging by the doctor's respectful address, the woman must be some local priestess or noble. Why here, in the hospital? Then he realised. Of course, this was Aquae Sulis, the renowned healing spring and temple of Sulis Minerva. The woman must be part of the Goddess's cult here.

Without hesitation she picked up the gory head, looking carefully at the severed neck. She even sniffed it; again Quintus was taken aback. She ran her fingers over the neck stump.

'One stroke, a clean cut of great force by an expert. I should say no more than two days ago.' The doctor nodded gravely.

Quintus twisted the bronze ring on his fourth finger in an attempt to still his suddenly shaking hands. Memories poured back, but he did not want to believe it. Could it be true?

His gaze shifted to the doctor. The little man seemed to fit here: the type of mediocre medical officer to end up in a clinic at the end of the world. Nothing out of the ordinary, apart from his respectful manner with this native woman. What had he called her? "Lady Julia"?

Quintus watched as the woman peered closely at the dead boy's face. She opened his mouth and, searching with her slim fingers, took out a small crushed sprig. It was mangled and bloody but two whiteish berries were still attached to the stem. She sighed, and closed her eyes fleetingly. Her movements had slightly disturbed the line of her white *stola*; it slid down a little, revealing the neckline of the brown tunic underneath. On top of the tunic lay an unusual necklace, a ring of yellow-gold owls. Minerva's owlets, linked together to form a circle of gold around her beautiful arched neck.

Quintus stared at her. He felt sick, a rising nausea that had nothing to do with the dead boy and the stuffy little morgue, and everything to do with long-suppressed memories of horror, pain and long slow recovery. It *was* her, the girl from the north. Damn her! He thought he had completely crushed the shock of his losses: first his brother, then the girl. *This* girl, now a beautiful disdainful woman, who had reappeared in utterly the wrong place and time. He forced himself to speak.

'Lady Julia, may I know your status here?' He tried to speak evenly but even to his own ears he sounded stiff and suspicious. The woman's glance dropped to his hand. Then she looked at him with palpable hostility. What right had *she* to be hostile? Quintus had never been raked by such angry eyes, scorched by such a gaze of burning blue. But yes, he had—once. A long time ago, a long way from here.

"Don't you know, Frumentarius? Shouldn't I be asking you — why are *you* here?'

Quintus turned abruptly and left the room, ignoring the startled call of the doctor and a whistle of surprise from Tiro. He couldn't stay in that room, where claws he had long thought sheathed would tear down the defences he had built with such effort. If he had stayed any longer all the calm control he had built over the years would desert him, and leave him to the mercy of his feelings. That couldn't be allowed to happen, not in front of her. There could be nothing between them now, once the business of the dead boy was resolved. Quintus was a senior Roman officer, and by Mithras, his pride would hold him together. At least till he got outside.

In the dark courtyard garden, faintly scented by rosemary bushes, he strode around until his leg struck a bench. He sat down heavily. His heart was racing and he still felt nauseous and light-headed. He tried to watch his breathing as he had learned in the east. It was no good; the thudding of his pulse and racing thoughts were too distracting. Unbidden, a long tunnel of memory opened and swallowed him.

It had been a golden start to his military career: his first active service in a staff job with his father's proud Praetorian Guard, campaigning with the great Emperor Septimius Severus in exotic Britannia. Then Septimius had died suddenly in early 211 while putting down yet another rebellion in the far north of the island. *I wasn't even on duty when they cremated my lord*, he reflected bitterly. *So many funerals I didn't attend. Too stupid to avoid that Caledonian warrior with the blue-painted face. I stood there, transfixed by the deaths around me, too slow to act. The Caledonian slewed sideways in the mud, dodged my gladius and slashed his long native sword deep into my leg. Had it not been for Gaius… And later I'd been too weak to mourn the Emperor, too near death myself even to be told.*

A prickle came from the mass of old scars scything slantwise down his thigh, a faint reminder of the time he had thought despairingly that his career was over. But as the harsh northern winter gave way grudgingly to spring, he slowly healed in the Eboracum military hospital.

There had been a girl in the forum. A girl who glanced at him as he hobbled around the square on his first foray away from the army medics. He hadn't got far. His bad leg collapsed under him, and he would have fallen had the girl not caught him. She was tall for a young girl, well-dressed. He was surprised that she had no escort. She told him later that she routinely slipped away from her grandmother's elderly maid.

'Caecilia is dull and slow. Anyway, what harm can I come to in my mother's beloved city?' The girl smiled, and he felt the cool northern light brighten into gold around her. She explained that she was visiting from the south, staying with her maternal grandmother while she trained as a healer at the new riverside Temple of Serapis.

Quintus saw the image of that girl, clear as cut glass. Her grey robe was plain and her long fair hair braided into a simple plait. But her necklace of golden owls proclaimed her high status, as did her educated voice and the grace of her movements. She smelled of rosewater. She sat with him, talked to him, walked with him every afternoon as the limp slowly lessened. It became a habit to find her waiting outside the hospital, chatting to the orderlies and even the younger medics. She seemed interested in everything around her.

It was a time of magic. The days lengthened into a perfect summer of swift-song and amber evenings. They explored the quieter parts of Eboracum, finding nooks in the pale grey-stone buildings that allowed privacy for a young couple intent only on each other. For a time he forgot his nightmares, forgot he was a Roman soldier. Until he received a letter from Rome.

His mother wrote that his father was in political difficulties. Enemies in the Senate were turning against him. His heart turned over as he read this. His father was a proud man of old Roman integrity. It was a deadly combination in those times under the new Emperor Caracalla.

His mother, however, was resourceful. She had made plans that would save the family, she wrote, even as her husband fell from influence. She had arranged an advantageous match for Quintus with the daughter of an old friend of wealth and high esteem. This marriage would restore the family's reputation, perhaps allowing his sister to marry respectably also. He must return to Rome immediately. She was sure his sense of duty would bring him back quickly.

Sitting in the dark on a damp splintered bench in Aquae Sulis thirteen years later, Quintus remembered how love for his father and anxiety for Lucilla had driven him home. The pain and loss of the Caledonian battle was buried deep, so it had seemed then. He reasoned he would still have his career and his family, no matter what he left behind in this distant grey province. His duty was clear.

The army medics discharged him reluctantly, cautioning him not to strain the newly-healed leg. He was to ship out with a cohort of Legion 11 Parthica departing Britannia the day after next.

He tried to tell her, tried to explain, but she wouldn't understand. She turned and ran, her fine-woven summer *palla* dragging over the paving of the forum as he stumbled and called after her, his voice rough over the lump in his throat. His leg let him down, he couldn't catch her. He waited in the forum all that day and the next, the last day, but she never came back. He wrote a note begging her forgiveness and had a messenger take it to the house of her grandmother. No reply ever came. So he rode away with the Parthica. He didn't even know her family name, or where her real home was. On that desperate voyage back to Rome he thought he was leaving Britannia for ever.

It was too late to save his father. While he was still travelling his father had slipped quietly away, his life ebbing with his blood into the warm bathwater. An honourable suicide, they said. But at least he arrived in time to prevent his open-hearted young sister being forced into a loveless match with some useful ally of his mother. His mother was so enraged and humiliated that she rarely spoke to him again. But he had done the right thing for Lucilla.

And now here he was, back in the one place that hurt more than Rome. On a mission rapidly getting dangerous and deadly. What would he give to just walk away, put it all behind him?

He laughed softly. Walk away from his duty? Leave that poor headless boy unavenged? Betray his Emperor? That was not the Valerian way. No, he was stuck here in this barbaric province until the job was over. No matter the cost in hiding his anguish from these strangers, the young centurion, his illiterate provincial assistant Tiro ... and Julia. Whatever and whoever she was now.

Chapter Seven

By the time Tiro came to find him Quintus was his usual reserved self.

Marcellus Crispus was waiting to accompany them to his small fort on the other side of the Abona, having left Piso and an orderly to their solemn tasks with the dead boy. There was no sign of Julia. Quintus told Marcellus about the attack at Calleva.

Tiro said, 'I still wonder if I've seen that bloke somewhere before. Bloody great hole he knocked in my head, though. No wonder I can't remember now.'

'I doubt we'll ever identify him now.' Such attacks at a well-run *mansio* were rare, and without more evidence they were left in the dark. As they walked the short distance along the riverbank, the centurion broke into the *frumentarius's* thoughts.

'Quintus Valerius?'

'Mmm?' Quintus was calculating the odds of it being a random mugging attempt, and not liking the answer.

'The Lady Julia,' the young redhead looked abashed, but ploughed on, 'she had to leave to see her patients before you came back into the morgue. Anyway, Surgeon Piso asked me to pass on a couple of suggestions she made.'

'Did he now?'

Discouraged by the dry tone, Marcellus paused. Tiro winked at him. Quintus took no notice. He really would have to put the Britisher in his place.

'Um, yes sir. She said the dead boy looked familiar. The lady is the sister of Magistrate Marcus Aurelianus of Bo Gwelt in the Summer Country. He's the ancestral leader of the Durotriges of Lindinis. She knows the local people well, having grown up there, and I believe she acted as her widowed brother's hostess until he re-married a few years ago.'

Quintus stopped dead, thinking. *Sister of a tribal noble; resident of the Summer Country near Vebriacum; thinks she knows this dead boy. Could there be links here, between this murder and Vebriacum's missing silver?*

'And, sir?'

'Yes?'

'She suggested we look again in his dispatch bag.' Quintus ground his teeth.

They entered the fort. Centurion Crispus nodded to his guard to shut the Principia doors. He laid out on his wooden desk a large leather bag with a shoulder strap. A dark liquid stain ran from the outer flap, tacky but evidently soaked well into the leather. Quintus wrinkled his nose.

'Blood.' He lifted the flap, reaching in to search the interior. 'Nothing in here. So much for the *matron docta* and her — ' His finger jagged on a rough sliver of wood wedged hard into the base seam.

'What …? Tiro, your tweezers.'

Tiro pursed his lips and glanced at Marcellus Crispus. He handed Quintus his toiletry set on a brass ring. Quintus used the tweezers to carefully pull a fragment of birchwood into the candlelight. Only a shard remained of what had been a thin note tablet.

'May I?' asked the centurion. Quintus grunted, and the young commander held the shard closer to the candle light. 'Very little to make out, but I think on the letter side I can see three characters: *TER*. On the address side—hmm, wait a moment.'

Tiro was frustrated. He had excellent eyesight, but without the magic trick of deciphering the little black ink strokes he could offer no help. Maybe the *frumentarius* was right; perhaps he should learn to read.

Marcellus Crispus looked again, angling into the light the splintered edge where the sender's address should be.

'Yes, I thought so. There *is* a bit more, perhaps part of a sender's name - *VEB*. Nothing more. Perhaps in better daylight, tomorrow?'

Both young men looked at Quintus. His eyes were half-closed, as if seeking inspiration from the Gods.

'Centurion Crispus — Marcellus, if I may? I think after all we are going be spending time working together.' The centurion looked puzzled.

'I would normally hand a case like this over to you, being the chance killing of a local boy of no particular status. We are already on an urgent Imperial mission. But this murder may have something to tell us about that investigation too. I think we should collaborate, if you agree?'

This was far and away the most gracious request Tiro had yet heard Quintus make. But Tiro had a pressing question of his own.

'Sir, Frumentarius Valerius — what have you found out about the dead boy?'

'The boy? Nothing. But we may be able to discover who sent him on his errand, and why. Marcellus, who runs the mines at Vebriacum in the Summer Country? Not the owner — I mean his manager there, his man of business?'

'I don't know, sir. We're in Dobunni territory here, and I have no jurisdiction with the Durotriges that far south. But,' he paused in thought,' the Lady Julia Aureliana might. Especially as she thinks she recognises the boy.'

Quintus groaned inwardly. *Mighty Mithras, why is this mission such a mess? Look on my years of service in your worship - surely they mean something to you? I will make whatever sacrifice is best pleasing, my Lord, if you can help me see my way more clearly. Preferably without involving the Lady Julia.*

'Right. Could we stay here at the fort for a night or two, Marcellus? Discreetly, though—from now on we should stay under cover. Tiro's horse has gone lame anyway, and mine needs to go back to the *mansio* here. Can you supply two horses or ponies? Not obviously of Army breeding, no Army saddles.

'We need to carry on looking like civilians, Tiro. But before we leave Aquae Sulis, we're going to pay a morning call on the *matron docta*.'

Quintus could hardly believe he had said this. He saw with resignation Tiro trying to keep a straight face. Julia was the very last person he wanted to see. But he had many years of professionalism to call upon, and he needed whatever local information she might have. He hoped he could remember that, and keep his bearing polite and proper when he saw the lady again.

As for Tiro—he'd be laughing on the other side of his face when they got up before cockcrow in the morning. He wanted to catch Lady Julia at home in private, early. He needed to know who to speak to at Vebriacum, and it wasn't going to be the owner Bulbo.

It was barely daybreak the following day when Quintus and Tiro knocked at Julia's front door. She owned an elegant little townhouse by the river, stretching back from a narrow frontage and embellished with skilful carvings. Bay trees in white marble stands stood duty on either side of a miniature portico. Quintus glanced down at his nondescript tunic, checked his cloak was arrayed neatly and stood straight. His hands felt clammy despite the morning chill.

Quintus Valerius, son of Senator Bassianus Valerius, scion of one of the oldest families in Rome, should fear no-one, he reminded himself fiercely. *This woman means nothing to you; you owe her nothing and can expect nothing back.* He pushed back at the shadows of past pain and loss trying to rush him. *Remember, you are a soldier of Rome!*

At his knock a sturdy young woman opened the door. Her chestnut hair was uncovered and she clutched a thick chequered shawl over her drab tunic. A scent of lavender clung to her skirts.

She frowned at them. Quintus felt taken aback, a feeling that was becoming too familiar since arriving on this forsaken island. It was unusual not to have a male porter, but this servant, judging by her confident bearing, was more than a common household slave.

'My name is Frumentarius Quintus Valerius. I am here to consult your mistress, Lady Julia Aureliana.'

'I know who you are. Sir.' The young woman blocked the doorway, rounded arms folded across her chest. Quintus found himself missing the deference of Roman slaves. A window shutter creaked over their heads. Someone else in the household was stirring.

The woman glanced up, and moved aside to let them in.

'Best step inside quick, you'll be waking up … ,' she hesitated, 'the whole household.'

Tiro saluted her with a nod. She looked straight through him while his best smile went to waste. She didn't ask his name either, before turning to stalk through the vestibule ahead of them. She threw open a door into a narrow pretty room at the back of the house. There was a dim dawnlit view through tall glazed windows, and a glimpse of a little courtyard to the rear.

'Good morning, gentlemen.'

Julia stood near a brazier, wearing a long robe. There was a bowl of spring flowers, daffodils and crocuses, on a side table, but the room held the faint scent of roses. Her owl necklet was on vivid display against the sky-blue of her *tunica*. She looked remote, untouchable. Quintus longed to rush to her; longed to dash from the room. He stood paralysed, stiff and cold.

'Some spiced wine, perhaps?' Julia nodded to the other woman. 'Britta? If you would be so kind.'

The door closed softly.

'I have very little time to spare, Frumentarius. Urgent family duties await me. Could we get to the point, please?'

That explained the more formal clothing today. Julia looked more the *matrona docta* this morning, and was clearly a wealthy woman. Quintus wondered about her husband. He hesitated, debating whether it would be good form to ask after her spouse. She wore no ring, he noted, twisting his own round his finger. Perhaps a widow?

She was watching him. A dismissive look crossed her face. What was it? Disdain, pride, impatience?

'Lady Julia, it's good of you to see us so early.'

There was a stony silence, broken when Britta came back into the room carrying a bronze tray with a carved glass decanter and four matching cups. Steam rose lazily as the housekeeper poured the wine. Despite himself, Quintus relaxed at the rich smell of cinnamon.

Tiro hurried forward to help Britta serve. She glared at him.

'Madam,' he murmured, grinning. She tossed her head and turned her back on him to set the tray down.

'I'll leave you in peace, my lady,' she told her mistress. Tiro bowed to Britta as she left the room. The plaid shawl slid off one plump white shoulder as the door shut. Quintus saw Tiro was enjoying himself, and felt irritated.

'Lady Julia,' Quintus said again.

'Frumentarius?' A rigid look.

This wasn't going to work. He was determined not to bring back the painful past. It was a long time ago, and there was nothing between them now. He had hoped they could have a polite conversation like the strangers they were. He tried again.

'Lady Julia, I need information, and think your connections in the Summer Country may be of help.'

'Help for *you*.' It was said so scornfully, that if he had not been looking directly at her he would not have known that she shook from head to foot. The most minor of movements, but it cut through him like a knife.

Tiro broke in.

'My lady, we seek - '

Quintus spoke across Tiro; his voice felt dry as sand in his throat. 'I'm told you recognised the dead boy.'

Julia hesitated. 'He looked familiar. I can't be sure, though.'

Quintus tossed the wooden fragment onto the table.

'Time is pressing, Lady Julia. As I think you know, this was inside his despatch bag. Can you tell me anything about the writing?'

She picked up the birchwood note, turning it over carefully. She seemed to arrive at a decision.

'If I tell you what I know, Frumentarius, can I rely on you to protect someone, an innocent party?'

Impatience rose in him; he shook it off. Full professionalism, nothing less. That was his duty.

'My job is to protect the Emperor's interests, and ensure justice is done in his name. I have the power to call up witnesses, and the power to protect them.'

Julia turned the fragment over once more, then handed it back to Quintus.

'The boy is — *was* — Catus. His father was a farm worker on my family's estate in the Summer Country. He and his sister lost their mother when he was born, and were eventually sold into slavery by their father, who soon after died of drink. I...' she sighed, and paused a moment. 'I got to know Catus and his sister Enica after Catus fell out of an orchard tree scrumping for apples and broke his arm. I was training with Demetrios back then, still living at home with my brother at Bo Gwelt. The injury took some time to heal, and I got to know the sweet little boy well. He was so affectionate to Enica. I felt really sorry when their father sold them to the Iscalis estate. But I kept an eye on them when I could. Later I helped Catus become apprenticed to the mines manager at nearby Vebriacum, carrying out errands and delivering messages. He was very close to his sister, who works in the kitchens at Iscalis villa.'

'Iscalis? Owned by Claudius Bulbo?'

'Yes. The letters VEB here could refer to Bulbo's lead mines at Vebriacum. And TER? I may know who that is, too.' She paused again, apparently weighing up something. Then she surprised him by veering away onto a different subject. Her voice seemed to harden.

'Frumentarius, tell me why you still wear that ring with the bronze owl.'

Quintus looked at Tiro. 'Tiro, go and ready the horses for departure.'

Tiro looked disappointed but left the room promptly. The Briton must now realise there was something wrong between the lady and his boss, but Quintus had no intention of revealing what.

Chapter Eight

It was cold outside. Tiro stamped his studded boots against the cobbles to shake the feeling back into his feet. Mist rose from the nearby Abona as daylight strengthened into full morning. He tried not to hear the raised voices inside the house.

The shuttered window above his head opened again. This time there was no Britta to prevent him from looking. A young girl peered through the open window, dark wavy hair escaping from a shawl over her head.

'Who are you?'

Tiro grinned. 'I'm Tiro. Who are you?'

'Aurelia. This is my Aunt Julia's house. I'm just staying here. I really live at Bo Gwelt with Father. And with my horrid stepmother, Claudia. Why do you sound funny?'

Tiro bowed. 'My excuse, pretty lady, must be my birth in the great city of Londinium.'

'Oh, Londinium! How I long to go there! Is it true the streets are paved with gold, and the walls stretch forever?'

'The streets *are* paved, but not with gold, Miss Aurelia.' Tiro frowned a little. Even he had to admit that Londinium's streets were often filthy, full of waste and mud after high tides and rain. And the city had shrunk somewhat since the plague of his grandparents' time, he had heard. 'But the walls are certainly tall.'

'Why are you here?'

Tiro puffed out his broad chest a little. 'I can't tell you that. Except to say I'm assisting Frumentarius Quintus Valerius from Rome.'

But the girl had stopped listening. Something else had attracted her attention.

'Hush! Over there! What's that?' Before he could look, the shutters were banged close. Tiro shrugged. No accounting for the nobility. Then the front door opened quietly, and a thin young girl slipped out. There was something at once engaging and arresting about her. She was dressed in a fine linen shift, with a thick plaid shawl clipped at her shoulder by a bronze brooch, and shiny leather slippers on her feet. Not quite enough clothing for the briskness of this March morning, but the girl seemed heedless of the cold. She darted across the road, her dark curls tangled and flying, and leaned down to peer over the stone balustrade towards the river path below.

'I thought so!' She pointed triumphantly. Tiro, joining her, saw something moving feebly in the reeds at the river's edge. Knowing his duty as a Roman soldier, he heaved himself over the balustrade and searched through the reed bed, emerging with a near-drowned little bundle.

'Is it dead?' Her face was a picture of dismay.

'No, I think not.' He stripped off his *birrus*, and folded it round the pitiful soaked creature. He had never until now appreciated quite how versatile a garment the *birrus* was. He hoped the mud wouldn't be as hard to shift as the messenger boy's blood stains had been. The girl grabbed the bundle out of his arms, cooing over the shivering animal.

'It's a puppy,' she said unnecessarily. 'Not very old. Some cruel slave has thrown him in the river. Poor little darling!'

Tiro forbore to point out that any slave tasked with ridding the world of an unwanted cur would have little say in the matter. Aurelia carried on crooning, holding the little dog tight against her bony chest. A small tongue slid out and licked her face. She giggled, then her face dropped when she saw Britta appear in the doorway.

'Britta, please say I may keep him! He is so little, and cold, and all licky. He needs a good home. I'll call him Cerberus, after the guardian dog of Hades.'

'Will you now, Miss Aurelia?'

Britta sounded stern, but Tiro saw her smile. The scent of lavender had followed her outside. 'You know we have no room for a dog here. He would have to go back home with you. Maybe Morcant has room in his kennels for another dog. Although,' her forehead wrinkled as she looked at the tiny creature, all damp fluff and wagging tail, 'I doubt this one will make a hunting dog. Or a guard dog.' She looked at Tiro reflectively. Once again, he knew his duty. He held his arms out for the bundled puppy.

'Leave him with me, Miss Aurelia. I'll look after him till we can either deliver him to your home, or find somewhere else for him.'

He saw Aurelia's face crumple, and added hastily, 'And then when you're old enough to have your own house, he can join you there, can't he, Mistress Britta?'

Aurelia nodded and handed the puppy over, partially assuaged. Just in time. A swift booted step sounded behind them. Quintus looked pale and taut-faced. Tiro doubted the interview with Lady Julia had prospered.

'Oh, sir! Are you the Imperial Investigator? All the way from Rome! Tiro's been telling me about Londinium, but I bet Rome is even more wonderful. I've never been anywhere bigger than Corinium.'

Tiro looked at his boss, expecting a thaw in the face of this artless charm. But Quintus was looking more wooden than ever. And staring at the young girl. Tiro looked again at the girl, then at his boss. He wondered—

Britta surged across, tucking Aurelia under her encircling arm. 'My lady, back with you out of the cold. You'll see Cerberus again soon, I'll make no doubt.'

As they went back inside, Britta turned to glance at Tiro. Nearly a smile, he was sure. The door slammed shut. Tiro sighed, admiration spreading across his face.

'Now that is my kind of woman.'

Quintus was still white-faced, his grey eyes fixed on the closed door. Voices had been raised, regrettably unclear. Tiro shrugged. Not for him to comment. He thought it best not to mention the dog, either. Or his promise to Aurelia. He slipped the sleeping puppy into his saddle bag and followed his stiff-faced master back to the fort. He was looking forward to a quiet afternoon. Maybe a few games of dice with the troopers, and a nap to make up for all the early starts on this trip.

The next morning they took delivery of two horses provided by Marcellus, a chestnut with a white flash, and a docile dun, and headed south. They didn't get far. In less than a mile Tiro heard the shortening thuds of a galloping horse pulling up behind them. A trooper with the badge of the Aquae Sulis cohort on his breast flung himself off his mount, and saluted breathlessly. Tiro felt the drag of déjà vu. What now?

'Greetings from Centurion Crispus, sir, and would you please come back to the fort urgently?'

Quintus frowned. 'We are on urgent Imperial business. What does your commander want this time?'

'There's been a death in the city, sir. Unexpected, like.' The guard shifted feet, his mouth twisting. 'It may be murder, sir. The commander was most anxious to catch you before you left the city. He thinks this death may be related to your inquiry.'

Another murder — related? Tiro gave the *frumentarius* a quick glance. Quintus was as grim and silent as ever. Tiro scratched his flaxen-haired head and turned his horse to follow the boss's chestnut.

Marcellus Crispus was waiting outside the fort, his horse saddled and ready.

'It's an old woman, sir, name of Velvinna. She was found this morning by her household slaves, lying on her bedchamber floor, unconscious and not breathing. Her heart was barely beating. She died within a few minutes.'

Quintus cut in. 'By Mithras, man! Old women die of heart disease all the time. Send for the priests, or the doctor, or even that Aureliana woman, and let me get on with my mission.'

Marcellus flushed. The young man had such thin pale skin under his freckles, every pulse of blood looked visible. But he stood his ground firmly.

'Sir, that isn't all. Velvinna may have been murdered. She came to me only a few days ago with rumours of a resurgence of Druidism in the area. Without definite information I couldn't act. Now I fear she has been silenced. You must see the evidence for yourself. I urge you to attend the scene, as the ranking investigative officer present in Aquae Sulis. Sir.' And he had the nerve to snap off a magnificent salute before mounting his horse. Quintus merely nodded once to the rigid young centurion, and followed his lead back across the bridge.

Chapter Nine

'Come on,' Julia said to Aurelia over a light breakfast of wheat pancakes and honey with a scattering of dried dates. 'It's time for Britta's gossip ration. Let's go to the baths.'

She forced herself to sound light-hearted. She barely picked at her breakfast. The recent second meeting with Quintus had left her fighting a rising tide of resentment, streaked with currents of longing. How dared he suggest she was at fault? He had abandoned her, left her to cope alone with Aurelia, (*whom he never knew about*), and ruined her for marriage *(would she really ever have considered marrying, once he had taken her heart away with him?).* And now she was so distracted she found it difficult to focus on Catus, though she was burning to track down his killer. Julia stared at the untouched beaker of warm milk in front of her, mulling over the poor boy and wondering how she could help uncover his murderer. The mistletoe berries: that was a curious touch, and not the only one. If she wanted to see justice done she would have to accept the official inquiry. But there might still be ways Julia could shed light on the murder, though that would inevitably bring her back into contact with the Imperial Investigator. She willed herself to shunt aside her resentment for now, and pay attention to next steps. Yes, the baths. Who knew what she might uncover in that hotbed of local telltales? It would be worth the slight delay in leaving for Bo Gwelt. And amuse Aurelia, while Julia thought more about her niece's troubles too.

Aurelia had been mooning around the house since the early morning visit, wondering aloud every five minutes how Cerberus was doing, and where Tiro and the Investigator were by now. The promise of the outing to the baths galvanised her, and they set off with Britta after breakfast.

It was a drier day, still chilly. The town bustled with visitors. They passed the theatre on the way to the baths. The noise of music clashing out on cymbals and a battered horn drew their attention, and they paused to see the fun. An actor was declaiming outside the entrance to the theatre, publicising the current production. It was apparently a jolly comedy by Terence. In contrast the actor looked thoroughly miserable, the victim of a streaming cold. In between wiping his nose on his robes and coughing, he was regaling passersby with snippets of comic dialogue and making exaggerated claims for the wit and beauty of the leading actress. A small crowd began to gather, laughing and making fun of the actor's red eyes and running nose. The poor man tried to rise above the teasing, pitching his hoarse voice higher.

'... with luxuriant red locks falling below her waist, and roving black eyes, she's the loveliest slave you'll ever see. And best of all, folks, she turns out to be a free woman of fortune. Our lucky hero has a lot to look forward to.' As he spoke a willowy young woman slid through the theatre doorway, moving gracefully to his side. Her face was obscured by a translucent veil, but as the actor reached the end of his pitch she whipped off her head-covering to reveal a pale face and a mass of tumbling auburn hair cascading down her back. The crowd gasped, and the actor beckoned them forward.

'Buy your tickets now, ladies and gentlemen. Don't risk the disappointment of a full house if you want to see the lovely virgin Fulminata on stage tonight!'

Julia laughed. The poor man needed a hot posset for his cold, not the charms of Fulminata, who Julia doubted was a virgin.

Aurelia, not a natural lover of literature or drama, was hopping from foot to foot despite the warmth of her cloak. Julia obediently walked on to the baths, where they joined a short queue at the entrance. A man with stubbled jaws in front of them was bewailing the poor state of commerce in the town.

'If you ask me, Docilianus, the town council have got it in for us local merchants. Will they lease me a decent pitch to sell my shoes and leathers? Will they hell! *Over there outside the forum is good enough for you, Septimus.*' Docilianus shrugged his big shoulders. He was shielded from the morning chill by a good-quality *birrus*. Julia remembered how she'd lost a scarf herself in these baths; he'd need to keep an eye on that *birrus*.

Inside the changing room Julia paid a slave to guard their

clothes. They headed through to the tepid and sweat rooms before relaxing with a scented massage. Julia greeted a range of acquaintances; it was a busy morning at the baths. Aurelia had gamely gone to plunge into the circular frigid pool. She rushed back.

'Aunt Julia, Britta—you'll never guess what I've just seen. Ladies paying to have pigeon dung and wee put on their hair!'

'Some people will do anything to get blonde hair, Miss,' said Britta. She ran her fingers through her own gleaming locks. It was her one vanity.

A loud slap, a shriek and the smell of burnt hair emanated from an adjoining salon.

'Ooh, look! It's that fat woman over there. She was having her hair curled. The bath slave over-heated the curling irons, and burnt off some of her hair. So funny! May I swim in the Great Bath, Aunt?'

Julia, who felt a little sorry for the slave, was preoccupied in looking around the Great Bath. She nodded permission for Aurelia to join a group of shrieking young girls splashing in the big pool.

Ah, there she was, her old mentor and friend, Velvinna. Julia's brow cleared. She asked Britta to keep an eye on Aurelia, then excused her way behind a loitering young woman, robed and hooded. Stray locks of a rich red escaped the hood. Julia muttered a hasty apology as the girl swivelled, glanced at her and edged away. She had remarkable black eyes in a very pale face, Julia noticed, now squeezing past an attendant bath slave who was carrying a basket of unguents and massage oils. Julia rotated her own relaxed shoulders, and thought she should come more often to bathe and enjoy a massage.

Velvinna was waiting for her in one of the alcoves. The two women embraced. Velvinna stepped back, apologising as she coughed.

'Sorry, my dear. Don't get too close — I seem to have caught this wretched cold that's passing round. How are you, Julia?' Julia glanced down at her friend's ankles, showing under her tunic. They looked less swollen than the last time the two had met.

Velvinna caught her glance, and laughed.

'Yes, yes. *Physician, heal thyself,* of colds and heart disease. And yes, I am being cautious with the correct dosage of the foxglove, just as you prescribed. I'm sure this cold won't kill me, Julia, but I am getting older and one day my heart will give out despite your excellent medicine.'

Julia summoned a slave and ordered honey cakes and watered wine with added ginger for Velvinna's cold. They settled in for a chat, catching up on news of mutual colleagues and general town gossip. Velvinna was well-liked, a respected wise-woman with connections across the Dobunni and other regional tribes. Their talk paused for a moment. Julia saw that Aurelia was still occupied in racing her friends across the pool, with Britta watching nearby. She took the opportunity.

'Velvinna, I wondered what you might make of this?' She reached into her bath bag, and pulled out a torn scrap of coarse white cloth. There were a few drops of some dried liquid, red-brown, smudged at one end. She also pulled out a piece of twig.

Her friend took them carefully. She sucked in her breath, and cast a glance around the alcove, pausing until the young hooded woman moved on. She looked worried.

'This cloth is Druid-woven bleached linen. Blood-stained. And a crushed branch of mistletoe, as I guess you well know. Where did you come by these, Julia?'

Julia held her friend's gaze. It wasn't necessary to explain that she had picked the fabric scrap up from the morgue floor where it had fallen unnoticed as the dead boy's head had been unwrapped. She was sure neither the Londinium *stator* nor his superior had fully understood the significance. Julia had, though, and was troubled enough to show Velvinna the worrying scrap.

'I don't want to upset you with all the distressing details, my dear. What I can tell you is that these were found at the scene of the death of a boy of my own people, someone I knew and cared for. He and his sister were of our Summer Country estate, and I feel some sense of continuing duty to them both. The boy was far from home, alone, and I believe was carrying an important message. He didn't deserve the cruel attack that ended his life.

He *does* deserve all my efforts as a noble of the Durotriges to avenge him.

'I wanted to ask you, Velvinna - have you heard any rumours of trouble brewing lately? After this, I am worried for our tribespeople.'

Velvinna took her younger friend's hands in her own.

'That's a terrible story, Julia. You must do the right thing in the eyes of the Goddess, and of course I'll help as I can. Well, I have heard a few stray murmurs. In recent weeks there have been mutterings that some of the young folk seem dissatisfied. Difficult to know why — times are no harder than usual. We've had several good harvests, and the awful plague of my parents' time seems to have died away. Thanks to the bountiful grace of our Lady the Goddess Sulis.'

Both women bowed their heads a moment.

'And?' prompted Julia.

Velvinna smiled. 'You know me too well, oh sharp-eyed pupil! I *am* uneasy. Parents worried about their children. Odd comings and goings at night. The young men of the town, the worse for a few beers, marching down the street, knocking over market stalls and frightening people, shouting 'Make the Dobunni great again!' Some of us older ones spoke to the centurion at the garrison here. He soon sorted that lot out — banged a few heads together and took the ringleaders in for a talking-to and a night in the cells to cool off. He's a good lad, Centurion Crispus, he handles matters well without causing resentment. '

Julia nodded and smiled. She too respected the quiet young red-headed soldier. It was Marcellus who had asked her to make discreet enquiries.

'Yes, Marcellus Crispus is a good commander, and knows the people of Aquae Sulis well. But I sense there is something else on your mind. You know your confidences are safe with me.'

Her friend had a worried look on her face. 'Well, Julia, I've heard there is a White One back here in our territory.'

Julia recoiled. The White Ones, the Druids of old, had once been all-powerful. But since Rome came they had been outlawed, and banished from public view. It was generations ago since the last one had been whispered of. Especially in this town with its sacred spa, the home of the mighty Goddess Sulis Minerva. The Lady Minerva was revered by both British and Romans.

'A White One?' She repeated the words, shaken. So perhaps a Druid *had* been behind the attack on Catus, as the mistletoe and bleached linen cloth suggested. But why? If Quintus was right, that attack had been to prevent news of a fraud reaching Londinium. Why would Druids associate themselves with such matters?

Velvinna blew her nose, and nodded. 'Only the merest word, my dear. Still, I've heard that same story from several sources, level-headed people I trust.'

Julia ran a smoothing hand across her forehead.

'I'm happy to go with your instincts, Velvinna. There is no-one I trust better. But I need to know more, and quickly, if I'm to prevent trouble. My brother Marcus will need to know, too.'

Velvinna stood, shaking out her skirts.

'Well, my dear, as always you remind me of what should be done. I will sound out some folk who might be in the know, including our Sisters here in Aquae Sulis. How can I best reach you with any news?'

Julia thought. She trusted Anicius implicitly, but all sorts came and went through his hospital wards. This had to be handled discreetly. She would need to send word quickly to Marcellus if she did uncover anything.

She thought briefly of Quintus, the Imperial Investigator with the authority she might need; could she get a message to him? That thought was instantly dismissed. He didn't trust her, and she wasn't sure she could bear to ever see him again. Anyway, she had no idea where he was now, or how to safely contact him.

'Send to my house, Velvinna. And keep Centurion Crispus informed too. I need to go to Bo Gwelt soon to see my brother about this and other family matters, but I'll delay leaving till tomorrow in case you need me. If I'm not at home, you can trust my staff to forward a message quickly.'

'Thank you. I wish I had spoken to you sooner. Sometimes I

think I'm just a silly old woman. But I know the Goddess Sulis Minerva is guiding our steps. Remember that, Julia, and have faith.'

Julia kissed the other woman, and went to fetch Aurelia away from her friends. Britta raised her eyebrows in mute question, and Julia nodded slightly. Rightly or wrongly, she'd set matters in train with Velvinna and the Sisterhood, and there was no turning back.

They left the bathhouse, heading to the marketplace to shop for supper. At the Sacred Spring a queue of people waited to send urgent messages and requests to the Goddess in her holy pool. A chattering flock of young women muffled up in bright mantles were in the line. They'd probably be wanting blessings for marriage or fertility, or both. Julia saw that another of the party was a man, tall and fair. His sky-blue cloak swung as he walked away. Julia smiled; one of those girls was likely to find her request of the Goddess answered if she wasn't careful. Then she spotted the burly man they'd seen earlier. Docilianus was angrily dictating a curse tablet. He leaned over a nervous clerk, shivering a little without his cloak in the fresh spring wind. *'Docilianus son of Brucerus to the most holy goddess Sulis. I curse him who has stolen my hooded cloak, whether man or woman, slave or free, that the goddess Sulis inflicts death...'*

Julia smiled at Aurelia, who grinned back. They both worshipped the Goddess, valuing her interventions. But Julia doubted Minerva would deign to deal death in this case, no matter how valuable the *birrus* was to Docilianus.

As they made their way back across the Sacred Precinct later, laden with warm bread and two fresh plump capons, Julia paused at one of the altars. She often slipped a few coppers into the hot waters of the sacred spring. Today she placed three eggs on the altar, bowed her head and prayed. She did not see Minerva's image, as she often did in prayer, but she left the temple with her mind more at ease.

Dinner was a casual affair. Julia had adopted the family preference for sitting upright to eat rather than reclining on couches. *How do people manage to carry on looking elegant leaning on their elbows?* After roasted capons and garlicky wilted spring greens from their own garden, followed by spiced plums and a handful of walnuts each, they relaxed over the local wine. Britta always insisted on eating in the kitchen with the rest of the staff, but she came back into the dining room while Aurelia was telling Julia about a boy who had swum alongside her in the Great Bath. She had challenged a boy she knew to a race, knowing herself to be a strong swimmer, and beaten him hands down.

'And do you know what, Aunt? Drusus just got out of the bath, and stalked away sulking!'

'Mistress? I beg pardon. An urgent message. Would you step into your bookroom for a moment?' Britta was frowning, and shrugging a shoulder in Aurelia's direction. Julia excused herself, and closed the door as she joined her worried housekeeper.

'It was Velvinna, my lady. She's gone now. She refused to come in and wait, or be announced and join you at table. She said she wouldn't wait for an answer. I don't know what kind of household she thinks I run, that my lady's friends wouldn't be made welcome, dinnertime or no. I wonder she didn't send a messenger instead.'

Julia soothed Britta's ruffled pride, asking her to make her excuses to Aurelia. Then she locked herself in the bookroom to read Velvinna's birchwood message. It was short, and written in haste.

My dear, I dare not stay. I worry that I am followed, and do not wish to bring trouble to your house. I have good information that a meeting has been summoned by a White One, but not here in Aquae Sulis. You were right to be concerned about your people.

Can you go, or send someone to a town meeting in the forum in Lindinis of the northern Durotriges, at sunset in two days? You might get the answers you seek there.

Your friend.

Velvinna had not signed the letter, a measure of caution that underlined to Julia the potential danger. She hoped her friend had got home unmolested. She would send to check at first light in the morning.

Julia moved restlessly round the room, picking up things and putting them down in the wrong places. She was worried by Velvinna's letter. More than that, she was unsure of how she felt after the difficult meetings with Quintus. The last time she felt this way was many years ago, when she came back from Eboracum heart-broken and sickeningly pregnant.

Naturally it had been Britta—ever-practical —who had come to her rescue then, travelling north to Eboracum to fetch her young mistress home. It was a difficult journey. Julia vomited constantly, unable to keep food down or travel far before becoming exhausted. Britta developed a variety of cover stories in which her mistress had been afflicted by the gods, or was homesick, or had drunk foul water.

On their arrival back in the Summer Country, Britta's parents had offered a welcoming haven at Home Farm while Julia recovered from the journey. She was heart-broken and feeling low in body and spirits. She needed time to decide what was to be done.

Julia hesitated to tell her older brother about the baby. Julia and Marcus's parents had both died suddenly when a plague swept through some years ago. Julia was still a young child then, so Marcus and his wife Albania had brought Julia up until she left to stay with her grandmother in Eboracum. Julia loved Marcus, and dreaded upsetting him. He was a generous and cultured man, with a strong sense of duty and more conventional Roman attitudes than Julia herself. Nothing had been said yet, but she guessed Marcus had been expecting to see his only sister married in due course to one of the local landowners. He would have welcomed a love match, of course, being very fond of his sister. For her to be seduced and abandoned by a young Roman legionary he had never set eyes on—that would be more difficult for Marcus to accept.

She was relieved when Britta offered to fetch Julia's sister-in-law from Bo Gwelt. Together they came up with a plan regarding the unexpected infant. The sweet-hearted Albania was just the friend Julia needed. She overcame her husband's initial shock and hesitation, pointing out the truth in her gentle way: Marcus and she had no children, despite a decade of marriage. Though they rarely spoke of it, no amount of prayer, sacrifice and pilgrimages to Aquae Sulis had improved their fertility. This child was undoubtedly of the Aurelianus blood, and they could give it the best possible start in life and still protect Julia from scandal. The old grandmother in Eboracum need never know, either. Secretly, Albania knew Marcus would soon need the comfort of a child, and she was right. Barely a year after they had announced the birth of their daughter Aurelia, Albania died.

Over the years since, Julia occasionally wondered at how she had coped. She had been so young, of course, barely sixteen. To have such a love and lose it and to give up the child of that love, felt at times more than could be borne. But she *had* borne it, and had been rewarded by seeing Aurelia grow into the spirited much-loved daughter of the doting Marcus. It was obvious to Julia that Aurelia was blossoming at Bo Gwelt. Marcus deserved all the happiness the young girl brought him.

Once the blow of giving up her child had subsided a little, Julia took up the dual roles of independent *matron docta* and indulgent aunt. With a handsome legacy left by her Brigantian mother she set up her own household in Aquae Sulis, completed her healer training, and never regretted her single life. Being independent, learned and well-respected in her community suited her in a way a conventional marriage to a noble husband probably would not have done. She did, though, keep a close eye on Aurelia. The loss of her child was an ever-present burden, though for Aurelia's sake she never let her distress show. The pain of telling her daughter about the betrayal by the young Roman officer was more than Julia could face.

She never knew whether to be delighted or heartsick that Aurelia had the same grey eyes as Quintus.

Julia re-read Velvinna's letter. Midnight in two days. Just enough time. She asked Britta to have their packing done and the carriage prepared for a trip to Bo Gwelt the following day.

'An early start. I need to consult my brother urgently. Pack for you and me, and Aurelia, of course. My maid. And two grooms. And spare horses for Aurelia and me. Unless you...?'

'No, thank you, my lady.' Britta spoke forcefully. Country girl or no, one thing she did not hold with was sitting on large dirty beasts, bouncing up and down in mud and dust. Obviously they had to use mules or horses to pull the carriage, but at least then the animals were a good breathing distance away and had postilions to control them. And there was a canvas roof of sorts over their heads to keep out the worst of the weather. 'My gratitude to you, Lady Julia, but I prefer to ride in the carriage with the maid.'

Julia laughed. She did not mention why they were leaving in such a hurry. That knowledge could be dangerous, and Britta was one of the people she wanted to protect. Along with Aurelia.

Grey eyes, dark hair, slight wiry build, compact energy betrayed by constant impulsive movement, all these reminded her of Aurelia's father. But this older Quintus was changed — restrained, measured, disciplined ... cold.

Damn! Why didn't he just stay out of my life? I'd finally begun to make peace with the past, and now he's back here and causing more trouble. I won't be dragged down into all that pain again — I'm not a silly lovestruck girl anymore. Any trouble coming to my people, including Catus and Enica, we'll deal with ourselves without his interference. The Aureliani are still the tribal leaders here. By the Goddess, I swear I'll do whatever it takes to get rid of Quintus. Even if I have to single-handedly scotch a rebellion to do it.

Chapter Ten

Velvinna's home was a small stone house in a respectable neighbourhood of the city, not far from the Sacred Precinct walls. Her elderly household was clearly upset.

'It was me who found the mistress this morning, sir, when she didn't answer the maid's knock. She's had a cold for a few days. Complained she couldn't taste her dinner last night. So at first I wasn't too worried. I thought she was sleeping late after a bad night coughing. Then the maid came back to me when she still couldn't get an answer,' said the steward, Silvanus. He was red-eyed and his hands shook as he led the three officers up to the old lady's bedchamber. She was wearing a night-shift and lying in a relaxed pose on the floor, head turned to one side. There was no distress on her calm face.

Quintus crouched down, taking her hand. It was still warm, but there was no detectable pulse. 'Was she alive when you found her?'

'Yes, sir, but barely. Her breath was very faint, and her heart beating exceptionally slowly. I did my best to rouse her, calling her name and trying to sit her up.' The steward's eyes filled with tears. 'She died in my arms, sir. She just stopped breathing.'

Quintus looked around. 'Tiro, could you take Silvanus downstairs and sit him down with a drink?' As soon as they were gone, Quintus motioned to Marcellus to show him the grounds for suspecting murder. The soldier picked up a glazed dish standing on a dresser near the bed. It contained powdered leaves, rather dusty. He handed it to Quintus, who cautiously sniffed. The leaves stank. It was a familiar smell, taking Quintus years back to a case in Dalmatia when he had investigated the suspicious death of a high-ranking official. That official had been poisoned with dried foxglove, *digitalis* as the local doctor called it. 'It has a characteristic smell, and the taste is hot, like black pepper. But don't ever try it unless it's prescribed specifically for you — it's quite deadly,' the medic had warned.

66

And so it must have proved for Velvinna. 'Foxglove. Enough of it to drop a horse. An overdose would certainly stop her heart.'

'Yes, sir, I agree.'

'That alone is not evidence of murder. She may have taken too much by accident. Still, it's potential evidence. Anything else of note in here?' They searched the room; there was little apart from two dresses and some ritual robes hanging from hooks, one of them a white full-length gown of a rough weave, with a matching hood. Quintus raised his eyebrows. Marcellus said slowly, 'I believe that to be the robe of a wise-woman, one of the local Sisterhood of healers and sages. Velvinna had that status. No longer connected with the Druids of old,' he added hastily.

Downstairs they found the dead woman's library. It was quite a collection, mostly books on medicine, native plants and herbs. On a writing desk near a window was a pile of papyrus. Velvinna was apparently writing a herbal treatise of her own. Quintus took up some sheets and looked through the text, written in a careful spiky hand in lampblack ink.

'I did look myself, sir.'

'What's the book about?'

'Native plants, and their properties for healing and poison, sir. And…'

'Yes?'

Marcellus looked away. 'She makes some mention about the old beliefs, sir. As I said, Velvinna was well-known hereabouts as a wise woman, a herbalist and healer. She trained other wise-women. She seemed also to have an interest in the White Ones, the old Druids.'

'Did she now? Any dubious friends? Or enemies among the local tribes?'

'Velvinna, sir?' The young centurion sounded shocked. 'Oh no. Velvinna was loved and highly regarded in the city and the surrounding countryside. She was a wonderful healer, and often gave her services free to those in need. She was a renowned teacher, too. I believe she trained the Lady Julia Aureliana.'

Quintus was moving around the room, searching carefully.

'Could you check the kitchen with Tiro?'

'What are we looking for, sir?'

'I'm not sure. I want to know more about Velvinna, her life and work. Who she knew, who's been here recently.' Marcellus left, and Quintus heard hob-nailed boots clack along the narrow tiled hall and into a larger room at the back. Voices reached back to him, muffled.

He picked up a tiny bone cup on the desk. There were a few drops of liquid at the bottom, whitish with pale brown traces caking dry on the sides. He sniffed, holding the little cup closer to his face. Ginger...and something else underneath, masked by the pungent Eastern spice. *Interesting.* He ruthlessly plundered Velvinna's book, using torn-out sheets to carefully wrap up the cup. The foxglove leaves he poured out into a separate twist of paper.

In the spacious airy kitchen he found his two colleagues inspecting hanks of dried herbs hanging from the ceiling over the big scrubbed kitchen table. There were amphorae stacked around the white-washed walls, and stoppered bottles and jars arrayed on shelves. Labels written in the same spiky hand had been stuck to each container, but beyond a few simples like lavender oil, honey, and marigold ointment, Quintus was none the wiser. There was a small locked cabinet on one wall, too. Tiro got the key from Silvanus. The cupboard contained a single glass jar, sealed and labelled *Digitalis*. The smell of the contents told them this was nothing but the truth. It seemed that Velvinna was as she had appeared to be: a wise-woman, herbalist and teacher.

'Marcellus, can you call the steward back in, please?'

The old man looked scared, but Quintus invited him to sit, saying, 'Don't be frightened, Silvanus. My job here is to find out what has happened to your mistress. You were fond of her, I think?'

'Oh yes, sir. We all loved her. So did everyone who knew our mistress.' It had the simple ring of truth. Quintus probed further, asking about her friends, business acquaintances, any unexpected visitors in the past few days. One or two people had called to collect regular prescriptions; a pregnant neighbour popped in for raspberry leaf tea and a chat; a young visiting herbalist had borrowed a book and brought a gift of powdered ginger for the mistress's cold. Nothing of obvious use there. The cook was summoned too. Had Velvinna been eating as normal, been given any gifts of food? None, said the cook firmly. In fact her mistress had been troubled with a cold for a few days and had lost her appetite, despite all the cook's efforts to tempt her. In any event, like so many old ladies Velvinna ate like a sparrow, and much of her mostly plant-based diet was supplied from their own garden. The cook herself and the steward were both freed slaves who had been with their mistress since childhood. The cook's assistant was her daughter. No strangers had called, no parcels of food or drugs had been received out of the ordinary. Her friends were for the most part herbalists and healers in the city, many of whom had attended Velvinna's school in their youth. No new visitors or anyone unknown to the staff had been to the house in months.

'The mistress retired from formal teaching and all but occasional healing consultations a few years ago, saying she was getting tired and old. She told me herself that her heart was failing,' confided Silvanus. 'It is thanks to the Lady Julia that she lived with us as long as she did.'

'How so?'

'Lady Julia had been treating our mistress for heart failure for several years. '

'What treatment did Lady Julia prescribe?' Quintus could feel his heart tripping.

'Why sir, the powdered foxglove in the little flat bowl by her bed. Just enough for a few days - it's very powerful, but toxic too, you know. The mistress warned us not to touch the powder when we cleaned the room. She's been taking foxglove for at least ten years now. Lady Julia would often come to see the mistress and check the medicine dosage, or meet her in the baths or for a walk. Our lady always said Lady Julia was the best pupil she ever trained.'

'When did Lady Julia last visit your mistress?'

Silvanus thought for a moment. 'Mmm, not since last week, sir, I believe. But the mistress went out several times in the past few days, and as she preferred to make her visits unaccompanied, I don't know if she and Lady Julia saw each other after that.'

'One last question. Where did Velvinna keep the rest of the *digitalis*, and any other dangerous drugs she had?'

'In the locked medicine cabinet.'

'We'll take that bottle with us, then.'

That was all. Velvinna must have either mistakenly taken too much of the digitalis, or had somehow been given an overdose to cause her heart to stop. Either way, Julia was now a potential suspect and would have to be questioned.

Is it possible that Julia is a murderer? The mother of my child, and the only woman I've ever truly loved? Quintus felt himself shaking. He desperately wanted to sit down and take stock. He breathed in, slow and deep, and exhaled.

What was it Cicero said? *Cui bono? Who benefits?*

How would Julia benefit from the death of her friend? It was difficult to see. Unless the old lady had information that she had shared with Julia, information that threatened or incriminated the younger woman?

Quintus compromised. He could take no further action about Julia before Anicius Piso had checked the body and confirmed how the old lady had died. There was no time to waste with moving on to Vebriacum. The mining fraud case was even more urgent since the death of the messenger boy, and his connection with the mine. The mines whistleblower was still their best bet to cast light on the plot. And if a Druid element was revealed, he would know then what to do about Julia.

Once they'd had left the house, Quintus held out the jar, the twist of paper and the wrapped cup to Marcellus. Then he changed his mind and handed them to Tiro instead.

'Tiro, stow these carefully in one of your saddle packs.'

Turning to Marcellus he said, 'Get Surgeon Anicius Piso to examine Velvinna's body as soon as he can. We need a confirmed cause of death.'

Tiro looked enquiry at his boss. Quintus remained distracted, thinking about Julia and the drugs in Velvinna's house before he spoke again.

'We can't delay the Emperor's mission any longer. Marcellus, I need you to do the preliminary questioning of Lady Julia in my place. She needs to be ruled out as a suspect before we can safely cast the net wider.'

It seemed to Tiro that Marcellus blanched at that; Quintus just looked calm and professional. Tiro scratched his chin, and marvelled. Had he merely imagined that recent heated scene between the *frumentarius* and Lady Julia?

Quintus continued, even-voiced as ever. 'Also find out whether Silvanus is correct about Velvinna's medicine and dosage, and try to find witnesses to when Julia Aureliana last came to her house, or met her elsewhere. And see if the visits by the pregnant neighbour and the trainee herbalist raise any question marks, although I doubt it. I'm heading south, initially to Vebriacum. Where is the nearest post station to Vebriacum?'

'Iscalis, sir, in the Great Gorge.'

'Right. We may need to make enquiries there as well, anyway. Use the Imperial fast post to keep me informed, but I authorise you to use your best judgement in this case, for now. If there is any connection between this new death and unrest in the regional tribes, I rely on you to keep me posted.'

He mounted his horse, urging the chestnut to a quick canter. Tiro scrambled to follow him. They were back to their main mission, on the trail of the Emperor's silver.

The road south of Aquae Sulis ran for several miles along a plateau, giving high views over the mist-filled valleys on either side. Tiro guessed their journey today would be barely twenty miles. They stopped at noon in Camerton, a small iron-smelting town whose only notable feature was a rough shrine to Minerva. Quintus paused for a moment to salute the Goddess of the shrine. This surprised Tiro, who had not thought Quintus a devout man. They found a tavern boasting glass in the windows and heating under the flagged floor. The tavern-keeper was watching the road anxiously. He bowed slightly to Quintus, who asked if all was well.

'Yes... Nothing stirring here at the moment, sir.' Quintus cocked his head in enquiry.

'Oh, just foolish youths coming into town every so often, sir. Too much drink, the usual thing.'

Quintus waited. The man said, 'You know how it is, sir, when idle youngsters have been drinking. Telling old tales, calling for the White Ones to come back and thrust all that's evil from the world. Wanting what they call the good old days. Predicting the end of the world, such nonsense. Good old days, my arse.' He gave a unconvincing laugh. Tiro smiled at him, clapped him on the shoulder. Quintus called for a table and two dishes of lamb stew. They sat in a dim corner, away from the busy entrance.

Tiro was keen to hear what his boss planned to do at Vebriacum, but at first the Imperial Investigator was quiet, concentrating on the stew. Tiro's mind drifted, thinking about some of the people who had crossed their path. To begin with, Marcellus seemed a worthwhile young officer. Then there was the household in Aquae Sulis. The fragrant and feisty Britta. And Miss Aurelia, who was certainly entertaining. His mind switched to Cerberus, still snug in the saddle bag. Was the pup old enough to eat bits of meat? He'd have a quiet word with the tavern-keeper, see what little scraps or maybe milk he could scrounge.

'Tiro!'

'Sir?' Quintus had clearly been speaking without his noticing. 'I beg your pardon.'

What was that he'd just said? Begging the Italian toff's pardon? Never mind; just this once.

'I asked how your head was. Is it healing?'

'Oh, yes sir.' Tiro rubbed a hand along the itchy red line of the healing slash. It felt like a lifetime ago. 'No problem.'

'Good.' There was more silence, a pause that stretched till Tiro thought that was all Quintus had to say. Then, 'I did get some further information... from Lady Julia in Aquae Sulis.'

Tiro decided Quintus hadn't realised how loud his conversation with the lady had been that morning. Truth to tell, it had been a full-blown argument. At the end, even through the solid front door, he had heard Quintus say sharply, 'I had no choice. I tried to tell you. I sent a message…'

Then Julia's higher voice,' …didn't my ring mean anything to you? I thought…'

'You never wrote. I left a message.'

'Your message didn't reach me. I had to go home, to hide … I knew my brother and sister-in-law would help. I came to tell you, that day. I couldn't stay in Eboracum, my grandmother would have been so upset…'

The voices softened; finally Quintus, in tones of palpable pain, had said, 'So —a girl? What happened to her?…Yes, I see.'

Shortly after, the Frumentarius had come out onto the doorstep and stood staring at Aurelia, rigid agony on his face.

Tiro shook his head, paying attention again.

'Sir?'

'Yes. Julia - Lady Julia Aureliana that is - thinks that the letter fragment we found in the dispatch bag was sent by a man called Tertius. He manages the mines at Vebriacum for Claudius Bulbo. Some sort of freedman, a clever Syrian accountant. And what makes it more plausible is the link with the boy Catus.'

Tiro was puzzled. Being a Londoner, he could easily imagine a Syrian being here in Britannia, but he didn't understand the close relationships and unexpected connections country people often had with each other. Quintus went on.

'The Lady Julia's housekeeper, what was her name …'

'Mistress Britta, sir?' Ah, the luscious, lavender-scented Britta. Tiro closed his eyes for a moment, breathing in.

'Yes. Britta. It seems she is a close friend of Enica, the sister of the dead boy. They lived near each other as children on the Bo Gwelt estate, before Enica and Catus were sold into slavery. Enica went to work at the Iscalis villa. That's the big villa downhill from Vebriacum. Enica became the property of Bulbo along with the house when he bought it, and she's now a cook there. And with Bulbo's sister Claudia married to Julia's brother, Magistrate Marcus Aurelianus, Britta and Enica see each other whenever Julia is invited to Bulbo's house. It was Julia who suggested to Bulbo that young Catus would be a useful apprentice to his mines manager. If Tertius is a talented man with numbers and languages, I suppose Lady Julia thought she was helping the boy into a good career and maybe towards his freedom someday.'

That all made sense. But -

'So why was Tertius sending a message so dangerous that the boy was murdered to stop it reaching its destination?'

'Why indeed? I think Tertius could be the whistle-blower who's been passing on information about the loss of silver to the authorities in Londinium. If he is, he's now a man in great danger. At all costs we must find out what more Tertius knows, and establish Bulbo's involvement.'

Something rang a far-off bell in Tiro's head, but he pushed it aside and rushed on with his next question.

'But the way the boy was killed, sir?'

'Yes, it's strange. There is a bad smell about that, Tiro. Fraud and rebellion often go hand in hand. The inn-keeper here is a worried man, and I haven't forgotten the attack on you at Calleva. We might be about to uncover a bigger stink than even Governor Trebonius suspects. But first things first. We have to find Tertius and question him, in secret.'

Quintus sat in thought, twisting the bronze ring on his finger and reflecting on his meetings in Londinium. Gaius Trebonius had been frank and welcoming, and Quintus knew where he stood with his old friend. But there had been that second meeting, in Southwark with the Provincial Procurator Aradius Rufinus. The pale-faced man had made an uncomfortable impression on the Imperial Investigator. He had spoken softly, but Quintus felt him watching with the eyes of a hawk. That sort of quiet could be ruthless.

Quintus seemed to realise Tiro was waiting. He flushed faintly, moving his hand to rest on his scarred right thigh.

'Right. Given what we've just heard from the host here I want to approach the mines unseen. We'll go by a less obvious route, check the lie of the land carefully before we find this Tertius. But first Marcellus Crispus needs to know the flavour of what our host here has told us. Outside his normal jurisdiction, perhaps, but I think we should keep him informed of our doings in case we need his backup.'

He called to the tavernkeeper for a writing materials. Tiro watched, something scratching away at his memory while Quintus signed the note, bound it round and sealed it.

'Have this conveyed immediately to the nearest post station,' he told the tavern-keeper, showing him the *hasta* token on his baldric, and dropping a few extra coins into his hand. 'It's to be sent urgently to Aquae Sulis, for the attention of Centurion Marcellus Crispus at the garrison.' The innkeeper bowed, assuring the investigator it would be dispatched immediately with his best groom. 'Ah, another thing — ' the man turned back, enquiringly. 'My *stator* here has care of a pup. It's too young to come further with us, but it is beloved by a … lady friend of his. Could you arrange to have the dog cared for and conveyed to the Bo Gwelt estate for the attention of the Lady Aurelia Aureliana?' Again the man bowed, and left them. No doubt he hoped they would go quickly, before any more onerous tasks came his way.

Tiro shuffled his feet.

'How long did you think I wouldn't notice the whimpers and snuffles coming from your saddlebag?' Then turning serious, Quintus said, 'Tiro, I don't like this combination of fraud, deaths, murder, restless local tribesmen. There's too much going on. It's more than coincidence. And talking of your saddlebags — have you got Velvinna's cup and dish still safe?

Tiro nodded.

'I asked Marcellus to send on the results of Piso's examination, as quickly as possible. I've been thinking about Velvinna's cold.'

Tiro was lost. 'Velvinna's cold, sir?'

'Yes. It might turn out to have been a very convenient time for her sense of smell and taste to be blunted. Velvinna was apparently a Wise Woman of influence and connections. She was interested in the old Druids, at a time when there has been another murder with possible Druidic links, and whispers of Druid-inspired rebellion across the region. We don't know her affiliations, but if she was mixed up in something she could have acquired deadly enemies who decided to get rid of her influence. I'm thinking about that drink with the ginger we found by her bedside, as well as the possible foxglove overdose.

'Tiro, perhaps you should go back to Aquae Sulis to support Marcellus. He hasn't got your experience, and may need help with his investigations and his interview with Lady Julia. What do you think?'

Tiro thought that he was amazed that Quintus would trust him with this task, especially given which lady was involved. He was also very taken with the chance to see Britta again. On the other hand…

'Well sir, what if you go getting yourself into bother at the mines without me? I mean, with Tertius being such an important witness and all. There are bound to be guards, and who knows what there. Plus I speak the British lingo; you might run into yokels there in the Summer Country who can't speak Latin.'

'True enough. We go together then. The mission at Vebriacum must take precedence, and where there is fraud on this scale, there will be people who will stop at nothing. All the same … I can't make the links join up yet, but I would bet a crate of best Falernian and a year's pay that this tribal unrest has something to do with the deaths of Catus and Velvinna.'

Tiro grinned. He was as fond of pay as the next Roman subaltern; and a sincere lover of any wine. Falernian, watered gut rot, and anything in between.

Quintus sat a moment longer.

'Right. On with our original plan. I hope you're up for more danger, Tiro?'

A rare smile appeared on the *frumentarius's* face, gone almost as soon as Tiro spotted it. Tiro grinned too, trying to remember how much he disliked his boss. As they stood to leave the taverna, Quintus lifted the red leather baldric off over his head, twisted the leather strap, and replaced it with the miniature *hasta* hidden.

Chapter Eleven

'Those must be the Mendip Hills. Vebriacum is over that ridge.' Quintus pointed south-west, directly into the sinking sun. 'Further along the Fosse Way there's a crossroads with the main road running west to Vebriacum.'

Tiro rubbed the healing knife-wound on his forehead, looking troubled.

'Cheer up, Tiro. We'll take the older British trackways. The main road is likely to be watched. I want to approach the mines from an unexpected direction so we can take stock before we enter the operations centre. It's a cross-country route, and you'll learn more about the history of your country, I'm told. A brisk night under the stars in the company of your ancestors. What could be better?'

Tiro's mouth turned down.

Leaving the main road, they began to scramble north-west up the hillside to the ridge-top. They turned due west towards the sea, following the highest line. It was moonrise and light enough to pick their way between tussocks and outcrops of pale grey rock. As the night advanced it grew colder and Tiro pulled up the hood of his grubby *birrus.*

The breeze had been blowing light but steady from the south-west, a sweet whistle across the sedges and rushes colonising the hills from the damp valleys below. As the night progressed the whisper turning to buffets of swirl, coiling and changing direction. Suddenly the cloud dispersed. Right in front of them a long dark hill reared up, taking Tiro's dun horse by surprise. She tried to shear away, but Tiro put his hand on her shaggy neck to reassure her. He spoke to her softly in the British tongue.

Quintus watched. 'She feels the old dead.'

'What?' Tiro spat on the ground against the Evil Eye. With the moon rising before them, the shadow firmed. No hill, it was clear. A long earthen barrow. Quintus was right – it was a house of the ancient dead, and full of dread to the Briton.

Quintus clapped his *stator* on the shoulder, making Tiro jump.

'Tiro, if you could only see your face! What harm can these ancient bones do us? Truly, your ancestors are our friends. None other of your countrymen will come up here at night, so close to the barrows. It's a perfect place for us to camp.'

And camp they did, right in the shadow of the long departed. Tiro's face grew even more miserable.

It was a cold supper. Quintus might laugh at Tiro's superstition, but he would not allow a fire to betray them. After supper Tiro seemed to struggle to settle. Not until the moon had set and utter dark dropped over them did he fall asleep.

Quintus lay awake as he often did, watching the crisp night sky with its scattering of starlight. He returned in his mind to the encounters at Julia's townhouse. He saw the engaging young girl with his rebellious dark hair, his grey eyes, and Julia's generous mouth. Was Aurelia really his daughter? It seemed so unlikely, a fantasy he might have dreamed up under the influence of the poppy syrup in the military hospital at Eboracum. *My daughter.* How strange that sounded! His daughter, Aurelia, and at the same time the daughter of Julia. Julia who had run away from him, knowing she was pregnant, knowing he would be unlikely to come back. She hadn't given him a chance. She took his child away, before he could get used to the idea. He felt suddenly resentful. Julia had ripped away a whole possible future in which he stayed in this strange northern country. All stolen from him by an impulsive younger Julia.

Really, Quintus? A sterner inner eye now shone a harsh light on that final meeting in Eboracum. Julia had run to greet him in the forum. She had looked so happy. He pictured himself ignoring her joy, unable to look her in the face while he told her he was leaving. That his family was in trouble, that he must return to Rome immediately. He gave her no chance to tell him her news, no reason to change his mind. He was the one who ran away — from his real family in Britannia. He was trying to run from the shame of his father's disgrace, from the horror of the Caledonian battle where Gaius had saved him, from the guilt of watching as Flavius died…

I did this to us, Julia, didn't I? I rejected you. And now I pay the price: not just thirteen years of trudging the Empire's roads, policing the Emperor's business, but also thirteen years without you. Thirteen years of missing my daughter growing from a baby into a wilful bright girl who calls someone else "Father".

Eventually Quintus slept, not knowing that he turned and groaned in his sleep as the same old nightmares clawed at him.

Quintus woke Tiro before dawn. A ribbon of bright sun hovered along the eastern horizon as they circled round to the southern edge of a sloping plateau already humming with activity. A tumbled mass of slag-heaps and the scattered buildings of the straggling mining complex stretched away into the distance. They crouched down near a small tumbledown fort, anxious to avoid being silhouetted by the rising sun slanting up behind them.

Beyond the old fort were long wriggling clefts in the bedrock, which Quintus guessed to be the rakes dug out by miners to follow the line of the lead ore. As they watched, miners began to hammer lead ore lumps into smaller piles. Fire and smoke showed where the raw ore was heated by workers swathed in big leather aprons to melt the silver from the lead. Even this early in the day, Quintus could see the sweat pouring off the workers as smelting fumes rose in plumes.

He touched Tiro's sleeve, pointing to a central brick-built block surrounded by a courtyard, with stables off to one side.

'There's the office. I hope our man Tertius will already be at work. No sign of horses or wagons, so Bulbo hasn't yet arrived from his Iscalis home. Quick as we can, and pull your hood up.'

Leaving the ponies hobbled in a copse of wind-sculpted ash trees, they slunk along narrow lanes to the mines administration block. Several men passed them, hurrying to work without any sign of interest.

They crept into the courtyard and round to the back of the building. Through rough window shutters Quintus spotted a swarthy man seated inside, papers and wax tablets scattered across the table in front of him. The man started at Quintus's rap on the shutters and came over to the window. Quintus flashed his *hasta* insignia briefly. 'Round to the front,' the dark man hissed, and went to let them in, bolting the door as soon as they were inside.

'Tertius?'

'Yes, sir. You have been sent by …?'

'Rome. The Castra Peregrina.' The little man anxiously smoothed both hands down his ink-stained robe. With his harsh desert nose Tertius looked every inch the Eastern Roman he was. Dark curling hair bulged in tufts from the top of his tunica. He was slight and stooped, an unlikely hero. He closed the front window shutters, plunging the room into darkness until he had lit a smoky tallow taper.

Quintus got to the point. 'We're investigating the possible theft of silver from these mines. We are told by Lady Julia Aureliana that it may be you who has been reporting secretly to Rome.'

'Yes sir. I am so glad my messages got through.'

'Sit down, Tertius. We have bad news.'

Tertius trembled, and his black eyes moistened as Quintus told him about Catus. He dashed a hand across his face and wiped it on his tunic. 'He was such a good lad. His sister Enica will be devastated. They were everything to each other.' Then Tertius straightened.

'What more can I do to help, Frumentarius? I must avenge Catus, and make his ending worth the dreadful cost.'

'Just tell us everything you know.'

Tertius knew a surprising amount. It was obvious he had been an effective investigator for some time. He'd realised the mine accounts were being falsified to cover irregularities in the silver smelting processes, and had kept his own secret records. He'd overheard the security manager Caesulanus talking. Then he'd gone searching in the old barracks in the crumbled Claudian fort, and found silver ingots stored illicitly. He'd witnessed a recent meeting between the owner Bulbo, his son Lucius, and two strangers.

'I have some written evidence too, a letter inviting my master to a meeting in Londinium last winter. He was instructed to bring with him samples of silver coins.' He passed a white wax tablet to Quintus, who quickly scanned it. Coins, perhaps to pay troops? Army pay was always in silver *denarii, and* keeping the army happy was of critical importance to the security of the province. He looked again at the letter. He was disappointed by the lack of any names or signature, but that would only have confirmed what he already suspected. With any luck Tertius would have other corroborating documents.

'Praise be to Mercury that you're so sharp and conscientious, Tertius. But how is the silver being sent out?'

'Normally the finished ingots, both lead and silver, are sent direct from the cupellation works here, lowered in sledges down the cliffside of the Great Gorge.'

'The Great Gorge?'

'Yes, it's a mighty chasm in the Mendip rock, splitting the hills in half. At the bottom the ingots are loaded onto wagons to be taken the short distance to the dockyard in Iscalis. The pigs are loaded onto river barges and rowed to the coast, where they're transhipped onto trading vessels heading to all parts of the Province and the wider Empire.'

'Right. Well, to escape notice I expect them to stick to normal patterns. That is, if the silver *is* leaving this area. Tiro, I want you to take up position in Iscalis by the docks. Watch the comings and goings, and try to trace back to where the silver is being coined.'

Tertius shifted nervously in his seat.

'Frumentarius, I believe the silver pigs are being offloaded nearby for minting into coins before leaving Iscalis.' He told of the meeting between Bulbo and Lucius and the two strangers. 'I, err…' he coughed, 'could hear some of what they said. The visitors weren't happy. Something to do with discrepancies between the weight of the silver and the amount of coinage produced. They seemed to think the silver was being debased. One of them made a threat. It was then my master offered to bring a sample of the silver coins to Londinium. By his voice, the threat came from the taller of the two strangers, the softly-spoken one wearing a fine blue cloak. Then—'

'Blue cloak!' A memory held back for too long flooded into Tiro's mind like the cool overflow of a drinking fountain on a hot afternoon. He leapt up, slapping his head. 'What a fool! If only I hadn't been drinking; I had such a hangover, it's just come back… Sir, I've seen that blue cloak myself. At the Palace of Procurator Aradius Rufinus, in Londinium. Two men, one tall, low-voiced and wearing a fancy blue cloak, on a roan; the other smaller, darker, with a scarred eye. They came out of the Procurator's headquarters while I was waiting for you on the day we left Londinium. And they spoke to another bloke, greasy-looking. I remember now – I'm pretty sure that third bastard was the low-life who attacked me in Calleva, the one you killed, sir.'

Quintus frowned at him, but Tertius nodded.

'Yes, the other man does have a badly scarred face — his eye droops from the pull of it. And I can tell you who is in league with them, arranging the coining of the silver. It's Caesulanus, our noble head of mines security. I'm pretty sure how they're stealing the silver, too. During the first phase of smelting, some of the lead pigs are being stamped as if the silver had been removed. Then they're stored away as if for future shipment.'

Tertius glanced up and must have realised he was making no sense. He stumbled on, eager to explain, 'You see, I know to a gram the exact production and destination of everything here: lead, silver, zinc. When I found some of our lead pigs stamped in the usual way and apparently ready for shipment, but stored in separate piles, I got suspicious. I weighed one of them. It was too heavy. You see what that means? The silver hasn't yet been removed from the galena ore. These pigs are smelted without the silver being floated off.

'They must be making the pure silver ingots secretly, later, after the pigs have supposedly left site for export in the usual way. Only then is the silver removed. The lead ingots are also then properly refined and sent for shipment as usual. The books are cooked to cover the delay. The retained silver is never recorded in the paperwork. And it's being made to look as if I've been colluding. If I hadn't got the wind up, copied the crooked records and checked the old barracks while everyone else was away on Saturnalia, you might well be investigating me now.' The accountant looked upset.

'Right,' said Quintus, ticking items off on his fingers. 'So now we know how the silver is being siphoned off; how the removal has been hidden by false over-stamping of some of the pigs; where the silver is stored; how the books are being cooked; and the possibility of silver *denarii* being minted locally from Vebriacum silver. I suspect these coins would be the samples requested in the letter from Londinium, meaning this business is well underway.'

Tertius continued eagerly, 'Yes, once the stolen silver has left the recorded production process, I believe it's being sent instead by Sextus Caesulanus to be secretly stamped into false denarii at —'

Tiro turned his head, but they all heard it at the same time: the clatter of hoofs in the cobbled yard, and the sound of an imperious young voice calling for the yard boy.

'It's Master Lucius! Quick, you must leave.' Tertius ran to the window and flung open the shutters once more, but Quintus caught him by the arm.

'That young man – that's Lucius Claudius? Don't worry. Look, he's going straight back out of the yard again.'

They saw a dark-haired, expensively-dressed young man hand his horse to the stable boy, and immediately leave again through the yard gateway, heading downhill into the town. Tertius dragged a hand over his sweating forehead, and sat down as heavily as his little frame allowed. 'By Astarte, that was close. My heart nearly left my chest!'

'Right, we may not have much time left. We'll have to split up. Tiro, don't worry about the docks; I'll go there. You follow Lucius. If Tertius is right and he's meeting Caesulanus, I want to know what they say and do.

'Tertius, we'll push our luck here a few more minutes. If your master Bulbo arrives, I'm here on official business, checking taxes paid or some such. You can leave the talking to me. Now show me your hidden records, and tell me exactly what you sent by way of messages to Londinium, and to whom. And why you suspect the mines security chief is behind all this.'

Tiro, moving with a speed and silence that would have surprised his drinking cronies in Londinium, pulled his *birrus* hood back down over his face and hurried out of the office after Lucius.

Chapter Twelve

Tiro approached the old fort cautiously. He'd kept Lucius in sight easily enough. Tiro arrived to find an open-topped wagon pulled up close alongside the dilapidated wooden building. A harnessed ox was feeding nearby. He squeezed himself behind the wagon to watch and wait. His heart was racing. This was where he belonged, in the action, getting on with the job. What if he pretty much solved this case single-handed? What would the *frumentarius* say? What would Britta think? A scene unfolded in his head: himself, modest, controlled; Britta leaning close to him, face turned up, her lavender scent in his nostrils …

The scene dissipated as Lucius came out of the barracks carrying a load wrapped in canvas. A big man, looking like a retired soldier but moving with the strength and grace of a gladiator, came out behind the boy. His load was at least twice the size. The big man — Tiro guessed it was Centurion Caesulanus — hoisted the bullion into the wagon with a grunt. Lucius struggled with his smaller load. Caesulanus laughed. Lucius looked angry, but glanced down into the wagon, and he smiled too.

The big man slapped Lucius hard on the back. 'Get a shuffle on, boy! Naught to amuse, everything to lose. We need to get these bars off to the boys at Chilton Polden, soon as. If that little rat Tertius comes snooping round, the fat'll be in the fire and no mistake! I might have to slit his scrawny throat, and you wouldn't want his blood all over your fancy clothes, would you now? So shift yourself, give us a hand with the rest. Then you can get off home on that showy nag of yours.'

The smile stayed pasted rigidly on Lucius's face.

Tiro tucked himself further down, and tried not to breathe until they'd both gone back inside. He reached through the slats of the wagon and wiggled out one of the metal bars. It was incredibly heavy, double axe-head shaped, with an incised stamp on one side. Tiro had no idea what the stamp meant. Not

85

his fault. He couldn't read, could he? But he knew the shapes were letters, which might tell a tale, and he knew someone who *could* read. He slipped the ingot into the pouch on his belt.

The pair returned with more ingots. Lucius dropped one, just missing his soft leather boot.

'Hecate!' the boy swore. He leaned over, then froze, looking under the wagon. 'There's someone here!'

It was Tiro's turn to swear, but no time for that. He stood, drawing his dagger. His *birrus*, so long his friend, now turned traitor and he got his hand tangled in the folds. There was a sudden thump on the back of his head. *Not again!* He thought, as his feet were swept away and he fell into a black pit.

Tiro woke an aeon later, the back of his head lanced by pain and his vision blurred and dancing. He was lying in the wagon, bouncing along a rutted road. A hood was over his face and his hands were tied together behind his back. Ah, Gods! — it was his own damned *birrus* wrapped round his head. He tried again to pull his dagger from his belt. It wasn't there, unsurprisingly. Moving cautiously to avoid alerting the two men, he felt heavy cold rectangular objects stacked all around his body.

At any event, he'd found the missing silver. And landed himself right in the proverbial.

The rough ride lasted a good couple of hours. Tiro was cramped, cold and bursting to piss when the swaying came to a halt. Two new voices hailed Caesulanus in the British tongue. Tiro could speak the language fine, but these men had a rough rolling accent that made them difficult to understand. Lucius answered in Latin, his voice high-pitched and nervous.

'He'll have to be got rid of. We can't have any witnesses.'

Rumbles of alarm from the two local lads, then the centurion weighed in.

'All in good time. I've a story to hear from him first. Maybe a score to settle. We heard from the Palace that this bloke and his boss were on their way to snoop, so a mate of mine was sent to Calleva to sort them out. My mate never came home, but this fellow seems to have got back on his feet just fine. I want to know why he's here, and where his boss has got to. Then I'll deal with him properly.'

Lucius broke in. 'There isn't time for your petty revenges now, Centurion. Get the money ready to move. Your story will have to be told later.' There was a pause, a sound of tearing fabric, and a high-pitched gasp. The boy's voice moved up an octave, coming quick and breathless. 'No need for violence, Caesulanus, we're partners — all in it together. I meant no disrespect.'

'No? Then keep your trap shut, and remember who's in charge.'

Tiro played dead while he was hauled out of the wagon and thrown onto the ground. More than ever, he wished he'd never left Londinium.

'Stick him in the shed for now,' Caesulanus said. He heard a door being dragged open. Tiro was bundled into a dark place and fell heavily onto his shoulder. The door was banged shut, and bolted from the outside. Muffled footsteps moved around and then a rhythmic metallic banging started up.

The smell in the shed was foul. Tiro guessed it had been the home of farm animals, probably sheep, before being pressed into use as a prison. He pulled the wretched cloak off his head using his teeth and lay back tallying his injuries. A sickening bruise at the base of his skull; pain erupting in bursts from the shoulder he'd just landed on; scrapes to elbow and hip. That was about it, with the infernally itching scab on his forehead. Apart from being locked with tied hands in a stinking shed miles away from Vebriacum with several criminals outside, and no way to let Quintus know. And a big ex-military thug who seemed to have taken quite a dislike to him. And his knife gone.

First things first. He looked around the hut. Empty, apart from a couple of sacks and the animal dung. Nothing useful there. On the plus side, the cloth binding his wrists was nowhere near as strong as the whipcord he routinely carried himself.

He wriggled his bound hands over a splintered wedge in the wooden wall, rubbing the fabric to and fro over the rough wood. The cloth tore and gave way, at the cost of a deep scratch. He spent a moment rubbing the feeling back into his numb swollen wrists and sucked the scratch to stop it bleeding.

Better.

He crouched to look through a knot in the wood. He had a narrow view of Caesulanus and Lucius in a dusty yard. A tall block of wood had been hammered into the ground. Set into the block was what he guessed to be a mould. A man sat on a stool before the block, holding a metal stamp in pincers. A second man wielded a hammer, and Tiro watched as he aimed skilfully and struck a hard blow, forcing the disk down onto the mould.

'Right, on my way,' said the centurion. 'If I'm going to be back again before dark, when our cockerel in there has softened up enough to start crowing, I'd best get a shuffle on.' Caesulanus heaved himself up onto the wagon.

'You can find your own way to Iscalis docks, can't you?' he called to Lucius. 'And check all the coins are there before you take them away. I don't trust these peasants to count right.' He shook the reins, and the wagon rolled out of the yard.

Tiro watched Lucius. He was the one to follow, now he had the *denarii.* The boy looked quite sick. His face had turned white, sweat was starting out under his eyes. His hands shook, and he stuck them under his armpits as if to hide them. Maybe he also didn't care for Caesulanus and his manners, thought Tiro.

'You heard, you revolting pigs! Get those coins laid out where I can see them. And they'd better all be true copies.' If Lucius was trying to sound as frightening as Caesulanus, he had a way to go. His voice was cracked and pitched too high to sound assured. But the counterfeiters seemed impressed, and moved quickly to lay out the coins. They looked anxious as he began counting, muttering under his breath. After a while, he paused to look at the scared men. He sniggered.

'Can't count, hey?' Lucius seemed to be getting some confidence back now the big man had gone.

Tiro wouldn't be surprised himself if the men were innumerate. He bet they couldn't read or write either. Just like him, dammit.

Another giggle, too shrill, burst from Lucius. The young man was back to counting the rolls of coins, grinning and laughing while beads of sweat rolled down his pallid face. The sound made Tiro's skin crawl.

Lucius wrote on the docket recording the acceptance of denarii struck against the bullion supplied. Tucking the money into his saddle bag, he let a full-blooded laugh rip out. The counterfeiters stepped aside, faces stricken. Lucius glanced at them. 'Don't you see?' They looked away, as if trying to avoid the infectious gaze of a madman. One man made the sign against the Evil Eye, provoking Lucius to more laughter. Tiro was amazed - had the boy been struck insane by the gods?

'It's such a joke!' Lucius was nearly gabbling now. 'They think it's all for the cause. Only Fulminata knows, and she's totally mine.'

He picked up the laden saddle bag, swayed and nearly fell. Even this seemed to amuse him, and he carried on sniggering while one of the men hurried to fetch his horse. Moments later Lucius had mounted the black stallion and cantered away. The two men looked at each other, one shaking his head. The other slapped him on the shoulder and fetched a jug left under a tree. He poured wine with a shaking hand into a cup. They sat down, passing the cup between them and taking gulps.

Tiro sat down, wincing as he rubbed the tender spot on his head and calling himself every name under the sun. Stuck. In a bloody country shed. What a fool he'd been, making himself so easy to catch. He winced at the sarcasm the *frumentarius* would fling his way.

But it was highly likely the Imperial Investigator would never know what had happened to him. Best guess? Tiro would end up a crumpled body at the bottom of a disused mining shaft. Unmissed, even by Britta. Why would she care? But if he did ever get back to Aquae Sulis, he'd call on her, casual, on his way home to Londinium. If only he could get out of this stinking hut, get rid of the two men outside... Hang on. With Caesulanus gone and the mad boy too, there might be a way after all. They thought him unarmed and helpless. What if they were wrong? He began to grin.

There's only two of them left now. Just need to attract their attention. So here's something that'll get them moving!

He'd already checked the back wall of the shed, which was too tough to break down without being noticed. Tiro set to, kicking the back wall and making as much noise as he could. Hopefully enough to get them charging in through the door.

It worked.

'Come on!' called one. 'Let's smash that noisy bastard into next week. Teach him a lesson. In together!'

Both of them at once. How thick can you get?

The bolt was dragged back, and there they stood in the doorway, both with raised hammers. Tiro was ready for them, and much, much quicker. He swung the heavy silver ingot low and hard into the hip of the first man. The man gasped and fell back onto his mate. The second man staggered, but made a recovery and came on. His reward was to get a nasty London headbutt, faster than lightning. A sickening crunch and he sagged like a sack, spark out. Tiro stepped over him to reach the first man, who was yelping with pain and trying vainly to get up. Tiro shrugged, picked up the man's dropped hammer and dealt a neat sideways blow to the man's temple. He wasn't aiming to kill, and he didn't *think* he had killed either of them. He hesitated a moment, then left them. They weren't going anywhere in a hurry.

Tiro was in a hurry, though. He needed to get to Bo Gwelt after that boy with the silver. But first, he needed to find out where Bo Gwelt was.

'Hey, mister! You got them men sorted. I'm glad. They were nasty to me once, when they caught me watching here. '

Tiro swung round. A child in very muddy clothes was sitting on the ground, hidden by a gorse bush on the edge of the clearing. How long had he been there?

'Can you help me, little boy?'

'I'm a girl, not a stupid boy!'

'Of course you're a girl. What's your name?'

'Narina.'

The young voice was a blend of suspicion and intrigue.

'All right, Narina. Can you tell me where I am?'

'By the coiners' hut, silly. '

Yes, silly. He tried again.

'Is there a town near here? Any soldiers? Or a magistrate?'

The suspicion on the little face deepened.

'Why should I tell you? Who are you?'

Tiro took a deep breath, and squatted down to look directly at the girl.

'My name is Tiro and I need to sort out some other nasty men, the ones these men work for. Will you help me?'

The girl pondered. Tiro hoped he looked trustworthy.

She seemed to think so.

'Yes, there's a magistrate. Dominus Marcus Aurelianus, he's a magistrate in Lindinis. Lindinis isn't really near here, though.'

'Oh.' Tiro resisted the urge to wail. Dear Jupiter, where in all this rural mud and muck could he get help, quickly?

'But his house *is* right near here, just down the road. You're already on his land, Bo Gwelt. I live here too, on Home Farm, cos my dad works for the dominus. Mum helps out at Bo Gwelt villa, and my dad looks after the estate.' A giggle. 'Nobody knows what those men you whacked do here, it's a secret. But I know. They're from the village. I've followed them before and hidden and watched. Other people from the mines bring stuff here in a big wagon, and the village men make coins with the stuff. For some posh gentlemen. And Master Lucius from Iscalis. I've seen him too, he visits a lot. Quite often he takes some of the money and puts it in his saddle bags when no-one's looking. But *I'm* looking, so I know.'

Narina tilted her head, considering. 'Is he one of the bad men you're trying to stop?'

'Yes,' said Tiro quickly. 'I think he's stealing that money. Narina, what else have you seen Lucius do?'

'He just comes to Bo Gwelt a lot to see Domina Claudia. Lady Aurelia runs away when he comes, and hides in the stable. I seen that Lucius sneaking round the house, though.

'And—' she paused to make sure Tiro was paying attention, '—and some other posh men come here, Master Bulbo an' that, to check the coins. And one on a big fancy horse. He talked to Master Lucius about taking money to show in Londinium.

Master Bulbo said he doesn't like going south of the river. Dunno what river that is. I heard him say he wouldn't cross the bridge without a guard, and Lucius said they could stay in the city once they'd done the business. Fancy Master Bulbo being scared of footpads! He's so big. I wish I could have an adventure in Londinium. Are those men sleeping now? They're having such a long lie down...'

Tiro's head was spinning by now. He managed to interrupt the flow of chatter.

'Narina, you're a brave girl. I bet you're clever too. Clever enough to help me. I promise you won't get into trouble.' He really hoped now he hadn't killed either of the unfortunate coiners. They were probably just doing a job to make ends meet.

'Mmm, well, I could, I s'pose. I like mysteries and adventures. Are you in a mystery, Mister, or an adventure?'

Both, thought Tiro.

'Thank you, Narina. What I need is to get to Bo Gwelt and speak to Magistrate Aurelianus urgently. Could you take me there without anyone knowing?'

The girl looked at him scornfully.

'Course I can. I live here, I know all the secret ways.'

Of course you do, Narina.

The urchin girl and her new friend left, heading cross-country through birch and alder trees along the low Polden ridge to the big house at Bo Gwelt.

Chapter Thirteen

Julia drew in a breath of pleasure as they approached the golden-hued courtyard villa. It faced north across the river Bruella towards the Mendips, overlooking marshland, arable meadows and low scrubby woods. Her sister-in-law Claudia complained the house was old-fashioned and drafty, and lately Marcus had given in and agreed to install a hypocaust system in the west wing. But Bo Gwelt remained Bo Gwelt.

Nevertheless, she was worried by Velvinna's reports. She had sent a message to her old friend's house before they left for the Summer Country, but no reply came back. Neither was she happy about leaving her patients at the clinic, although Piso had assured her that he would try not to kill anyone in her absence. Underlying all these lifted a swell of confusion about the return of Quintus. The independent life she had built since Aurelia's birth was showing cracks. Had she really been content, alone? She pushed doubt aside.

She passed the ornamental pond in the front garden with its red-gold fish flickering in the water, and walked through the house to the sunny garden at the back. Several bee-hives, abuzz, were dotted among the clipped hedges at the end of the garden. Above the loud honk of swans in the valley came the soft hoot of an owl. She found her older brother seated in a high-backed chair, dozing in a pool of sunshine. He was togate as usual, with a woollen shawl over his shoulders She watched as he drowsed in the warmth. Next to Marcus sat a thin olive-skinned man with a long nose, books heaped on his lap.

'My lady,' he nodded to her, smiling.

'Demetrios, how good to see you! How is my brother?'

'Much the same, although I fear his eyes are deteriorating.'

'You are still making sage tea for him?'

'Of course, my child. And I strive constantly to keep your brother away from honey cakes, sweet compotes, and too much bread.'

'His urine?'

'Still dark and sweet-smelling, I am afraid.'

'I may be going blind, but I can hear you clearly, Julia.' Marcus was awake and smiling at her. She was taken aback at how tired he looked. 'May I remind you that Demetrios is *my* employee?'

The Greek laughed. 'And as your servant, I am surely entitled to worry about your health, *Dominus*.'

'No need to pretend respect for my sake, Demetrios, old friend. We both know I am not getting any better. Now let me have a private talk with my sister before my wife appears to organise us all.'

Once the stooped tutor had departed, Julia sat and took Marcus's wrist to check the pulse. Marcus humoured her until she let his hand drop.

'Now,' he said, 'I imagine your sudden desire to visit us means Aurelia has been telling you how awful her life is, and begging you to intervene?'

'I *was* worried when I heard about the projected marriage with Lucius Claudius.'

'Then let me reassure you about my arrangements for Aurelia.'

Some time later Julia had heard all about his recent will bequeathing all his property to his "*beloved daughter Aurelia, under the guardianship of her aunt Julia Aureliana until she comes of age*".

Julia was surprised. 'What does Claudia think of that?'

'She doesn't know. She will have some income from the estate, which will then revert to Aurelia and her heirs on Claudia's death or her departure from this house. I have made my wife many valuable gifts during our marriage. Claudia will not go hungry. And we will never have a child between us now.'

On the subject of Aurelia's marriage, Marcus put Julia's mind further at rest. 'While I am alive, Aurelia will not marry before I think best. That age has not yet arrived.' They both laughed, picturing the impulsive Aurelia streaking across a meadow with head down low on one of her beloved horses. 'When I am dead, Julia, you as her guardian will be the best judge of a suitable marriage for her. She will be mistress of Bo Gwelt, and I hope she will have your support until someone she truly loves shares that burden with her. I have made provision for the servants. With your approval, I would like Demetrios to continue as tutor and advisor to her.'

Marcus closed his eyes, his face very pale. Julia stood quietly, but he roused again. 'One last thing: I am fully aware that Claudia wishes Aurelia to marry her nephew. Lucius Claudius is a troubled and dangerous young man. It is plain to me that his father Claudius Bulbo cannot control his wild fancies and unpleasant acts. I do not envisage Lucius ever making a suitable husband for my daughter.' His eyelids drooped back down; he said softly, 'I am tiring, Julia, and can't spend my remaining energies openly fighting Claudia. Rest assured that Aurelia will not marry Lucius against her will.'

Julia took the chance to mention Velvinna's fears of discontent among the Durotriges, and her warning about that evening's meeting in Lindinis. Marcus nodded, sighing.

'Since I have been ill with the Sweet Sickness I have largely withdrawn from public life. Perhaps Demetrios and Morcant will be better able to advise you.'

Julia pressed his hand reassuringly and stood to leave, wanting Marcus to rest.

'Julia? One more thing. I should have said this to you years since, but I didn't want to upset you, or my darling Albania who was so devastated at not giving me a child. I supposed when we decided to adopt Aurelia that she was the offspring of a villager in trouble. But I knew the moment I set eyes on our tiny newborn that she was your daughter. I want to thank you for bringing us so much happiness. I hope the Gods will reward you with your own joy one day.'

The laundry door at the back of the house flew open with a bang. A child of eight or so ran into the garden, followed by Britta and another young woman, red-faced from steam and shyness. 'Narina! Narina! Come back here, you naughty girl!'

Narina ran straight to Marcus, and climbed up onto his lap. He smiled; it was clear he was fond of this little girl.

'Oh, Dominus! I've been having an adventure!'

'Have you, little menace?'

'Yes sir, but it's a secret, so you mustn't say anything. Specially not to the *domina*. I promised.' Marcus frowned a little at Julia.

Julia lifted the child, muddy tunic and boots unheeded, and settled her onto her own lap. 'You remember me, don't you, Narina?' Narina's mother was standing nearby looking worried. 'It's fine, Gwenn, she's no trouble. Let her stay with us a while.' The young woman ducked her head, and went back indoors.

'Now, then, little monkey, tell your story.'

They soon heard that Narina had brought home a fighting man with a funny accent called Tiro, who was chasing bad men. He was now with Morcant at Home Farm. The man wanted to speak to Magistrate Aurelianus.

Julia stiffened. *Tiro? What happened at Vebriacum? Where is Quintus?*

'Come on, Narina.' Julia held out her hand. 'Let's go and see your father and your new friend.'

Marcus grasped Julia's sleeve, speaking in a low tone. 'Julia, I am sorry I can't take on this burden for you; I no longer have the strength. I think one of our family must go to the meeting at Lindinis, and I suppose with Aurelia so young, it must be you in my stead. Promise me you will be careful, and take a bodyguard.' Julia nodded, but she wasn't at all sure who to take. Rufus was too inexperienced, Morcant had family and estate responsibilities; who else was there? The Imperial Investigator might have been able to use his authority, but he was not of the tribe. *And not here, anyway,* she thought with resignation.

Britta had stepped back discreetly, but Julia beckoned her.

'Britta, I think after all you will need to know what was in Velvinna's message...' The two young women walked away with Narina towards Home Farm.

Tiro was also pleased to get to Bo Gwelt. There was everything to like about Britta's brother Morcant, firm-handed and broad of grin, as dark as Britta was russet. And his wife, shy Gwenn, made the most delicious drop scones and kept topping up Tiro's mug with home-brewed beer. Tiro persuaded himself that it would be best to consult Britta discreetly before he decided how to deal with Lucius. *Not to put the wind up the lad - let's find out quietly why he's here first, with all that money.* So Tiro sat on a bench by the fire, drinking with Morcant and roasting his feet while dusk cooled outside. *Ah, these beers sink down just right.*

The farmhouse was a large comfortable roundhouse of the old British style, with a low door, and a hole in the roof to let out the smoke from the big hearth-fire. Nevertheless, Morcant was not a man to spurn Roman luxuries when they appealed to him. He had made sure his house was built on solid foundations, and had a good tiled floor. There were beds with woven sheets and thick bedcovers of new wool. Gwenn had a proper Roman kitchen in an adjoining building, and there was even a tiny bathhouse next to a stream. Just perfect, thought Tiro, stretching out his aching limbs and nearly forgetting why he was here. He could fit right in with this family.

Morcant was interested to hear what Tiro had to say, an edited version leaving out Lucius or Velvinna. He quickly picked up on the innkeeper's remarks at Camerton, and the circumstances of Catus's death. Gwenn was openly distressed. Morcant sighed and shook his head.

'Well now, that fits in with what I've been hearing roundabouts. Quite a few of the younger men seem dissatisfied, saying loud they don't see why Britannia should be ruled from Rome. I do hear rumours of secret meetings, and changes to come, and even - ' he lowered his voice, ' - I've heard tell that White Ones have been seen locally. Not had none of them causing trouble since … well, since before my Grandfer's time. I'd put it all down to idle gossip, but that Drusus lad over to Bawdrip villa seems cock-a-hoop that some big White One is coming to shake us up in Lindinis. I overheard him saying so to young Rufus only yesterday.'

The door opened to let in a draught along with the faint scent of lavender. A buxom young woman in a swirl of tartan shawl walked in and looked straight at Tiro. His heart leapt up to bang under his breastbone.

Morcant laughed. 'Britta! Always a sight for sore eyes!'

Tiro stood rather too quickly, and found his feet not as firm under him as he would have wanted. *The curse of Hades on the home-brew!* He was overcome with the desire to impress Britta, but found the words wouldn't come.

'I see the Londoner has got his fist round your beer, Gwenn. That was quick work.' Tiro heard — surely? — a note of warmth under the sarcasm. *Jupiter Best and Greatest, but that woman is a sight to cure any eye sickness.*

'Mistress Britta,' he managed. She flicked a smile at him, before hugging her sister-in-law.

'But where is that little monkey, Narina?'

'Here, Auntie!'

The door swung open again, and his little friend hurled herself in, followed by a tall elegant figure. Julia Aureliana. *Jupiter!* Tiro wasn't sure whether he was now better or worse off without his boss. Either way, trouble beckoned.

'Auntie Britta! We've been having such adventures! This is Tiro — the man who talks funny. Ooh, I nearly forgot— we followed Domina Claudia's nephew here, that Lucius. He's been down Chilton Polden—'

Julia pounced on that. 'Lucius! Here?'

Tiro found his tongue at last, although it felt oddly too big for his mouth.

'Yes, Lady Julia. I tracked him from Vebriacum and we believe he is involved in a conspiracy…' *How much should I reveal? Yes, she knew about Tertius and Catus, but then there was Velvinna's death. Quintus suspects — actually, what* did *Quintus Valerius suspect?* Not for the first time Tiro cursed his superior. Fact was, Tiro had no idea what he could safely share with Lady Julia.

Julia frowned, cutting through his beer-damped doubts. She took Narina's hand again, and crouched down beside the little girl.

'So you and Tiro followed Master Lucius Claudius from Chilton Polden to Bo Gwelt, just now?'

'Yes, my lady! Isn't it exciting?'

Julia said nothing, turning on her toes. The door banged closed behind her. She was gone so quickly that Tiro wondered whether she'd actually been there at all. Just a draught and the flickering light of the oil lamps marked her departure. Britta glared at Tiro, and turned to follow Julia. He grabbed her arm as she was leaving.

'I must talk to you, outside, Britta - it's urgent!'

'Mistress Britta to you.' But she didn't pull away as they left the roundhouse. Tiro had no idea how to open the thorny subject. So he just let it spill out.

'It's about the old lady in Aquae Sulis. Velvinna.'

'How do you know her?'

'She was found dead in her house. Meant to look like natural causes. Me and the boss went to investigate, with Commander Crispus. We think it may not be accidental. Your mistress might be in the frame, as she'd been giving Velvinna a medicine that could have killed her.'

Britta turned pale, and would have fallen had Tiro not caught her. He steadied her and led her to a bench, saying guiltily 'Here, sit down a moment. Sorry to give you such a shock.'
Fool you are, Tiro, letting it out like that. Now she'll hate you, and you'll never have a chance.

But Britta rallied.

'What do you know so far?'

Tiro could never work out how he came to trust Britta so quickly. He just did. He explained about the powdered foxglove; their questioning of the household staff; Quintus's request for a medical examination. He didn't mention Quintus's instructions to take Julia in for questioning. Irrelevant now the boss and Lady Julia had both headed to Bo Gwelt at the same time. Quintus could do the questioning himself when he arrived.

'Of course, it could be a natural death — old dear, bad ticker …' he said hopefully. Britta shook her head, looking upset. ' 'Fraid not. Tiro, can I trust you?'

He moved closer to her, and felt a momentary yielding towards him, he thought. Her eyes were a warm hazel, but her face was paler than usual, drawn with shock. He hoped she wouldn't ask anything he couldn't answer.

'That poor old lady! Velvinna warned us the night before she died that there was trouble brewing. Druid trouble, she said, if you can believe it. She told Lady Julia she'd heard that a White

One was coming to stir up the tribe at a meeting to be held in Lindinis tonight.'

Her lips trembled, and Tiro put his arm back round her shoulders and squeezed gently. Britta seemed not to notice. 'That's why we left Aquae Sulis so quickly. Julia sent a message to Velvinna, but we never heard back. We couldn't wait any longer. My lady needed to talk to Magistrate Aurelianus, and decide what's to be done about the meeting tonight. And sort out the mess with Miss Aurelia too.'

The reference to Aurelia was too obscure for Tiro; he elbowed the comment aside. So Velvinna had known about the tribal unease? That seemed good grounds for murder but not, he was relieved to think, by Julia.

Britta smoothed out her tunica as she stood. She was shivering in the cold evening breeze, but looked more composed.

'Tiro,' she said, 'best you stay here with Morcant for now. No point risking more trouble in the house with that Lucius if he's with Domina Claudia. I'll see what's what, and tell my lady about Velvinna before she goes off to that wasp's nest of trouble at Lindinis.'

Tiro caught her arm. 'Britta, she mustn't go alone. The *frumentarius* will be here soon. He's the right person to get to the bottom of all this. There may be a connection between the silver theft and the Druid uprising, although the Gods know what.'

He threw caution to the wind. 'We do know that Lucius Claudius has been involved in plundering silver from the Vebriacum mines. Let my master accompany Lady Julia tonight, perhaps even go in her place. I can go too.'

Britta looked him full in the face now. 'You really have no idea who you're dealing with, do you? You folks up there in the big smoke must be daft in the head. This is Lady Julia Aureliana, not one of your soft painted Roman ladies. She and her brother, they're the leaders of the northern Durotriges. That's the tribe that nearly fought Vespasian to a stand-still when Rome came to Britannia. If anyone can stop this trouble, it won't be your Roman boss with his mouth full of pebbles and his fancy badge. My lady is the only person who can make this right. You just try stopping her.' Britta dragged a hand across her reddened eyes.

By Jupiter, what a woman! Lucky Julia, to have Britta at her side.

'Well, tell her I'm standing ready to come with her. It isn't right for such a great lady to go into town alone with all this unrest. She needs an escort, some bloke with fighting skills. Like me.'

Britta nodded once, and squeezed his arm before hurrying away. Her lavender-scented warmth lingered on his skin. He felt tired as he trudged back into the roundhouse.

Morcant winked at him. 'Pour the lad another beer, Gwenn. He looks as if he needs it.'

Chapter Fourteen

Tertius peered between the shutters, gasped, squeaked out, 'It's the man from Londinium!'

Tiro had gone after Lucius, and Quintus and Tertius had been packing away evidence in a deep leather carryall when they heard horses' hoofs on the cobbles of the courtyard. The little Syrian crouched down to hide. Quintus stood near the window, and saw a close-shaven fair rider wearing a cloak of summer-sky blue. The man slid gracefully off a striking roan horse, as a second horseman clattered through the gateway. This man was shorter and darker. A long puckered scar dragged down the corner of his right eye. Both men were armed. They were looking back along the road, apparently waiting. The dark one rattled the locked door. He called out, 'Tertius! You there?'

Quintus took his chance. Moving carefully, he blew out the tallow candle and crossed the room to open the rear window. Ignoring Tertius's muffled indignation, he picked the little man up wholesale, bag, papers and all, and bundled him out. He motioned to him to stay down, closed the window shutters, and took up position by the door.

It crashed open.

'Tertius! Where are you, you treacherous little rat?' It was a low deadly voice; one that would brook no argument. Quintus had his sword out. He stabbed low and hard, feeling a satisfying resistance at belly height. The unlucky droop-eyed man swayed, making a sobbing sound. Quintus knew it had been a fatal stab, but before the gladius had sucked free the second man leapt into the room. The cloaked man's movements were balletic in their strength and grace. His sword flicked out, searching. Quintus was momentarily unbalanced and stumbled backwards. Only the luck of the dawn light being behind his attacker saved him. For a scant second the tall silhouette paused while he searched for Quintus in the sudden gloom of the shuttered room. Quintus dropped onto one knee, slid sideways on the dusty floor and brought his weapon up to thrust at the man's groin.

This time his sword did not pierce flesh, but snagged in cloth. The blue cloak had fallen from the man's shoulder as Quintus slashed out. It whipped his gladius out of his grasp.

Blue Cloak seized the advantage.

'You've come a long way from Rome for nothing, Frumentarius. A shame.' He lifted his own sword overhead into both hands, and drew breath to bring the blade down with full force onto the unbalanced Quintus.

Two things happened.

The tall man bellowed in pain, dropping his sword to clutching his right arm. Quintus paused in surprise. A slender knife was sticking out of the man's upper arm, wedged into the fleshy triceps muscle. There behind Blue Cloak was little Tertius, who had ignored Quintus's instructions and crept right round the outside the building and up the steps to the front door. He'd even found a knife from somewhere. He stood trembling now, totally defenceless but with his hands balled into fists anyway. The tall man swivelled to stare unmoving at Tertius. Quintus suddenly understood that his attacker must be momentarily confused, puzzled by pain and with his eyes screwed up against the low east light coming through the office door. This was a single precious moment of pause.

Quintus struggled to reach for the hilt of his sword, still wrapped in the cloak on the floor He found the pommel, pulled the sword free and in the same movement leapt to his feet.

Too late. Blue Cloak recovered, picking up his own dropped sword with serpent-like swiftness. But he seemed to know the odds were against him now. There were two of them facing him, and he was wounded. The blood ran down his sword arm making his grip slippery. He leapt past Tertius, knocking the Syrian over, slammed aside his dead companion and jumped off the porch to reach his horse in a few paces. Quintus had to admit he'd never seen a better running mount. Within seconds the roan was gone, only dust and the clatter of its passing bearing witness to the encounter.

And there was the body on the floor.

Quintus ground his teeth, wishing there were two bodies.

'Where in Hades did you get that pathetic knife?'

'It's my qu…quill-sharpening knife.' The little dark man was brushing his tunic down after picking himself up off the floor. 'I had it all along, in the pocket on my belt. I just forgot, I panicked. I'm sorry, sir.'

Quintus clapped Tertius on the shoulder, hard enough to nearly knock the accountant over a second time. 'So you should be, my friend. You just put me in your debt, saving my life And my name's Quintus, not "sir". I hope you can ride?'

It transpired that though Tertius had little experience of horses, he had ridden camels in his desert youth. That was good enough for Quintus. They headed off to retrieve the two horses hobbled outside Vebriacum.

Quintus had been thinking about whether he should follow Tiro, wherever he had gone, or catch up with Bulbo. He decided Tiro was able to look after himself. And since Blue Cloak apparently knew him for a *frumentarius,* despite the lack of uniform and identifying *hasta,* Quintus was now sure the plot stretched all the way back to Londinium. The time for being subtle was over. He needed to catch Bulbo, now.

Plus there might be news from Marcellus at the *mansio* in Iscalis. Perhaps the news he dreaded: how Velvinna had died. For a moment he pictured Julia dressed and hooded in Druid robes, a White One raising rebellion against the Governor. She was closely linked to both Catus and Velvinna. But why would she murder her own people? To overthrow Roman rule, when her own family had prospered so? Then again, she had strong connections with Bulbo and his son, who seemed well and truly mixed up in the silver theft. He saw afresh that scornful look on her face when she'd demanded to know why he was back here in Britannia. The way she'd spat out his title — *Frumentarius* — as though he was a snake emerging from under a stone to slither across her path.

He shook his head, making an effort to put the scene out of mind. *Push it all away till the time comes to deal with her. Remember who you are. Carry out your sworn duty as a Roman officer.*

He opened his eyes to find Tertius watching him.

'The master will be at his Iscalis villa at this time of day, sir. We can catch him there.'

Quintus took a deep breath and mounted his horse with his accustomed calm, he hoped. Tertius seemed eager to set a fast pace despite his lack of horsemanship. Quintus had to suppress a laugh when he saw the little man on Tiro's dun, arms clutched round its neck, head buried in the rough mane of the British gelding. Neither graceful nor comfortable, but it worked.

The short route southwest to Iscalis led Quintus and Tertius past the ancient barrow mounds. In the full light of day they seemed diminished, dwindled into an old superstition banished by the mighty Roman gods. They entered an awe-inspiring gorge which grew deeper, more winding and imposing as they picked their way down. The gorge sides were pockmarked with caves. A bright young river chuckled along with them, broadening beside the road as they entered the town.

The gorge opened out onto a busy scene. Smoking hearths and furnaces were scattered on either side of the road, mixed in with small houses and shops. A large modern villa was set down amongst the little businesses right in the heart of the town, like a brood hen with chicks clutched round it.

'Master Bulbo likes to keep a close eye on his money-making, so he lives here. He owns the leaseholds of most of these businesses.' Tertius steered Quintus round to the rear of the walled villa, insisting they left the horses discreetly tethered out of eyeshot. Quintus bridled.

'I am on official business.' The little spearhead *hasta* was back on display on his red leather baldric. 'Bulbo must be in no doubt about who I am and my authority to investigate.'

'I know, sir, I know, but first there's someone you must meet— quietly.'

Tertius looked about cautiously before stepping into a large kitchen. Quintus followed to find Tertius sweeping a slave girl into his arms.

'Enica, I came as soon as I could.'

The girl was younger than Tertius, not yet out of her teens, tiny and plump. She burst into tears and hugged the Syrian back. Her only claim to beauty was a magnificent mane of golden hair springing loose from her headcloth. Tertius stroked her face tenderly. Quintus began to see the real importance of coming to Iscalis.

Tertius was speaking softly. 'I'm so sorry, Enica. I know he was everything to you. I blame myself for letting him go. But he insisted on carrying the messages. You know the way he was — eager to make his mark in the world. Such a brave, bright boy.'

Quintus could have sworn the Syrian's dark eyes were glistening too. He looked away tactfully.

Tertius pulled himself together and made introductions. The girl looked scared on hearing that Quintus was an Imperial Investigator. Quintus hastened to reassure her.

'Your brother was courageous, an example to us all, Enica. He will be given a proper burial. I see that Tertius is your —' he hesitated, wondering about the relationship between them, 'good friend. But you can't stay here now. Tell me where your master is. I'll deal with him, and make sure you and Tertius are safe.' *Gods above, what am I saying? Where can I hide these two innocents from the enemies that keep springing up around us?*

The little slavegirl unwrapped herself from her friend's embrace.

'Master Bulbo isn't at home, sir. But he's not far away, just down at the docks checking on some freight. He's arranged a special shipment to Isca Silurium, due to catch the afternoon tide.' The girl hesitated, and one hand crept into the other, fingers twisted together. 'He seems put out today. There was an argument with Master Lucius. This morning.'

Quintus knew only one thing about Isca Silurium: it was a vast army base, home of the famous Second Augusta legion for near two centuries. He doubted the fort needed secret supplies of lead pipes or pewter dishes. That left only one possible product from Vebriacum —silver, coined into money. His heart sank. This mission was getting worse all the time, and now he was beginning to doubt his ability to handle it by himself. He wished fervently that his British *stator* was with him. Well, till he caught up with Tiro he'd have to deal with matters alone.

'Can you tell me what the argument was about, Enica?'

'I've heard them having a few rows lately, since they came back from a recent trip to Londinium. I think there is a girl involved... someone Master Bulbo doesn't like. And they've quarrelled about money, too.'

'Any idea who the girl is? And why would they be fighting about money?'

'I dunno the girl, sir. Master Lucius, he's—' the young girl blushed deeply, and seemed on the point of fresh tears.

'Got an eye for the ladies?'

'Yes, sir.' She twisted her hands again in front of her apron. Tertius stiffened, and took the girl's hands in his. Quintus nearly smiled at the fierce protective look on the little Syrian's face.

'And the money — well, it's no secret that the young master gambles and owes money all over the place.'

'Right. Thank you. Now, Tertius, I'd like you to help Enica to pack her belongings as quickly as you can so we get her out of here.'

'I got nothing to pack, sir.'

Enica's admission touched Quintus. He'd never thought about the belongings of slaves before. They were simply belongings themselves. He hadn't given a moment's consideration to the institution of slavery. It was the way the Roman world worked. But Enica was barely older than his own daughter Aurelia. With her parents and brother dead, this young girl was entirely alone in the world apart from her faithful friend Tertius. It was a novel and chilling thought. He was profoundly grateful that Aurelia had loving security around her.

It's this strange province. Things feel different here. I'll get used to it when this mission ends, and then I can go back home to normality. The thought crossed his mind that he was no longer sure what normality was. He twisted the bronze owl ring on his finger.

'My talk with Bulbo shouldn't take long,' he told Tertius. 'Take Enica and wait for me at the Iscalis *mansio*. Be careful out there on the streets, and look after that bag of documents!'

The little dock on the Iscalis Yeo was a mere couple of hundred paces south of Bulbo's villa. As Quintus approached the bend of the river where a wharf served the local shipping traffic, he saw a small rivership moored up. It was well past noon, and Quintus guessed the ebbing tide would soon force the ship to weigh anchor. Raised voices at the dockside reached him.

'Show me the bloody money, Bulbo!'

Quintus knew that voice. Its cultured tones still had a threatening edge. He dodged out of view, staying within earshot.

Bulbo's muttering reply was lost in the clatter of sailors readying the ship to sail, but he heard Blue Cloak say with finality, 'You'd better find it, all of it, by this evening Bulbo. Or I'll kill you slowly, and then I'll catch that spoilt son of yours, and kill him too. Even more slowly. You know I never make idle threats.'

Quintus thought hard. Despite his arm wound Blue Cloak had managed to get here ahead of him. He was still full of menace. Bulbo had plenty more trouble than just a problematic son. There was little chance now for Quintus to interrogate or arrest either of them, not without armed help. *Tiro, you damn useless Britisher!* Quintus smacked his fist against his other hand. He didn't care that he was being unfair. He himself had sent the *stator* off to follow Lucius, but now he really needed Tiro's martial skills and street smarts. He had to admit he was beginning to worry about where Tiro was.

Right. There must be some sort of army guard or *vigiles* presence here in Iscalis, given the value of the ore passing through the port. His authority as *frumentarius* enabled him to call on official aid at need, anywhere in the Empire. He turned to a local passer-by, a farm labourer carting vegetables in a wheelbarrow.

'You, man! Is there an army guardpost here? Or a *vigiles* station?'

The man, dirty, solid, fair-haired, stared at him. Then he replied slowly in a lyrical but incomprehensible language.

Hades and all the Furies! Why isn't bloody Tiro here to translate?

Quintus gave up, turning back to the altercation on the dockside. He swore when he realised Blue Cloak had already gone. It was no compensation to catch sight of a fat sweaty man struggling to climb up into a gaudy red-painted cart, toga gathered up in one hand. Before Quintus could catch him, the man had whipped up his mules and departed in a low cloud of dust. In this dirty little industrial town there was no doubting that the fat toga-wearer could only be Claudius Bulbo himself.

Deodamnatus!

Chapter Fifteen

Britta caught up with Julia before she could storm into the villa.

'Mistress - Julia! One moment, please.'

Julia bit her lip. There was only one reason why Lucius would be at Chilton Polden. Julia knew as well as her brother did what was made there. The Aureliani had long since tacitly agreed to turn a blind eye to the odd bit of local counterfeiting, on the basis that what the Londinium taxman didn't know wouldn't hurt him. It was the magistrate's responsibility to make sure taxes were paid regularly by the northern Durotriges, but it wasn't his job to check where the demanded *denarii* came from.

The involvement of Lucius changed things. He was the son of local magnate Claudius Bulbo, an entrepreneur with fingers in many local pies. Lucius was also the nephew of Claudia, Julia's sister-in-law. Too many connections already between Bo Gwelt and the spoilt unworthy Lucius. A small black-market enterprise to cheat the taxman smelt a lot more criminal once Lucius was coupled with it.

Julia turned to listen to Britta with as much patience as she could muster. Britta explained what Tiro had told her about Velvinna dying barely hours after coming to Julia's house. Julia was shocked, at a loss for words.

'I'm so sorry, my lady, about your friend. But you also need to know — the *frumentarius* and Commander Crispus think it may be murder. Your name was mentioned ... being as how you had been giving Velvinna your own herbal preparation.

'But —Lady Julia,' Britta hastened on, before Julia could reply, 'they know you've been treating her for heart disease for many years. And that Velvinna came to warn you about trouble in the tribes, and to ask you to intervene. I told Tiro about the messenger you sent to check Velvinna was safe the day we left Aquae Sulis.'

Julia felt the last shreds of her temper squeezing away from control.

'And how does the Imperial Investigator know all this, if he is not here yet?'

Britta opened and shut her mouth, looking unhappy.

'He doesn't, my lady. But,' she added quickly, before Julia could unleash her full fury, 'Tiro has asked you to wait till his master arrives before you go to Lindinis. Or at least, let Tiro himself come with you if you can't wait. He says you mustn't go alone.'

Julia could hardly believe that Britta was urging her to wait for Quintus. Of all the maddening, insulting suggestions—and coming from her best friend!

Her voice was frigid now, and she found herself holding her hands bunched down by the side of her robe.

'Britta, have you forgotten what that man did to me? Have you really forgotten how he abandoned his child, left me his, his…' she swallowed, and for a moment couldn't drag in breath, such was her rage. 'He broke a sacred promise to me, sworn at our Lady Minerva's shrine in Eboracum. He left me without explanation or reason, just disappeared out of my life —'

'Julia…'

'Be silent, Britta! If you want to keep our friendship, you — will — not — utter another word about that man. Or his dirty sidekick. The Londoner can't even read. Enough. The Imperial Investigator can't or won't do his job, so I, as lady of the Durotriges, must protect our people.'

Julia felt herself boiling over. She knew it was unreasonable, but she made no attempt to rein in her anger.

'Go and make yourself useful, Britta. Go back to Tiro if you like. No — better than that — find Aurelia and keep her safe from Lucius. Now get out of my way and let me save our tribe.'

Britta looked badly hurt, but Julia couldn't help herself. She swept aside Britta's protests, and surged into the house. Anger and pride got her on into the west wing. There she was stopped by her sister-in-law's nasal tones coming from the estate office.

'Lucius, there's no time to get it all out. Julia and Aurelia are here. I saw the carriage arrive. Any moment now they'll come into the house. Just leave the rest of the money hidden where it is till another time, after Julia's gone. It will stay safe, just as it's been all these months. I'll make sure the hole is covered over, plastered back the way it was. It's too risky now.'

Julia paused, trying to work out what she'd just heard. The anger powering her since she saw Tiro drained away, leaving her shaking and cold. What money was Claudia talking about? *But you already know that. Why else would Lucius be in Chilton Polden? Why would he come to Bo Gwelt so often and spend so much time closeted with his aunt? It was never just about marrying Aurelia. He's been stealing forged money for months, money diverted and minted from Vebriacum silver. Oh, Lady Minerva, help me! He has to be stopped.*

The Lady's cool hand seemed to smooth itself across her feverish brow. Julia whipped her mind back under control. She leaned against the corridor wall, listening intently.

Lucius spoke, impatient. 'There *is* no other time, Aunt Claudia. Don't you understand? Much bigger things are at stake than this family. They are all disposable if they get in my way: your precious husband, your step-daughter, your sister-in-law. I'm sorry if that shocks you, after all the effort you've made to become mistress here. But you must help me, or all your scheming will be for nothing. You'll lose Bo Gwelt and your position here. I must have that money now.'

Julia kept her ear pressed to the wall, and was rewarded by a steady scraping noise.

What was she to do? There was no point bursting in to confront the pair. It would be her word against theirs. Marcus was so delicate it might kill him to hear that his wife was aiding and abetting her nephew to steal money hidden in his own estate office. Time was pressing. She must get to the Lindinis meeting, and try to stop the rebellion. She knew very well from history lessons with Demetrios how terrible Rome's retribution against an uprising would be.

Julia closed her eyes, one hand tugging gently at the string of little gold owls round her neck. Shadows chased across the inside of her eyelids. She saw the flutter of silent wings, swooping low, here for a moment and then gone into darkness. In their wake followed a calm realisation. There was no time left to follow Lucius, *and* stop the rebellion. The Lady Minerva was telling her to choose carefully. She remembered Velvinna, and the anxiety in her old friend's eyes. Velvinna's death must not be in vain. Only by reaching Lindinis in time to turn her people away from revolt against Rome could Julia hope to avenge her. The money would have to wait.

From that decision she now made her mind up to let Tiro come with her. She supposed he might have his uses if things went badly. That made her think again of Quintus. Her mouth tightened, and her face screwed up.

Damn you, Frumentarius, wherever you are.

It took a while to persuade Britta to remain behind as cover. Julia would have a headache — this much was still true. Would Claudia kindly excuse her mistress from dinner, as she really needed to lie down? Britta would take up a snack to her mistress later, thank you, *Domina.*

More time was wasted while Britta separated Tiro from the Home Farm beer, and Rufus saddled two of Julia's horses and brought them out of the stables. Tiro was obviously taken by at the quality of her horseflesh, mounting Julia's high-spirited bay with alacrity.

Julia had been born and brought up at Bo Gwelt. She knew the countryside intimately. They made good time to Lindinis, tethering the horses near the centre of the muddy little market town just as cheers began to ring out from the forum. Julia touched Tiro on the arm, and pointed across the torchlit square, signalling that they should make their way discreetly towards the basilica's open-sided portico. Her face was well hidden, and Tiro could move silently when it pleased him. They positioned themselves among the shadows, where they could see the speakers without revealing themselves.

A slim lithe woman with strands of long red hair straying out of a white hood was addressing the crowd. They enthusiastically greeted her with chants of 'White One! White One!' Julia listened in dismay as the woman appealed to the tribesmen to throw off Imperial rule and take back control of their own country.

'Remember the Druids! Remember your heritage, your old

Gods! Throw down the Eagles, and the falsely-divine Emperors who keep you enslaved! Join your brothers the Dobunni, and follow me to freedom and victory over our long oppression!'

Standing as they were to one side, Julia couldn't see the speaker's face clearly until the woman suddenly swept off her hood. She raised her fist to punch the air and turned round in a slow circle, mesmerising the audience. Julia bobbed down, holding her own hood in place. She dragged Tiro into a crouch beside her.

What? his startled look said.

'I know her. That's the actress Fulminata. I've seen her — where have I seen her? Yes, yes, outside the theatre in Aquae Sulis. And again at the Great Baths. The day I met Velvinna there, she came right past us.'

'If she was hooded, how do you know it's the same woman?'

'Because I saw her face clearly at the theatre. Look! How many redheads have you seen with such black eyes?'

Tiro stared at the woman on the stage, and nodded. Then it was his turn to grab Julia. He put his mouth right next to Julia's ear, and breathed, 'That bloke standing with her is the man who killed Catus, Tertius's Blue Cloak, who I also saw in Londinium. What the hell is he doing here?'

Julia watched the tall blond man intently. She was rewarded by the sight of the tall man turning as a second man approached into view. Young, with long dark curls, wearing a saffron-coloured cloak. He had an arrogance of look and posture that failed to cover his fear of the fairer man. Lucius Claudius, again. Very eager to talk to Blue Cloak. The older man drew Lucius away to speak. Julia waited till they had both disappeared from view.

'Come on,' she hissed. 'Now is our chance.'

Julia had always been fit and athletic. She put on a turn of speed, keeping the hood of her long white robe up. She weaved through the crowd and leapt up onto the portico. Fulminata turned in surprise, and Julia pushed her, hard. The girl lost her balance, teetered, and fell into the crowd below.

Julia pulled off her hood to show her face clearly.

'Listen to me, Durotriges!'

The crowd pushed forward to see who was causing the fracas. There were gasps, and voices cried, 'Julia Aureliana! It's our own Wise Woman, the noble healer, Lady Julia. Lady Julia of the Durotriges!'

Julia took a deep breath, and began to speak, loudly and firmly.

Chapter Sixteen

Quintus was never one to cry over spilt milk. He boarded the small ship anyway, catching its master readying to depart. The man was in a hurry, but the sight of Quintus's official *hasta* made him pause.

'All I know, sir, is my sailing orders. I do a regular run across the Severn Sea. I was to dock in Iscalis as usual, and load a mixed cargo including a special consignment for Isca. But the cargo hasn't come, and I can't wait now, tide's on the turn.'

The man had been told only to hand the special cargo over on docking at the legionary fort of the Second Augusta, to a soldier who would show authorisation from the legate's office. Quintus looked round the ship but found nothing out of the ordinary.

He headed back into town. At least he now knew that the special consignment for Isca had not arrived at the docks. And he knew Blue Cloak was mightily put out with Bulbo. Quintus saw an opportunity to drive a wedge between these conspirators. The edge of a turning tide, perhaps.

He found Tertius and Enica waiting at the snug little posthouse on the western outskirts of Iscalis. They looked relieved to see him, but he ignored Tertius's questions and the waiting jug of wine until he had collected his mail. In small rural establishments like this, mansio-keepers doubled as Imperial postmasters.

There were two letters addressed to Frumentarius Quintus Valerius: one bearing the stamp of the Aquae Sulis garrison; and a short tablet of a few lines only, signed by the innkeeper at Calleva. Quintus broke the ties on that tablet first, and read:

Hail and greetings, sir. The dead man stayed here three nights in total, but as I told you, the other two men left after the first night. My stable boy saw them depart for the west. They came back the following day, heading east. They stopped briefly to speak to the other man again, before moving on. That was two days before your honour arrived here.

I hope this helps. My duty to you and salutations.

It certainly did help. It meant that Blue Cloak and his companion had been travelling westbound from Calleva, nicely in time to ambush and kill Catus, and had then come back east the following day. Perhaps to report to Londinium? To Procurator Aradius Rufinus at his Londinium headquarters, perhaps, where Tiro had seen them?

The letter from Marcellus was longer. Piso's examination of Velvinna revealed that she had long suffered from a heart condition, but had apparently died of an unknown poison. Not digitalis. The surgeon said it was a skilful murder, with no signs of struggle or spasm. That reminded Quintus that he too had thought the dead woman blessedly calm. From what Quintus knew of poisons, that would rule out powdered foxglove as the cause. The unfortunate Dalmatian tribune whose death he had investigated previously had suffered appalling nausea and vomiting, and died in obvious distress.

Velvinna's elderly steward had remembered something more, and faithful to his promise to Quintus had reported to Marcellus. The trainee herbalist of a few days earlier had attracted his notice, the old man said. She had been wearing a long hooded robe, not surprising in the cool weather. But Silvanus had noted the remarkable eyes under her deep hood, impossible to miss. Unfortunately, Marcellus commented drily, that was all he could remember — not the colour, or shape, or even some defect. Just that they were "remarkable eyes". *Well, that's indeed helpful. Thank you Silvanus! I'll just cast about the Summer Country until I meet a pair of striking eyes, and then all will be solved.*

There was a final item that Marcellus had witnessed himself, although he couldn't see how it was linked in any way to the death of the old herbalist. Being a conscientious young man he reported it anyway, at length.

You may remember, Brother, that my garrison is a vexillation detached from the Second Legion Augusta, based further west at Isca. I keep in touch with my fellow legionary officers, and recently attended the birthday party of one of the tribunes there. The wine and beer flowed, of course, and the officers were in high spirits. Surprisingly high spirits, I thought, as my fellow officers have often made it a point to complain about being buried out there in the backwoods of the Empire, with no glory to win and not even good hunting.

This time there were no such complaints. I also noticed that money was flowing even more freely than the wine, and high stakes in denarii were being offered at every table. The bets concerned mere pranks for the most part, such as a fence-jumping dare for the cavalry decurion. One young officer was heard offering his colleagues odds on how long the young Emperor would last on the throne. I was shocked to hear the camp prefect say, 'Who cares? It won't matter soon, after all.'

I covered up my disapproval, Brother, but know you will share my distaste. I was amazed that the legate, a man of rank and experience and successor in that post to our esteemed Governor Trebonius, uttered no word of chastisement. Perhaps he didn't hear the prefect's remark. He looked very pale, and left the party early.

I have no idea what is at the root of this, but doubt it bodes well. I enclose something that might help you to the truth.

Farewell, Brother, in hopes of your success and swift return,
Centurion Marcellus Crispus.

Quintus smiled as he pictured the upright young officer and his shock at the lack of respect for the Emperor. It seemed, as Marcellus admitted, unlikely that any of the birthday party behaviour was more than high spirits and boredom. Nevertheless, Quintus thought he would report in due course to Governor Trebonius, who would discipline the legion as he saw fit.

He read the report through again. The business of the flowing money troubled him. Silver *denarii,* of course. In itself, that wouldn't be unusual. The army was always paid in silver. The bit he didn't like was the sudden abundance. Where there was unexpected money, there was invariably trouble. And in this case, he suspected, silver was at the root of all the evil. He shook the wrapper of the letter, and tipped a small coin into his palm.

Quintus looked at Tertius, who was sipping his wine

appreciatively.

'Just before we got interrupted at the mines office, Tertius, you were telling me something about the stolen silver bullion being made into coinage.'

'Yes, sir. Counterfeiting is an old trade here in the Summer Country. I believe Sextus Caesulanus, as I told you, has revived one of those forges, but I don't know exactly where.' The dark little man spread his hands in a gesture of regret.

Quintus thought. Caesulanus might well be liaising with local forgers, but someone else who knew the area, with more authority and freedom to move around, was playing a bigger role. That someone must be either Bulbo or Lucius Claudius. Or they could be running the scam together. Lucius had left the mines office in a panic just before the arrival there of the man in the blue cloak; and now Bulbo had driven away from Blue Cloak at the Iscalis docks, sweating and in a whirl of dust. What were they hiding, and where had they gone? Well, there was nothing for it. Tertius would have to help once more.

'Tertius,' he said to the accountant, 'I hesitate to ask this of you, but I can't think of a more reliable help than you. Would you be willing to deliver an urgent message for me? I'll cover your costs, and I promise you'll be able to take Enica with you to a safe — very safe — place. You'll both be well-treated by a colleague of mine.'

The freedman looked up eagerly. 'What more do you know, Frumentarius?'

'We already know the silver is being shipped away from the mines by Caesulanus, in league with Lucius. I have discovered that a secret shipment of money expected at the Iscalis docks for shipping to Isca Silurium has gone missing. That has made Blue Cloak very angry, and frightened Bulbo into melting away like a streak of yellow snow in sunlight. And now Commander Crispus at Aquae Sulis has sent me troubling news of the Second Augusta. With this.'

Into Tertius's outstretched hand he tipped the silver *denarius*. It looked a perfectly ordinary coin, bearing the face of the boy Emperor Severus Alexander on the obverse. Quintus hardly knew a clever counterfeit from a true coin. But maybe Tertius knew better.

It was Enica who spoke up. Tertius held the coin out to her. She looked carefully at it.

'I believe this could be a local counterfeit, as Tertius says. I have seen such before, when I was a young girl in Bo Gwelt. Making coins is an old industry in the Polden Hills. Folks are not too fussy about whether it's lawful or not. To find out for sure you need to go there, sir. There are people there who can tell you.'

'People where? Where are the Polden Hills?'

'Bo Gwelt, sir. You need to go to Bo Gwelt.'

The list of Quintus's concerns was growing. Added to two murders, the report of Imperial fraud, his missing aide, potential tribal rebellion and continuing attacks by ruthless criminals, he now had rumours of disloyalty within the Province's most famous legion. Even the slightest risk of the Second Augusta being suborned needed urgent action, well above Quintus's head. Or even Governor Trebonius's level, although of course he had to be informed. The Frumentariate Commander at the Castra in Rome would also need to know, such was the potential peril to the Emperor. But Londinium was distant, and Rome even more so. There would be no help from either any time soon.

The trouble was, the evidence he had was still mostly circumstantial. He hadn't yet joined the dots enough to know for sure. Just straws in the wind, the evidence of a little Syrian freedman, reports by worried countryfolk of a Druid revival. And a roiling in his guts that he had learned to trust over the years of investigating crimes.

Quintus asked the innkeeper for a birchwood tablet and ink, and sat down to write back to Marcellus. He saw off Tertius and his little girlfriend with an escort to Aquae Sulis, taking with them the signed and stamped letter in a stout satchel. Then he joined a local guide, hired with the help of the mansio-keeper. Heading back east to pick up the Fosse Way, south to Lindinis, and west again along the Poldens to the Bo Gwelt estate would take too long. Not enough time before dark. Quintus followed his guide due south across country instead, along the narrow droves crossing the fens of the Summer Country. The pale spring sun was already beginning to slant, reddening, towards the west. His scarred leg grew cold, itching and prickling as they rode on between stunted willows and into thin fog across the sodden levels. He prayed to Mithras that the guide knew his way.

He also found himself praying to Minerva, and thought he heard the low hoot of Minerva's sacred bird in answer. Perhaps that was just wishful thinking. Then again maybe not, he thought, when their horses crested a low ridge above the fen fog and he saw the large honey-coloured villa ahead. He paid off the guide, and dismounted to take a path round to the stables. All was quiet, but as he led his chestnut to the stable entrance, he heard a young voice murmuring inside.

'Here, boy. Come. Milo won't hurt you. That's right, just let him smell you a little. Then you'll be great friends.'

A thin dark-haired girl in a rough woollen cloak crouched in the straw near a pony, stroking a small white dog with brindle splashed across half of his face. Cerberus was already looking bigger than when Quintus last saw him.

'Hello, Aurelia.'

The mobile face looked up quickly. Grey eyes met grey eyes. The girl remained crouching, holding the wriggling puppy to her chest defensively.

'Sir — I mean, Frumentarius Valerius. Please don't tell my stepmother Claudia I'm here. She hates me spending time in the stables, and it's my favourite place. And she makes me keep Cerberus kennelled!'

Quintus heard the nervous passion in Aurelia's voice, and couldn't help a slight smile. All that energy, that lack of discipline reminded him of the boy he had once been, desperate to be freed from the shackles of his tutor and to be roaming his family's country estates in Etruria. So long ago. He sighed. Aurelia cocked her head and stood up, holding out the little dog. 'This is Cerberus, sir. Tiro rescued him for me. Isn't he wonderful? He's a fine tracker already. I'm training him, well, me and Rufus are training him.'

A little pink tongue darted out to lick his hand.

'Cerberus and I have met before. I thought it would be better for him to grow up here with you at Bo Gwelt rather than in Tiro's satchel. I see I was right about that.' He studied the girl more closely, seeing familiarity in the quick movements and dark wavy hair. He also recognised the wide mouth, quick to smile and just as quick to harden into fierce reproof. That sensitive mouth was all her mother's. I can spare one moment, he thought, feeling tired. They sat down together on the muddy straw, Cerberus nestled between them, and chatted. He felt strangely as if they were old friends.

Aurelia told him of Aunt Julia coming to rescue her from a despicable marriage. She spoke of her beloved father, who wasn't very well; of Demetrios her tutor, who taught her wonderful things about the world, and the heavens, and truth and justice, and how machinery like pumps worked, and the marvels of Roman engineering, and Greek art and medicine. She talked of Rufus, the groom and her friend, who looked after her horses and taught her how to medic and curry them.

Quintus winced at the mention of her beloved father. He knew he should be grateful to Marcus for giving his daughter such a loving home. He stopped listening while he dwelled on the times he'd missed: Aurelia as a baby, clapping and smiling to see her father; as a toddler, sitting on a pony for the first time while Quintus held her chubby little body safe and steady; as an older child, full of curiosity, asking endless questions as she showed him her books and written assignments, with the tutor Demetrios looking on, smiling. And on and on.

He switched back to attention when, a little shyly, she told him about Lucius Claudius.

'Do you know, sir, how I first met Lucius?' Quintus looked encouraging, and Aurelia told her tale.

She'd been out riding, and had paused on the brow of a ridge, spotting something shiny in the grass. She dismounted, and found a brooch under a dusting of dirt.

'This brooch, sir.' She touched the little bronze owl pin that kept her cloak fastened.

As she been remounting her pony, Milo gave a start and tossed his mane in sudden alarm. A bright rust-coloured flash passed right under the pony's belly and dashed down the soaked grass towards the meadow. Aurelia heard the baying of hunting dogs, and nearly lost hold of the pony when two huge brindled hounds charged by within a few feet of them. The baying of the dogs rose to a climax, their long shaggy ears streaming back as they raced to catch the fox. Aurelia struggled to control the plunging pony, and had managed to calm him somewhat when she heard the shrill scream of the little russet animal, caught and tossed in the air. Sickened, she let go of the pony's halter and turned to run after the dogs; to do what, she didn't really know. It was madness to come between such highly-trained dogs and their prey. Before she had taken more than a few steps a black horse ridden by a gangling youngster appeared over the crest of the ridge, charging downhill so recklessly it nearly trampled her. She grabbed hard at Milo's reins and managed to swing him away. There was a curse, and the rider yelled, 'Out of the way, girl!', as he swept past. Aurelia caught a flash of metal and glimpses of dark tossing curls, a flowing bright-coloured cloak and long breeched legs as the horse and rider charged after the dogs. Two slower horsemen followed over the ridge, a well-dressed fair-haired boy and a slave groom. The fair boy vainly called after the other.

'Lucius! Lucius! Halloo, slow down a bit, wait. We're on Bo Gwelt land here ...'

Aurelia saw the dark boy dismount, shrugging and shouting at the dogs who were baying in a frenzy and darting around in a tight circle. He bent, knife in hand, giving a shout of triumph and brandishing the unfortunate fox's tail. Aurelia ran as fast as her trembling legs would allow.

'Stop, stop, you lout! How dare you!'

The dark boy, young but much taller than her, turned as she neared. He narrowed his eyes, apparently recognising the bedraggled little girl. She saw his look move up and down her muddy dress and the shabby cloak she had hastily fastened round one shoulder.

'Get back to work, girl,' he said,' before I report you to your owner for impertinence and laziness.'

For a second she was shocked into silence. Then she drew herself up, twitched her cloak round her, and spoke to him.

'This is the estate of Magistrate Marcus Aurelianus. You and your — ' Aurelia glanced for a second at the other young man, now hanging back ' — companions, are trespassing on our land. Leave this instant, and do not return if you wish to avoid my father's anger at the way you treat his daughter and his property.' The fair lad, who Aurelia recognised as the eldest son of the Sorio family at Bawdrip, looked away awkwardly.

There was a momentary stillness. From a nearby tree, Aurelia heard the hoot of an owl in the sudden quiet. Then the silent swoop of the tawny bird passed above her head as the tension spooled out like a wire between the stranger and her.

Lucius stared at her, his brown eyes hard as pebbles. He threw back his head and laughed shrilly. 'Well, I see I have met your neighbour, Drusus,' he said. 'I apologise, my lady Aurelia. Next time I will await an invitation before hunting on your father's estate.' He clicked his fingers, swerved his horse around, and was gone so quickly Aurelia had no choice but to crush down a bitter retort.

The next month, her father told her he was soon to marry Claudia, Lucius's aunt.

Not till the stable had grown nearly dark and the air chilly did Quintus realise how long he had been held there, enchanted by this daughter he had never known. At last the energetic irruption of Britta in search of Aurelia brought him back into time. Aurelia slipped away before she was scolded for messing about in a stable instead of dressing for dinner. Britta let Aurelia go with no more than a distracted nod. She glared at Quintus as if he was a turd trodden in by the puppy.

Quintus felt tiredness seep into his bones. His scarred leg was itching ferociously. He had no desire for a confrontation with Britta.

'Whatever you've come to say to my mistress, you're too late. She's gone off to Lindinis to do her job as the high lady of the Durotriges. That *stator* of yours went with her. Fancy, he wanted her to wait here for you.'

This was said so dismissively that Quintus blinked, struck speechless. At least he now knew where Tiro was.

'Tiro did say as how you weren't looking to arrest my mistress any more for the murder of her dear friend. So that's summat, I suppose.'

Britta summed up her feelings with a loud sniff and left the stable, throwing over her shoulder, 'If that horse is any good, you might catch them up before they get to Lindinis. I'll have some bread and cheese made up for you.'

Chapter Seventeen

The lessening light and unfamiliar way delayed Quintus. By the time he entered the forum in Lindinis a sizeable crowd filled the square up to the front of the town's scruffy little basilica. Full darkness had fallen and flaring torches held aloft by groups of young men showed a mixed assembly. Townsfolk, housewives, merchants and innkeepers were in holiday mood. Mobs of roving youngsters, some of them dressed in traditional chequered woollen clothes handed round jars of beer. Excited slaves huddled together. A tight group of people was gathered at one side of the basilica's open portico. Quintus was shoving his way on foot through the crowd when he caught the mention of a significant name. A richly-dressed young man, fair-faced and flushed with drink, was laughing with his friends and about someone they all apparently knew.

'So I said to him, *If I had a father rich enough and soft enough to take me carousing in Londinium, I'd want my friends to come too. I wouldn't fancy going alone to visit the whorehouses of Southwark. Where's the fun in that?* You know what Lucius said? He told me his father wouldn't go south of the river, saying that he was frightened of being mugged there, day or night. Claudius Bulbo apparently refused to cross over Tamesis bridge, no matter what.' They all laughed, the hilarity of very young men who were secretly envious of a bolder friend's adventures. 'Anyway, Lucius did go, on his own. And here she is, the lovely lady!'

'From the Londinium whorehouses, Drusus?' gasped his friend as a swaying slender figure in a floor-length white robe emerged into the lamplight, greeted by cheers and tossed-up swords among the crowd.

'No,' said Drusus, 'she's actually a famous actress from the theatre. Called Fulminata, they say. But I can't see Lucius with her. Where is he?'

'I wouldn't leave one like that alone, hey Drusus?'

They tried to push their way further forward and were hushed down, as the graceful figure spread her arms wide to gain attention. She began to speak.

'Durotriges! Great hearts! British heroes!' It was a clear modulated voice, projected with professional skill to reach all parts of the square. The crowd roared approval, and the woman pulled back the deep hood to reveal a long mane of rich red hair. But it was her eyes that captivated. They were as black as midnight, bold and searching.

Quintus stared until a movement at the edge of vision caught his eye. *Behind her, right at the back. The man in the blue cloak.* He slid his gladius silently out of its red leather-covered scabbard. Breath coming faster now, Quintus swerved and dodged between townspeople towards the basilica steps.

'Hey, where d'you think you're going? Stranger! Spy! Hi, Drusus, stop that man with the sword!'

Two of the young men ahead swung round and tripped him. One grabbed hold of his arm.

'Not now,' Quintus growled, sliding easily out of the young man's grasp and twisting his gladius up in a lightning move to slice across the other's knuckles. The boy cursed and wrenched his cut hand away.

Quintus had no time for these fools. '*Frumentarius*, on Government business! Stand aside!'

'Is that right?' said Drusus's friend. 'Our fathers are the Government round here, the *decurions* on the town council. Where's your authority to break up a tribal gathering, eh? *Frumentarius* — tax collector! Grab him lads. Oi, Lucius, look what we've caught!' The boy called up to his friend on the stage, then swore, realising Lucius was no longer there.

There came a sudden roar near the front, and a ripple of movement as those further back pushed and jumped up to see what was happening. Laughter arose: 'That one must be drunk. She's just fallen off the stage! This is better than the comedies in Aquae Sulis!'

Attention shifted away from Quintus. He kicked out, catching the lad Drusus on the side of his knee and getting away into the crowd.

He heard more roars, of surprise and approbation this time.

The red-haired woman had disappeared from the stage.

'Julia Aureliana! It's our own White One, the noble Lady Julia. Lady Julia of the Durotriges!' The name spread like a spell, and the mayhem and good-natured noise abated. Heads craned. Children were picked up to see better.

Quintus swore. It *was* Julia, his Julia, dressed in Druid robes and taking up a commanding stance centre stage. *Jupiter and Minerva, no! This can't be happening.*

His heart drubbed, and he felt sick to his core, but the long years of legionary training kept him moving. Then his cursed bad leg, already tired and prickling, suddenly hesitated. He stumbled. Leaning on his gladius, he stooped to rub his scarred thigh. He was close enough now to hear her, the melodious voice he knew so well sounding full and proud.

'Listen to me, Durotriges! People of Lindinis! People of our tribe! You know me, Julia Aureliana, and you know my brother, Magistrate Marcus Aurelianus. You know our family, who have led this tribe since before Rome came. We have always cared for our people, always been proud to protect you, to lead you into battle and out of danger.'

Why was she here? What in the name of the Gods was she doing here, tonight, on the eve of a rebellion?

Despite everything — her disdain, her anger, her possible involvement in the deaths of Velvinna, and perhaps Catus too — and despite the evidence of his own eyes and ears, he couldn't quite believe what he was hearing and seeing.

What has happened to you, Julia? Is this really you, this strident barbarian, this treacherous daughter of Boudica?

Julia spoke again. Her voice was full of pride, her bearing tall and fearless.

'Durotriges! Listen to me now. That woman is no White One, not one of us at all. She is a mere actress from Londinium, paid to prey on your tribal pride and rouse up old enmities. Take no heed of her or her fellow conspirators here. Do not let these wicked criminals lead you into foolish paths. Please, I beg you, go home peacefully, back to your homes and families.'

Quintus reeled. What had Julia said? He saw sudden movement in the shadows. The redheaded woman had rejoined the gaggle of robed men. With a rush of horror, he saw how wrong he'd been. Of course this was his Julia! A lioness protecting her own. Just as Britta said, she'd come to single-handedly stop a doomed rebellion that would leave her tribe decimated or enslaved.

The man with the blue cloak jumped up onto the porch and grabbed Julia by the arm. A big man in well-worn army kit reached for Julia's other arm, twisting her around and dragging her away despite her struggles.

Mithras, lend me speed!

Quintus accelerated into a run as if his life depended on it, pushing through the crowd like a dolphin through waves. His leg was forgotten. A familiar feeling of narrow focus and intense rage rose. He welcomed the anger. There was no room for anything now but the urge to attack. He saw the steps ahead, the big man looming. He raised his sword to stab, and heard a voice he knew well.

' You take Blue Cloak, Gov, leave that arse Caesulanus to me!'

It was the most welcome sound in the world, Tiro in all the glory of his flat London vowels.

Quintus left his *stator* to deal with Caesulanus in a whirl of fists and kicks, while he chased after Blue Cloak. The tall fair man was bundling Julia into the shadows beyond the intermittent flare of the torches. Somehow Blue Cloak had found himself two confederates, a hard-faced man with a knife, and a youngster, less eager but well-armed with a long sword. They both stepped forward, crouching into fight positions. Quintus launched himself at them, all fatigue far away. His sword flickered between the two men as his feet danced an intricate pattern of deception. He snared the youngster first, seducing him into trying an open swing at his head with his long sword. Quintus brought his shorter, deadlier sword up to pierce deep into the youngster's belly. He was vaguely aware of cries and bellows behind him. He moved his attention to focus on the older man. This hard-faced one was more experienced, and although he had only a knife, it was a good long one. Quintus twisted his sword free, and stepped back. The lack of light made the footing treacherous. Quintus pressed the man, forcing him swiftly round and casting his own shadow over them both. Sweat ran down the man's face. He was gasping now, and Quintus knew one more feint would allow him a deadly stab.

A cry of pain came from nearby. 'You bitch! Bite me, would you?'

Julia screamed, a short sharp sound cut off suddenly. For a tiny moment Quintus was distracted, and felt his concentration seeping away. His opponent smiled, and swerved to the side to bring his knife back into deadly play.

But the *frumentarius* had one more trick up his sleeve. Quintus spun round on his heels, with his sword held in tight and angled upwards. It was a nasty move he had perfected in training at the Castra in Rome many seasons ago. As he completed the turn his sword lashed out with momentum and slashed at the man, wide and deep into his side. It was a difficult manoeuvre. There was a real risk of catching his weapon on the others' ribs instead of finding a vital organ. But the training and his sword held true. The man gasped and toppled dead into the darkness at Quintus' feet. He glanced round. No Julia; no tall man in the blue cloak either. Quintus moved back into the lamplight, searching.

The crowd had broken up into small bickering knots. Punches were being thrown, and he heard shouts of consternation and grunts of pain as blows landed haphazardly. He looked around, trying to work out what was happening. A small group of youngsters was heading towards him. In the lead was that friend of Lucius — Drusus, that was it. His eager look had changed to concern, a frown lowering his brows. Quintus saw a plump middle-aged man, an older version of Drusus in a gold-fringed mantle, reach out to grab the boy's sleeve, saying something urgent. Drusus shook the restraining hand off, and plunged back into the crowd. His father failed to catch him, his trailing toga swamping his movements.

Quintus's attention was caught by Tiro on the ground behind Caesulanus, crouching, filthy and panting but triumphant. One meaty arm pinioned the other's sword arm and the other was crooked tight across the centurion's throat. Tiro called out to two approaching men in relief.

'Morcant! Rufus! Catch hold of this villain and tie his hands and feet up, would yer? I gotta help the boss.' He scrambled to his feet, winking at Quintus and looking smug.

'Pancratium move, sir. Works every time.'

No sign still of Julia, but it was a fair guess that wherever she was, Blue Cloak would be too. Quintus tossed the dice on his choices and began to run, calling over his shoulder, 'To me, Tiro.' He didn't wait, but soon the clump of feet and the puffing behind told him his assistant was following.

The gamble was on. Quintus was betting Blue Cloak had a horse tethered somewhere outside the forum in the high street. There were precious few other places you could leave a horse in this scruffy little civitas. Instead of trying to force his passage back through the market place, Quintus led Tiro at a run along the side of the basilica. They found a narrow passage past the end of the building, probably used as a discreet alleyway for magistrates and decurions on council business. They turned the corner and raced on towards the road behind the basilica. Quintus's heart was straining now. Not so much from the fighting, or the running. He was used to that after long Imperial service of the dangerous kind. What goaded him was a glimpse of Julia being dragged, struggling, ahead of them. Tiro shot ahead. He threw himself into a curious dive, hitting the man in the blue cloak from behind, low and hard. His shoulder hit the back of the tall man's knees, and he threw his arms round the long legs, jerking the man off his feet. Blue Cloak fell like an oak, bellowing as he hit the ground. Julia fell too, landing on her shoulder and crying out, but free. Quintus crouched down and checked her with a quick glance. She wasn't badly hurt. He joined the panting Tiro, standing over the enemy with drawn sword until his assistant was back on his feet and could take guard.

The Lindinis rebellion was over.

Chapter Eighteen

Quintus gently helped Julia back onto her feet. The familiar scent of rosewater reached out to him. Silently, she moved into his arms, shuddering and weeping. Tiro tactfully looked away and busied himself tying up the prisoners. After a moment Julia stepped back, brushing dust and leaves off her torn robe. Quintus looked her over for injuries. She smiled, saying, 'I'm tougher than I look. Shame the robe isn't.'

'It was a good choice of robe,' Quintus conceded. 'Although you had me confused at first.' The robe reminded him of the old wise-woman.

'Have you got that little cup, Tiro?'

'Of course, sir.' Tiro fetched his saddle bag, reached in and handed the tiny wrapped cup to Quintus.

'From Velvinna's house.' He held it out to Julia. She sniffed the contents, and dipped a cautious finger into the flecked milky fluid.

'Juice of poppy, mixed into a little wine. With added honey and ...ginger? Thank the Lady, at least she died peacefully and without pain. The actress masquerading as a trainee herbalist, I suppose.'

He nodded agreement. He saw a tear glimmer in the stray torchlight as it rolled through the pale dust on her face. There was so much to say, but not now.

He contented himself with, 'I was wrong to doubt you, Julia. Here — you'd better take care of this too.' He held out the bottle of dried foxglove. She nodded, recognising the medicine, and tucked it away.

The square was clearing now. Many of the older citizens had taken their protesting younger folk away home. Two men, one big, the other young and slight, were standing guard over the furious Caesulanus. They nodded greetings to Tiro.

'Frumentarius Quintus Valerius, this is Morcant, brother to Britta and estate manager for Marcus Aurelianus; and Rufus, groom to the Lady Aurelia. They came to help when the *dominus* and Britta told them where Lady Julia had gone.'

The black-haired man, broad and sun-darkened by a life on the land, grinned crookedly. Quintus immediately saw the resemblance to his younger sister. Rufus gave him a shyer look.

'Groom to Aurelia, hey? You'll have your hands full then. I hear she's quite the horsewoman.' The boy, not much older than Aurelia, smiled shyly.

Quintus turned to Morcant. 'I'm grateful for your timely help, Morcant. I wonder, did you recognise anyone here tonight?'

'Well, sir, there were lots of local folk, of course. That girl from the theatre, Fulminata, had got some of the foolish young men riled up and raring to go. Like Master Drusus Sorio and his gang. No fault of theirs, I hope you can see, no harm meant.' Quintus made no reply; rebellion against the Empire was a capital offence. There had been a narrow escape for this little town tonight, mostly thanks to Julia's intervention.

Morcant hurried on. 'And the old codgers at the back, they never expected anything to come of this, just venting they were. Habit of a lifetime. Would've been pretty horrified if they'd been taken seriously, I do believe.'

Perhaps there was something in that. Morcant wasn't educated or army-trained, but being the manager of a large estate he would know what was happening in the local community. There never had been anything to be gained for the tribe in this trumped-up rebellion. Only those inciting the trouble could gain: Fulminata in league with Lucius, Blue Cloak and Caesulanus too. That placed them all at the heart of the Vebriacum fraud.

Quintus swung round, eyes quartering the forum. No Lucius — and no Fulminata, either. Damn! That boy kept slipping through his fingers. He squinted across the emptying forum into the failing light of the sputtering torches. A gold-edged mantle caught the guttering lamplights. Councillor Sorio was leaving. Quintus hurried over to catch him. The older man looked chagrined when he saw Quintus's spearhead badge.

'*Frumentarius*! Well, I am ashamed of our town, and of my son too. I had no idea our young men were planning any such foolishness, attending an illegal meeting like this. Good job I got suspicious and followed Drusus. Of course, boys will be boys, but I blame that Claudius youngster. He's the real stirrer, him and his floozy from Londinium. Actresses! I don't hold with the theatre. Wait till I speak to Claudius Bulbo - I'll give him such a piece of my mind. He needs to keep that boy of his in check—'

'Thank you, Decurion Sorio. But I need to speak to your son. He may be able to tell me more of young Lucius's involvement in this affair. Do you know where Drusus is?'

A troubled look passed over Councillor Sorio's face. He flicked up his gaudy mantle and used a fold of fine wool to wipe the sweat off his plump cheeks.

'I tried to persuade him to leave with me earlier. He wouldn't come, saying he had plans to join up with Lucius after the meeting. And now I can't find him anywhere, and his horse has gone.'

'I see. Well, if either Drusus or Lucius turns up, send word to me at Bo Gwelt. And I'm afraid there are two dead confederates of the plotters behind the basilica. May I leave them for you to deal with? I need to continue my investigations urgently elsewhere.'

The older man nodded, still looking embarrassed. He was clearly grateful to be given responsibility fitting his town council role. Quintus saluted, and moved off quickly. He drew Morcant and Tiro into a huddle, leaving Rufus, knife drawn and standing guard over the shackled prisoners. Julia joined them.

'Lucius has gone, probably with his friend Drusus Sorio. And maybe also taking his girlfriend, our fake Druidess Fulminata. I need them all in custody.'

Julia broke in. 'Velvinna told me the Druid rising also involved her people, the Dobunni. They may be heading north to try to stir up that tribe too, in which case we should follow them along the Fosse Way.'

Tiro scratched the scar on his forehead. 'But the stolen money, sir. That must have something to do with the plot too, and I'm pretty sure Lucius has hidden some or all of it at Bo Gwelt.'

Julia nodded. 'Yes, that's true. I overheard Lucius asking Claudia to help him dig up some money they've hidden

134

somewhere in the house.'

'Right.' Quintus went over to Rufus and his little chain-gang. He drew his sword, pulled Blue Cloak up onto his feet, and pushed the tip of his gladius into the soft skin under the man's chin, pricking it hard enough to force a bead of blood through the skin. He nodded at Tiro, who sauntered over to Caesulanus and twisted his arm forcefully right up behind his back. The centurion gave a squeal, high-pitched for such a big man.

'Look away, Julia,' Quintus said. He jerked his left knee up into Blue Cloak's groin, hard. Blue Cloak doubled over, gasping, and Quintus followed up with a crash of the pommel of his sword into the man's ribs. There was a sharp crack, and a gurgle, and the man slumped back to the ground. Quintus put one foot on the broken rib, and pressed down.

Julia kept her face turned away.

Blue Cloak forced out, 'I don't know where the money is, or the boy. Both gone. I told his father I'd kill them if the missing money wasn't back by sundown.' He refused to say a word about why the silver had been stolen. 'Go ahead and kill me. My life is over anyway. You'd be doing me a favour. The one I report to will do far worse than you can. But I will not die unnamed. I am Antoninus Cassius Labienus.' Quintus got nothing more out of Labienus.

And Caesulanus, though he appeared to favour staying alive, could tell them nothing about the hidden silver.

Quintus motioned to Tiro to step aside.

'Any ideas?'

Tiro scratched his chin.

'Well, sir, they might want to raise the Dobunni, as Velvinna said. But if Lucius is planning on running away with Fulminata, like I heard him say while I was locked in that bleeding hog-shed, and he's got money hidden at Bo Gwelt as the lady thinks —' he nodded at Julia, '— then I reckon he'll make his way back there. So maybe they'll split up for now, and each go their separates.'

Quintus nodded. 'There is one thing our friend Labienus has told us that we didn't know before. There's someone else, much bigger, controlling this whole plot. And I don't mean the pathetic Claudius Bulbo. He's as much of a pawn as anyone. The theft of the silver had a purpose, but the real plot is more than theft. So, I wonder *cui bono*? This little charade tonight doesn't convince me that a Druid rising is the whole story either. Maybe that's a smokescreen. My job is to stop the treason, for the sake of this province, the Emperor, and the Empire.'

He thought for a moment. 'Well, we began by following the money, Tiro. Something in my bones tells me to keep following the money.'

'Bo Gwelt, then, sir?'

'Back to Bo Gwelt, yes.'

'What about our prisoners? Might slow us down if we have to drag them across country with us.'

'Indeed. I'm reluctant to let them out of my sight, but it might do them good to cool their heels in the Lindinis lockup. Perhaps they'll have more to say tomorrow. I'll arrange for Decurion Sorio to take custody of them for tonight.'

Rufus came running over, his face chalk-white. He gasped out, 'Frumentarius, come quickly! It's the prisoner, the tall one.'

Quintus groaned, knowing immediately that Antoninus Labienus had spoken the truth when he said his life was forfeit. The fair man lay still, his tunic a bloody mess. A slim blade protruded from his chest. His hands were still pinioned.

Quintus glared at Caesulanus, whose freed hands were covered in blood. 'You're a dead man, you know that.'

The man shrugged, his scarred face non-committal. 'Your peasants didn't search me properly; your loss. You heard what Antoninus said about the boss. I just did as he asked, one comrade for another. He didn't want to risk spilling the beans under torture. And before you ask, I have no idea who the boss is. Don't know, never knew, never wanted to know. Keeps it all clean that way.'

Quintus was furious, but he didn't show it. He would likely never find out whether Labienus's death was an act of mercy or expedient murder. Caesulanus was now the sole witness.

He would try one more thing, though. Before turning back to Tiro, he said softly, 'Capricornus, eh?' and watched in satisfaction as the former soldier's eyes brightened momentarily. He veiled them again almost immediately, but that was enough for Quintus. Now he knew the man was formerly of the Second Augusta, whose symbol was the Capricorn, birth sign of their founder the Emperor Augustus. The troubled Second Legion again.

'Tiro, we'll take this one with us after all. Search and restrain him yourself this time. I'll fetch another horse.'

Decurion Sorio had gone, but the night watch was still hauling away the bodies from behind the basilica. It took a while to negotiate the loan of a horse from the slow-thinking local who was apparently Lindinis's finest. Eventually Quintus lost patience. He dragged the man up by his dirty tunic, eyeball to chest, rubbing the man's nose into the spearhead badge of his authority.

'I never did see that before, though I heard tell of such fine officers as you, sir,' the watchman said, shaking his head. Eventually he found them a sorry nag from the town stables, gave lengthy instructions about its return, and headed off to resume his watch rounds.

The night was well advanced by the time the little procession headed west out of Lindinis. Julia was shivering but upright on her beautiful white mare. Tiro rode alongside, mounted less showily on his army horse. Quintus smiled briefly, watching the pair. They were equally matched in horsemanship, but still looked funny together. Julia so slim and tall, an elegant patrician to her fingertips despite her torn and bedraggled robe. And stocky eager Tiro, straw hair sticking up all round his head, filthy tunic and *birrus*, but vibrant under his nonchalance. The ultimate Londinium soldier, if only he knew it.

Quintus kept the horse carrying the bundled Caesulanus on a short rein alongside his own chestnut. He was infinitely weary now, as much from the evening's emotions as his exertions. He would not let himself think about what had happened between Julia and him. That would have to wait till another time. Or whether Aurelia and he had a future together, father and daughter.

Caesulanus had slumped into stillness now. All the fight seemed to have left him now Labienus was dead. Good. Pray

Mithras it stayed that way. Bringing up the rear were the solid reliable Morcant and young Rufus, swaying occasionally in his saddle, and furtively looking around in case anyone had noticed how exhausted he was. Another fine horseman, Quintus had to concede. All these Britons, Tiro included, knew their way around horses.

It was a clear night and the waxing moon had risen, swinging up to faintly light their way. It might have been that, or the low mists lapping over the road and onto the ridge that fooled his eyes. He became aware that the pale mist had taken on a pink, then red, tinge. As they approached the turn off the Polden ridge road to enter the Bo Gwelt estate, Julia reined her mare in sharply and gasped. The wind changed and he too knew. Smuts and smoke streamed towards them, and he heard the unmistakable crackle of flames. Julia held her reins motionless a second only, then galloped ahead at a reckless speed along the dark stony track. Tiro turned in astonishment, but Quintus wasted no time.

'Here, take this!' he shouted at Tiro, tossing him the halter of the prisoner's horse.

Rufus and Morcant were passing Tiro, too, both spurring their horses from canter to full gallop.

'Bo Gwelt! The villa - it's on fire!' the boy yelled, as his horse bolted past Tiro.

Chapter Nineteen

Tiro tied up the horses outside the villa, near a bright red cart with two distressed mules harnessed to it. The trussed Caesulanus lay motionless on his horse. Tiro tugged tight on the cord securing the prisoner's wrists. *You never knew though, did you?* He whacked the centurion over the head with a stout stick. Not too hard, didn't want to kill him—not yet. He left the manacled man slumped over the unfortunate horse, and hurried into the courtyard.

A wall of heat and sound nearly bowled him over. Tiro stood aghast, getting his bearings. All three of the house's main wings were on fire. The south block containing the atrium and reception rooms, and the north kitchen and servants' wing were blowing gouts of smoke from some of their windows, and Tiro could see lines of fire crawling along the ground floor corridors.

But the fire must have started in the west wing. Still scaffolded at its south end where the new hypocaust was in progress, the wing was well ablaze, a red mass of heat and crunching blasts of noise. There was a tearing sound as an avalanche of clay tiles slid off the roof and hurled themselves into red ruin on the paving below. The holed roof let out a sustained belch of flame, lighting up the courtyard.

People were rushing around everywhere. Near the kitchen was a water fountain, and a well where a line of servants had assembled. They were passing buckets slopping water, hand over hand towards the flames, directed by a thin old man with drooping shoulders. Tiro realised this was Demetrios, the Greek secretary and tutor. A richly-dressed woman sat wailing in a highback chair. That must be Domina Claudia, Aurelia's stepmother. Julia's dresser was leaning over her. The two women seemed helpless in the face of the disaster. A fat man in a smoke-stained toga was trying to grasp passing servants, apparently urgently questioning everyone. Marcus? No, too fat, too strong.

Ah, there was the boss. Quintus had joined Demetrios in

directing the flow of buckets, leading groups of servants close to the flames to point out critical spots to fling the water, and diving in and out of rooms not yet ablaze to rescue missing people.

Julia had found a mattress from somewhere, and had Gwenn with her, helping her to treat staff with burns and injuries. An old woman sat shaking on the mattress, crying as Julia smoothed a salve on her face and neck. To his relief, Tiro spotted Britta nearby with his little friend Narina, dipping drinking jars into clean water from the fountain and pressing them into the hands of thirsty people.

Morcant was working with a red-faced man, gasping in the smoke-filled air as they tried to carry a large wooden beam from the carpenter's quarters across the courtyard. Tiro hurried to help them.

'We're going to break down the front door. The *domina* thinks her nephew is trapped in the main block.'

With Morcant in the lead and Tiro anchoring the end, they swung the wood against the doors. The double doors groaned but held. Tiro bellowed over the crackling of flames, 'We need to get nearer. Morcant, really swing the beam back this time!' The three men hefted the wood as hard and high as they could. Morcant's big muscles bunched and he gave a mighty roar as they swung again. Tiro pushed his shoulders and hips into the action, nearly losing his footing in the process. The leading end of the beam crashed into the doors. There was a satisfying crunch and explosion of splinters as the doors shattered inward. Tiro rushed forward, but was immediately beaten away by billowing smoke and flames taller than himself reaching greedily for the outside air. He fell back, coughing and slapping at clinging cinders on his tunic. There was no going in that way.

Someone else was missing too, he realised.

'Have you seen Lady Aurelia?' he called to Morcant. The noise thrusting out from the main wing nearly drowned his shout, and he coughed as he sucked in smoke. 'Aurelia? Has anyone seen her?'

The other two shook their heads. Tiro ran over to Julia, who was directing a small boy to fetch more honey for antiseptic salve.

'Aurelia? No, I haven't seen her … oh Minerva, where is she?' Panic filled Julia's eyes as she jumped to her feet. Tiro fought his own confusion, thinking.

'Don't worry, my lady. Leave it to me.'

He was sure he knew where Aurelia had gone, but he had sense enough to tell Quintus too. 'Sir, I'm heading to the stables to look for Aurelia. Lady Julia knows. I'll get Aurelia all right. Oh, and Domina Claudia thinks Lucius is trapped inside the main wing. The fire has well and truly blocked that entrance.'

Quintus was smeared in black ash, sweating and dirty. He shot out a hand, red and scorched, grabbing Tiro by the shoulder.

'Your arm, sir!'

'No time. We can't find Marcus Aurelianus either. We must find another way into the house. Morcant! Take over here!' Tiro heard Morcant's deep bellow as he took charge in the courtyard.

'This way, sir!' Tiro led Quintus at a run to the stables. Aurelia was crouched down by a locked cage. She'd managed to get the terrified horses out and tied to surrounding trees by their halters. Some of them were still plunging and attempting to kick out, but Tiro saw at a glance they were securely tied. Back in the stable Quintus snapped the shackle on the cage with a single twist of his gladius. Aurelia screamed with delight as her puppy tumbled out.

'Right, Aurelia, out of here. Into the courtyard with Julia and Britta,' said Quintus; but the struggling puppy had scrambled out of Aurelia's arms and dashed away. With a sob, she flung herself after him.

'Hades and all the Furies!'

Cerberus was scampering straight for the scaffolding at the end of the west wing, with Aurelia at his heels. Tiro tore off his *birrus* and plunged it into the stableyard water trough. Quintus was soon with him, soaking his long red cloak. Demetrios had followed them, hobbling as fast as his arthritic hip would allow and holding up a small glazed lantern to light his slippery way across the ash-marked cobbles.

'My master? Lady Aurelia?'

'We'll find them. Give me your lantern, Demetrios.'

Quintus licked his finger, and paused with it lifted up.

'North of west. Pray to every god you know, Tiro, that the wind doesn't back much. If the smoke catches us in the hypocaust we're dead, along with anyone we manage to rescue.' He strapped his soaked cloak over his shoulders and back.

Tiro spat surreptitiously to allay the Evil Eye. He prayed as hard as he could. It seemed the goddess Minerva heard him. As they neared the doorway to the new hypocaust system, a small tawny owl emerged from the furnace room. In the dark Tiro heard it swoop over their heads, circling and hooting in a plaintive voice. It was the sign they needed.

They plunged into the hypocaust.

The height of the underfloor was knee-high to an adult man, forcing them to wriggle along on their arms. Plus it was pitch-black in the narrow space.

Tiro's heart sank. How were they to find Aurelia? They had no idea where she'd headed, and the light from Demetrios' lantern was feeble and uneven. He suspected the small girl would crawl much faster than they could, driven by fear for her precious dog.

Quintus led the way with apparent confidence, and Tiro tucked down in his wake as they slithered across the broken subsoil, scraping and scratching themselves despite the soaked cloaks. Quintus kept calling 'Aurelia!' but his cries seemed to fall leaden and be sucked into the darkness unanswered. After what felt like an age Quintus stopped, and Tiro glimpsed the lantern light rocking from side to side.

'There's a divide in the way here, Tiro. Wait a moment.' He moved forward, leaving Tiro blanketed in stifling blackness. Tiro felt his forehead prickling. Sweat was running down into his eyes, spreading dust and particles of building rubble over his face. His breath came short. Waves of panic rose in him. This was a hideous type of Hades, suffocating, dark, without escape.

Jupiter Optimus Maximus, please, I beg you, I'll make any sacrifice to get out of here.

No sign came, and Tiro couldn't help himself. He moved

forward jerkily, scrabbling like a beetle and slamming into something warm and solid.

'Stop! Tiro, stop! It's me. Just calm down and follow. I found Aurelia's owl brooch. I know the way now.'

His boss's voice was calm and commanding. The remnant of trained soldier left hiding under the blanket of Tiro's claustrophobia surfaced and took control. Tiro reached out to touch the hob-nailed boot in front of his face.

They wriggled on and on. The air became stale and warmer. Tiro had long ago given up hope of ever seeing light again, or pulling into his chest a breath of cool clean air. Suddenly the heels in front of him disappeared. Quintus said, ' You can stand up now.'

To his amazement, he could. Quintus lifted the lantern and revolved it. They were thigh deep in a hole in the floor of a small room. Part of the floor, a tiled segment on wood a couple of feet square, had been lifted up and dragged clear using a cunning arrangement of levers and wheels.

From a collapsed table had fallen a scatter of scrolls, an inkpot and several pens. A locked strongbox and a candelabra lay on the floor. Bookshelves lined the walls. A chair had fallen onto a brazier lying tipped on its side. The coals had evidently fallen out and charred the chair legs, but not burnt much beyond. More books, wooden tablets and birchwood letters remained untouched on the shelves and heaped here and there on the floor.

'Strange — there's no fire in here,' Quintus muttered. An oil lamp, still alight but dim, hung on a bracket from the wall. The light reached the corner of the room, and Quintus paused. 'Thank your gods now, Tiro. Here she is.' They scrambled up into the room.

The young girl was sitting on the floor in a corner, dark hair curtaining her face. She neither moved nor spoke. The body of a man lay next to her, his blood-soaked head in her lap. Cerberus was frantically licking her hand, but she ignored him. The puppy began to whine when it saw Tiro, and wriggled across to him. He picked the dog up.

Quintus laid his lantern on the desk, and sank down on his knees next to Aurelia. Still she did not move or look up at him.

143

He gently raised the man's head. Tiro gasped, letting the puppy drop to the floor.

It was Marcus Aurelianus. His toga was splashed with massive gouts of blood. The side of his head was cracked open, the bone caved in and splintered in a huge ghastly wound. He was obviously dead.

Quintus gently moved Marcus's head aside. He stooped to pick Aurelia up in his arms, and carried her across the room away from that terrible sight. He was murmuring to her, his voice so low Tiro couldn't catch what he said. The girl turned her head against Quintus's chest, and began to sob. Tiro looked away, feeling awkward.

They were obviously in the estate office, a strongroom where Marcus kept his accounts and records, and his library of books too. The floor was tessellated, plain and unadorned. Tiro looked curiously at the hole cut into the floor. He considered the dragged-away tiled cover, wondering which had come first — the secret hole under the floor, or the hypocaust. He remembered that the heating system was not yet complete. Chances were the hole was dug first. Putting the lantern on the floor, he reached his hand in to feel around inside the hole. Nothing … nothing — yes, there *was* something hidden here. Smooth uncharred leather bags, not large but heavy. Three of them, stacked at fingertip reach under the floor.

Grunting, Tiro heaved out the bags. They were sealed with thongs round the neck. He tugged one open and reached inside, not sure in the poor light what his searching hand had closed round.

Heavy stacked rolls, wrapped in cloth. Tiro closed his eyes for a moment, sucking in a long breath. He felt light-headed.

'Sir.'

Quintus stirred, looked up.

'The Vebriacum silver? We've found it. Some of it, anyway.'

Quintus seemed to come back to himself. He rubbed his face.

'We need to get out of here. The wind could switch at any moment and trap us. Aurelia, we have to leave your father here for a little while, but we will come back for him when it's safe.'

He nodded at the puppy, who was waffling around him, trying to climb up. 'Shall I carry Cerberus, or will you?'

Aurelia gathered up the puppy. Quintus moved to the door, but recoiled, startled, before he reached it.

'By the Gods, that's scorching! The fire is still too fierce out there. Marcus must have had a bronze security door made for this room.' Quintus picked up his damp cloak, wrapped it carefully around his hand, and tried to turn the metal door-handle. In the gloom he accidentally brushed the door with his burnt arm. He yelped and cursed, stumbling back.

'No good. We'll have to go back the same way we came. Get a move on, Tiro.' He nodded at the hole leading to the hypocaust. Tiro felt his heart beginning again to jiggle in his chest. His legs quivered. Quintus looked at him.

'Take this other lantern, Tiro. Have a last look round in here while we sort out Cerberus. You know the sort of thing we're looking for.' Quintus handed the lantern on the bracket to Tiro, then wrapped his cloak carefully around his shivering daughter. They quickly bundled up the puppy before lowering themselves back down the hole in the floor, and disappearing.

Tiro directed the lantern's gleam carefully round the room one last time. He was looking for a weapon capable of causing the crushing head injury, which might provide clues to the identity of the killer.

The ink pot? No, too small and made of breakable ceramic. The brazier ... mmm, not enough coals spilled to cause a fire in here, but too hot to be lifted at the time it was burning. No other obvious weapons, anywhere. Maybe the murderer took the weapon with him when he got away. Wait a minute —

Tiro dragged up the long heavy candelabra. It had a stand at the bottom and a tripod flower arrangement at the top for holding candles. One of the triple prongs was sticky with blood. There was also a discarded garment lying on the floor under the desk. He pulled out a cloak, a short one of exceptionally fine saffron-coloured wool, and slipped it behind his belt. A final look round, and a straightening of his shoulders. Then he picked up the lantern and lowered himself into the hole to follow the others.

Chapter Twenty

Julia pulled the lamp closer to examine the injured woman. She'd not really pushed aside her terror for Aurelia. While she worked some remote part of her mind worried at a nugget of reassurance, like a terrier pulling at a rat in a wall. Quintus would find her daughter — their daughter — and bring Aurelia back safely. *He must find her.*

She concentrated again on the injured woman, Totia, who had broken an arm. She'd tried to go back into the servants' wing to rescue some little belongings, and a beam from the ground floor portico had fallen on her, knocking her to the floor. Julia set the broken bone and bound the arm into position across the woman's body.

Totia sucked her teeth in pain as Julia tied the final knot.

'I'm sorry to hurt you, Totia. The arm is straightened and set now, and I'll put on a herbal salve for the pain. Don't touch the salve, though, it's not good to eat. Go and get a cup of mead from Britta to help you sleep. I'll see you again tomorrow.'

Julia lamented all the herbal remedies sitting useless in the dispensary at Aquae Sulis. Fortunately she knew where comfrey grew in clumps near the house. Britta had collected some of the early leaves at her direction, and now at least Julia had a supply of healing poultices for breaks, sprains and torn muscles, as well as honey from the beehives for infection, and mead to dim trauma and pain.

Again her mind flitted away to dwell on images of Quintus and Aurelia. Somehow she was sure he would find her. Just as he had saved Julia from the man Labienus last night. That had been the most confusing event she had ever experienced, leaving her now cycling between resentment, amazement and reassurance. In the midst of washing a cut or smoothing honey over a burn, her mind kept drifting back to the warmth of Quintus's shoulder against her face, the smell of his skin.

She stood up to stretch out her cramped legs before making her way across to her sister-in-law, sitting with Bulbo. He stood, rubbing his hands nervously down his toga as Julia approached and leaving sooty marks. His florid face was alive with anxiety and fear.

'Ah, Lady Julia. Have you seen Lucius? My sister says he was here earlier this evening. I'm concerned he may have come back for some reason, and got trapped in the fire.'

Julia looked at them both, puzzled. Why would Bulbo suppose his son to have returned to the villa? She studied Claudia's face. The panic she had shown when Julia arrived seemed to have been set aside. Now Bulbo looked much the more troubled of the two. It was clear Claudia knew something Bulbo did not.

Julia was suddenly overwhelmed with anger. It wasn't just the turmoil of that very long day, or even her own agony of worry about her brother and her daughter. She threw caution to the winds.

'Lucius? Yes, I *have* seen Lucius. I saw Lucius tonight, consorting with thieves, traitors and murderers in my own home town. I saw him next to a duplicitous woman I suspect of poisoning a dear friend. I saw him talking confidentially to a vicious man who killed a boy of my tribe. A man I think you know well, Bulbo. A man you're in fear of, who tried to kidnap me — Antoninus Labienus.'

Bulbo looked astonished. *So you don't know yet, do you Bulbo? Not about the missing money, nor about the death of your fellow conspirator Labienus.*

'And you, Claudia? What have you told your brother about Lucius? Don't bother lying. I *heard* you. Out of your own mouth, colluding with your nephew to hide theft and Imperial fraud on a grand scale. I'd say your lives, the lives of all the Claudii, are worth nothing now. Did you know a *frumentarius* from Rome has tracked you down, right here to Bo Gwelt? Yes, dear sister-in-law, your plans have failed. Aurelia's legacy will never be yours.'

She had the satisfaction of seeing Claudia turn white, gripping the arms of her chair with her bony jewelled hands. Julia had never liked or trusted Claudia. But Bulbo? He was dishonest, weak, easy to manipulate. He'd allowed himself to be dragged deeper and deeper into the plot. Nevertheless, Julia felt a tiny amount of compassion for this fat social-climber, who so wanted his son to be accepted into the upper-classes.

Julia's eye was caught by a slight movement, and her heart lifted. She looked beyond Claudia into the smoke-veiled courtyard, hoping her voice would reach.

'Bulbo, did you know the dangerous game your son was playing, hiding stolen Vebriacum silver at Bo Gwelt? What do you suppose his reward would have been? Trial, conviction and a short lifetime of slavery in the salt mines for conspiracy to steal from the Emperor, along with you? Or simply a knife between the ribs from your friend Labienus, when he discovered who was purloining his money?'

Another quick glance. They were closer now; she need no longer shout. 'Ask your sister where Lucius is now, Bulbo. He came back late tonight, didn't he, Claudia? To retrieve the hoard the two of you had hidden? Money even your brother knew nothing about?'

'Even so, it's a shame,' said the *frumentarius* from behind Bulbo, 'that we didn't manage to rescue Lucius Claudius. He would have made a fine spectacle in Rome, in chains. I'm sorry, Claudius Bulbo, your son must have been caught in the fire. We couldn't get to him in time. But we did find this.'

Quintus, clothes ripped and filthy, left arm red-raw, face soot-marked and exhausted, held out a saffron cloak in his right hand. Bulbo cried out in recognition and distress.

'Claudius Bulbo, you are under arrest. I am Frumentarius Quintus Valerius, Imperial Investigator, sent by the Castra Peregrina in Rome to investigate silver missing from your mine. I think this cloak belonged to your son, with whom you conspired. I found it just now in Marcus's estate office in the west wing. Along with a body, your son's murder victim.'

Claudia remained immobile, her ring-laden hands clenched like claws.

Bulbo gave another despairing cry. 'No! It can't be. My boy, my only son! I promised his dear mother on her deathbed he would be the great success I never was. He's everything to me. I don't care about the money. It was all for him, everything I've ever done. But it's not too late. I'll save him! Lucius, my darling son, Father is coming!'

Before Quintus could move, before the watching Tiro could let go of Aurelia's hand and spring into action, Bulbo was lurching across the courtyard. He burst in through the smashed front doors, brushing aside the flames as if they were gauzy curtains. They could hear him shouting —'Lucius, Lucius!'— until the shouts turned to screams, and then fell into silence.

It was the longest night in Julia's memory, even longer than the night Aurelia was born.

Quintus told her gently about her dead brother. She listened as if from a vast distance, calm. Because she already knew. She had known that Marcus was dead from the moment she saw Quintus, exhausted and white-faced, burnt left arm hanging at his side, holding out the saffron cloak to Bulbo.

Perhaps it was better so. In truth Marcus had been leaving them for a long time, with only a drawn-out death to look forward to.

After hugging Aurelia until the girl protested, and then allowing herself one session of unbridled painful sobs seen by no-one but Britta, Julia composed herself. She insisted on treating Quintus's arm before he did anything else. From the wrist to above the elbow his left arm was scorched and beginning to blister. Julia alone guessed the agony he was suppressing. She sent Britta to plunder Julia's own baggage for the small bottle of essential lavender oil she took everywhere, poured a few drops into a bucket of cold water and forced Quintus to sit with his arm plunged into the water for as long as he could bear. She would have liked to smear hypericum and marigold ointment onto the blisters then, but lacking provision here at the villa she had to settle for honey instead. Ripping up the hem of her linen *tunica*, she soaked a length of fabric in Bo Gwelt's own garden honey, and wrapped the bandage round Quintus's arm.

'There, pull your sleeve down tight over that. Try not to let it move or slip down. I'll renew the bandage when you next rest.' Quintus said nothing, but she fancied the greyness of his face warmed a little.

Morcant and the other farmworkers had managed to extinguish the fires in the servant's and reception wings, leaving part of the two blocks a broken black devastation, but still standing. The west wing was a lost cause. They simply left the fire there to burn out, and a merciful rain fell in the early hours to hasten the end. At dawn, Quintus, face still shadowy with fatigue, searched carefully through the cinders and soot. He found a smashed oil lamp on the portico by the estate office, and trails of oil baked on the bronze door.

Tiro helped Morcant and the stableman carry the body of Marcus out of the smouldering west wing. Julia immediately confirmed the cause of death when she saw the head wound. Britta and Aurelia went to keep vigil over their master and father, laid out with love on a slab in the cool dairy room. Julia knew her silent white-faced daughter needed to be with her father, and asked Britta to sit with Aurelia for a while. Julia herself would follow to be with her beloved brother once there were no more injuries to treat.

Then Morcant, Tiro and Quintus went off together through the ruins, searching. In the corridor outside the office they found another body. Morcant recognised him as a young servant, probably lighting the evening lamps when he was unfortunate enough to get in Lucius's way. He had been fatally stabbed, and was long dead when the fire caught him.

The other body they found felt even more tragic to Julia when she heard. He had been a big man, slumping to fat, with aspirations proclaimed by the charred remains of a toga. At least, thought Julia, Bulbo had escaped the worst consequences of his actions. He would not now have to live to see the downfall of his son. Quintus said very little, his face cool and still as Tiro turned Bulbo's body over.

'I wonder where you are?' Julia heard him mutter. She knew he meant Lucius. Like her, he believed the culprit had got away and was still alive somewhere.

Claudia was locked into her sleeping cubicle, with two stout men hand-picked by Morcant posted outside.

'What will happen to the *Domina,* mistress?'

'I don't know, Britta. Tiro may have a better idea.' Britta needed no more encouragement, moving close to Tiro and touching his arm while they talked. Eventually Julia took Aurelia to her own bedchamber, and tucked her into bed beside her. The room stank of smoke, but at least it was untouched by the fire. Aurelia, who had hardly spoken since seeing her dead father, sank into a troubled sleep, turning and mumbling in her sleep. Julia was desperately tired, but sleep kept dodging away. Her mind churned between periods of dozing. Every time she woke she found she had been chasing down impossible corridors to unlikely sunlit endings. There was Aurelia to think of. Aurelia, who had just lost the father she adored. Aurelia, the new mistress of Bo Gwelt, who was now responsible for dozens of servants and hundreds of tenant farmers and their families, as well as her own future.

No, she's too young to take on that burden yet. I'll speak to Demetrios about Marcus's will. When I'm not so tired — then I'll think about what's best for Aurelia. Maybe she'd like to live in Aquae Sulis with me for a while?

Julia drifted off at last, tears pressed between heavy eyelids and the image of her brother before her, sitting as she had last seen him in pale spring sunshine in the garden, with the books he loved.

When they had all managed a few hours of rest in the least damaged rooms, Gwenn roused them with a hearty soup and fresh bread made in her own kitchen. Tiro smacked his lips, and slurped the broth down as fast as he could. Quintus gave him a poker-faced look.

'It's not proper Roman food, sir, not the fancy stuff you're used to,' Gwenn apologised to Quintus. She was still shy of Quintus, even after her husband had told her roundly there was no better man in an emergency. Julia was diverted into a fleeting smile, remembering a much younger Praetorian's grumbling about army marching rations during the Caledonian wars.

After breakfast, Demetrios led the household in paying their respects to Marcus, whose body now lay in a splendid lead sarcophagus arranged on a stout table in the garden. Julia stood with her arms wrapped round Aurelia, wiping her eyes. Demetrios explained in halting words how the master had insisted on having the coffin made to his design some time ago, when Julia told him his illness would be terminal. His funeral and interment in the Aurelianus cemetery near the river would take place in a few days, when friends and associates from Lindinis and the neighbouring estates would be able to attend.

Julia was grateful for one thing. The ceremonial structure of the funeral process that would deliver her brother into the loving arms of his ancestors and the gods was something she could share with Aurelia. It would channel the grieving the bereft girl badly needed. Aurelia was crying openly now. It was so hard to know how to comfort her. So difficult to convince her the world would still turn without her father. Julia wanted to cry too, overwhelmed by the terrible loss of the brother she had loved so much. How could Julia put the crushed world back together for Aurelia? While Aurelia sobbed in her arms, Julia asked herself if now was the right time to tell her daughter about her true parentage.

Absolutely not. I have to let her mourn Marcus unreservedly as her true father, the man who loved her from the moment he set eyes on her. It's what he deserves, and what she needs. Much better for Aurelia if she believes I am still her loving aunt. Marcus, wise and fore-sighted, has gifted me a continuing guardian role in her life. I'll always be here for her, whatever she calls me.

They sat together in the sunny salon, Aurelia with legs curled up on the sofa and her head laid on a cushion in Julia's lap. Julia spoke gently to her about Marcus, how much he loved Aurelia, how proud he was of her, his hopes and plans for her future. As Julia added that she would always have her aunt, the thin shoulders gradually ceased shaking. Julia realised Aurelia had sobbed herself to sleep. She left the exhausted girl, knowing Aurelia would sleep for hours more. It was the start of her recovery, she hoped.

Later in the afternoon Quintus called a meeting.

'This is how the fire started, I believe. Lucius, having killed Marcus and knowing Marcus's body would be found at dawn when the servants stirred, left the office by the bronze door. He threw a lit oil lamp against the door to set a fire that would cover his tracks. I also believe he was not lost in the fire. He got away quickly, probably leaving by the garden exit in the north wing. He's long gone now, I fear.'

Julia, Britta and Demetrios were all sitting in the garden behind the villa, gathered in consultation with Tiro and the *frumentarius*. It was an absurdly beautiful day, balmy and still with all the promise of a warm spring. Only the occasional waft of smoke and glimpses of the crumbled west wing and ash-strewn courtyard hinted at the horrors of the previous night.

Julia watched the bees, busy among the opening spring flowers. Quintus followed her gaze.

'Where does white wax come from?' he asked abruptly.

'What?' He had shattered her train of thought, still focussed on Marcus.

'Where does white wax come from? How is it made?'

He seemed intent. She paid attention.

'White wax. Well, it's quite rare. The vast bulk of wax is yellow, as bees naturally produce it from coloured pollen. To make it white you would have to boil the beeswax in salt water, according to Pliny. I've never bothered to do that, as I find the yellow wax from our bees here makes excellent candles and wax finishes.'

'You don't make any white wax here, then?'

'No. I just explained. It's a fiddly business, for little purpose other than snob value.'

'I see.' He said no more. She knew him well enough not to press him. Even when she first met him Quintus had preferred to keep matters to himself until he was sure of something. And now? He was so difficult to fathom these days, almost as if he had been smitten silent by the gods.

Tiro broke in. 'Sir, what about that Fulminata? Shouldn't we be trying to find her?'

'I've set matters in hand about her. She won't get far. But I heard something at Lindinis last night that puzzled me. You

154

might know, Tiro, as it concerns Londinium —'

Demetrios broke in respectfully, 'Sir, we have a visitor. Decurion Sorio, I believe.'

Sorio entered the garden, accompanied by his son. The councillor looked sorrowful and ashamed. In the bright sun Drusus looked hangdog and very young.

Britta and Demetrios tactfully withdrew.

'Good afternoon. If it can be called "good", at a time of such sorrow. Lady Julia, we heard about the fire and your brother. We came to bring our commiserations on your huge loss, and to offer what help we can.'

Sorio, despite his flashy tastes, was a good-hearted man and a friend of long-standing. Julia took his hands and pressed them, willing back the fresh tears pressing behind her eyelids. Sorio's few kind words had released the dam of her emotions again, and she was swamped by feelings of loss. She thought of Aurelia, and made the mistake of looking over at Quintus. So much pain, the waste of years. The tears came hot and unstoppable now. She let them fall.

Sorio was muttering, 'Oh my dear Julia. We're all so sorry, so sorry…' She withdrew her hands from his, lifted her head, and forced herself to say, 'Decurion, you have met the *Frumentarius* Quintus Valerius?'

'Indeed. I am relieved to find you here, sir. Although sadly not in time to prevent the death of my great friend Marcus.'

They sat in the seats Julia offered, Drusus still unwilling to raise his eyes. Quintus looked at Julia, who nodded.

'What can you tell us about the meeting last night, Drusus?' His voice was not unkind.

The boy looked up, coloured, and began to stutter. At first it seemed he had little new to tell, and Quintus had to patiently drag the facts out of him. He eventually confirmed Lucius had bragged of being part of a gang stealing a pile of silver. He'd told Drusus, laughing, that he'd squirrelled away a handsome share for himself. Some silly boy's notion of using it to fund a life of honeyed bliss in a love-nest with the red-haired Fulminata, away from his controlling father.

'Can you tell us why Lucius went out on his own in

Londinium, against his father's wishes?'

Sorio scowled, and the boy muttered something inaudible.

'Again, louder please.'

'He told me he went to visit the whorehouses a couple of times. But not once he'd met Fulminata. He said she's high-class, with important and powerful friends. He met her at some meeting in a very big house, a palace, and that was when he agreed to help set up the rebellion among the Durotriges. When he got back home, he called all us boys from the big estates together. He said —' Drusus swallowed and shot a look at his father, who was black-browed '— he said we young men should stand against our old-fashioned parents. That the White Ones would help us, we should take control, rouse the tribe against the tax-collectors and the civitas council...'

'Yes?' Quintus's voice was low, but Julia heard the new firmer note. She began to feel sorry for Drusus Sorio.

'He promised us there would be money and weapons, a chance for glory, and that if we backed him and Fulminata at the forum meeting, we could be part of the big victory to come.'

Tiro leapt to his feet, tipping over the chair he sat on. His hand strayed to the long dagger strapped to his side. Quintus waved him back down. His voice was harsh and peremptory.

'The big victory? A battle, then? When, and where?'

'I don't know, sir. Truly I don't.' The boy's voice cracked. He looked up, frightened, flicking away the fair hair drooping over his forehead. 'Just somewhere up north, and soon. That's all I know. He said once the final payload of silver had been shipped there would be an armed uprising of all the western tribes, and we should get ready for the call.'

'Did he say where the silver was being shipped? Think, boy!' Quintus was standing now, facing Drusus. 'Did he name a port?'

Drusus looked desperate. Perhaps he understood at last how dangerous the position really was.

'Yes — no. That is ...' A bead of sweat rolled down the boy's flushed face. 'I'm not sure, I'm trying to remember -'

Now Quintus spoke very quietly. It was almost a whisper. Julia felt the flesh on the back of her neck crawl.

'Was it Isca Silurium, Drusus? Was the silver being shipped from Iscalis to the fort at Isca Silurium?'

'Yes, yes, that's it. That's what he said.' Drusus looked immensely relieved to have told the Imperial Investigator what he wanted to hear. Quintus had one more question.

'That meeting in the palace, where was it? Where in Londinium?'

Drusus looked puzzled. 'Umm, he didn't say. Just that it was a meeting of important people in a big fancy building. He said it was all a big secret, and he and his father were honoured to be in their company. He only told me about Fulminata because she was coming to Lindinis.'

There was a moment of silence. Quintus pushed his bronze ring round his finger, unseeing.

Sorio broke in, looking lost. 'Does it matter, Frumentarius?'

'Yes, Decurion. It matters very much.'

Julia drew a ragged breath. Her eyes were fixed on Quintus. She'd rarely seen a more distressed look on his face, not even on that day in Eboracum when they'd parted in mutual anguish. He thanked the Sorii, dismissing them back to Demetrios to confer on the help their estate could bring its neighbour.

Then the Imperial Investigator walked out of the garden, leaving Julia and Tiro to stare after him.

Chapter Twenty-one

The battlefield feels empty. It seems to the young officer that he is alone, in a valley enclosed by bare bleak hills. And yet there is movement all round, flashes of brightness sliced by sound. Listen, listen...

Yes, there it is, the cut of swordsong carving the air round him into jagged chunks. Or is it just his own breath he hears? Ragged, gasping, getting louder. And with each breath, the increasing thud of his heart.

Next to him is a sudden swirl of movement. It's another young man, lithe, leaping, darting his sword around in attack. His segmented cuirass is wet with hill mist, and Quintus watches as a cluster of droplets join and roll into one, a thin channel of silver flowing down the man's armour into his elaborate leather belt. The man's dance is a frantic one, designed to stop the enemy's weapons reaching him. His intricate footsteps, swerving left and right, weave a magic pattern. A Roman defence against the northern barbarians. The young man dances on, while the light dims. His armour is drained of its brightness to a dull sheen.

Who are you? I know you.

The young man makes no answer, and now Quintus sees the enemy confronting them. Many men bursting out of a hidden defile, spilling out to range up against the young man and himself. Could this be Flavius? Flavius, his brother—wiry like Quintus, but a little shorter, a little younger, a little less experienced. Flavius, who was mad to join the Praetorians like his big brother. Flavius, who Quintus begged his commander in the Second Augusta to appoint as a junior aide-de-camp so he could keep an eye on his eager little brother.

He sees that a superior officer, his friend Gaius Trebonius, is now at his side. As should be. He knows that Justin is somewhere on this battlefield too, leading a company of the Praetorians. Tall, calm, cutting the Caledonians down with measured deadly swings of his *spatha*.

A small wedge of the Second Augusta legion moves about him now, his new British colleagues. They pass him by and surge ahead. He frowns. A sudden barrier of enemies emerges from his left and separates him from the armoured Romans. A sideways manoeuvre of northern tribesmen: bare-chested, tartan-breeched, long hair swinging. All barbarian cries and long heavy swords. They come from nowhere and everywhere, flowing down the sides of the wet-grassed hills, filling the little glen with a deadly rising tide.

He yells to his colleagues. They take no notice, moving further away beyond the screaming barbarians, out of sound and reach. And now he can't find his brother. The clamour of battle deafens him as he uselessly shouts his brother's name. He cuts and slashes, pushing forward, frantic to regain sight of Flavius.

Then he sees him, holding his oval shield up. The Capricorn insignia glimmers through the rising hill mist. Flavius has outstripped his fellow soldiers, gone too far forward. The young man is alone, forlorn, with a circle of warriors closing round him like wolves. Quintus cries out, 'Flavius!' but still his voice fails and only the noises of battle and death answer. His brother has disappeared into the mists again. Then the curtain parts for a frozen moment. He sees one of the plaid-cloaked wolves slash at Flavius from behind, slicing into his brother's hamstring so he falls, landing heavily on his knees in the mud.

Quintus leaps forward. Gaius advances with him, covering his sword arm. Quintus cracks the metal edge of his shield hard against a naked back covered in blue circles. The Caledonian falls away, and Quintus reaches his brother. Flavius, still on his knees with a puzzled searching expression on his face, looks up and opens his mouth to call to Quintus and then jerks, as a spear is thrust through his body from behind. A gush of bright blood rushes out of his mouth and down his chest. Flavius seems to look down to study it. His body is pinioned by the blade of the man who has just killed him. Quintus gasps, unbelieving. Time freezes. Silence blankets the field once more.

Quintus never sees the warrior who trips him, slashing open his right thigh from knee to groin. Gaius Trebonius tells him much later of how he rescues Quintus, how his brother's body is snatched up by the retreating legion. They leave the mountains and glens to the swirling fogs, to the half-naked savages and their curved calyx war horns.

Quintus struggled in his sleep to ward off the scene, fighting to open his eyes and return. *How long, oh you gods? How many times will you inflict this horror on me? I thought my punishment was over.*

He lashed out, seeing with the eye of dreaming while knowing himself to be awake. A hand, smooth and firm, gripped him by the elbow.

'Quintus! Quintus, come back. None of it is real. Let it go, Quintus …'

His head swam. Now there was bright light on his face. The mists had withdrawn. The sounds of battle were gone too, along with the dreadful metallic stench of his brother's hot blood. Instead there was a faint scent of roses.

He was sitting on the ground, back propped against the stable wall in Bo Gwelt. Now he remembered: he'd wandered out here after leaving the garden. He'd sat down, just for a moment; must have fallen asleep.

He drew a hand unsteadily across his eyes, and when he opened them, Julia was there. She released his arm, and sat down on the muddy grass next to him, heedless of her pale robe. She looked at him intently.

'Still the nightmares after so long, Quintus?'

There was nothing to say. These visions, sent by the gods as waking trauma too —these were his punishment. Ever since Flavius was butchered in front of him in Caledonia he had denied the truth. He had tried to flee his guilt as he rode the long boundary roads of the Roman Empire. If he turned his back on anyone who tried to get close to him, surely they would know his unworthiness and leave him alone.

Julia was watching him with an uncertain look on her face as if she didn't know him. What did that matter? She'd abandoned him, left Eboracum without a backward glance, never replied to his letters. He was alone in the world, alone with his duty to his work and to his Emperor.

Yet she kept watching him.

'Quintus, you can tell me. Maybe I can help.' There was a look on her face of …what? Pity, of course.

He stood abruptly. He needed to get away. But she trapping him there with her coaxing hand and low voice.

'Quintus, come to the Sacred Spa. There is healing there.'

What could he say that she would understand?

'I can't walk away. It's my sworn duty to uncover the plot and bring the culprits to justice.'

'But … I thought you had done that already. You've recovered the silver, and with most of the conspirators dead and Caesulanus in custody, surely the plot has failed? You've solved the murders of Catus and Velvinna, and put down the Durotriges' unrest. Lucius and the girl may have gone for now, but what more can one young lad do? Don't you see? Your mission is over! You can come to Aquae Sulis with me.'

Quintus stared at her. She had no idea, of course. How could she know about the blow that had just fallen, bringing the ghosts of his past back to life?

He turned to leave.

She called after him in a breaking voice, 'What about Aurelia? She needs her father, more now than ever. You can't leave her!'

'Aurelia *had* a father, who she will never stop loving. She has you, and all her establishment here to help her. What she doesn't need is a damaged man, someone who can never be a proper father to her.'

He left, not looking back. She must see now that he had failed all his life. He was worthless. Wounded too deeply to heal. There was only his duty left: to reveal the ultimate betrayal, and finish the mission. If he survived. And if he didn't? No-one would care.

He hurried into the stable. The chestnut whickered on seeing him. Someone else saw him too.

He should have known. If he'd thought about it, he might have supposed that Aurelia was sleeping, as Julia thought. Or sitting mourning the man she loved as her father. But here she was, arms flung round the rough neck of her pony. The puppy Cerberus crouched at her feet. Her slight body shook with sobs. He was struck by the naked sorrow on her face.

'Aurelia. You shouldn't be alone. Does your aunt know you're here?'

She lifted her head.

'Sir?'

'Quintus. Just Quintus.'

She stumbled across to him, falling on her knees at his feet.

'I had to be with the horses and Cerberus. Now Father has gone, they are all I have. Mother died when I was little, and since then Father has been everything, both parents at once and my best friend. And poor Aunt Julia, who has her own busy life in Aquae Sulis—now she's stuck with me to care for. I c-can't do that to her, sir. But how can I go on without my darling father? I'm so alone!'

He sat with her, holding the child in silence for as long as she needed. She was right about one thing. Marcus had been the centre of her universe when her true parents gave her up. Marcus had given her secure love and a warm happy home here at Bo Gwelt.

He flinched as the reality hit him. *We hid the truth from Aurelia, Julia and I. My fault. If I had listened to Julia that day in Eboracum, it could have been so different.* What if Aurelia found out now, he wondered. He looked down at his child, the grey eyes so like his own red with grief, her wide mobile mouth so like Julia's now crumpled and trembling. *She would hate me. I've given her nothing, never been a father to her. Best she remains Julia's niece and ward, and forgets me.*

And yet—isn't this a chance, the *chance, to change all that?*

He allowed a vision to build, piece by piece, in his mind. What if he could repair the damage, make up for the mistakes? If he reclaimed his British family, Julia and Aurelia, wouldn't that make up for his failure to save Flavius and his own father? Perhaps the Gods might finally forgive him, and he would be worthy of grace.

He was holding Aurelia still. After a time she quietened, pulling herself upright and wiping a grubby hand across her wet face. She stared up at him, looking puzzled. Then a sound broke into the stable from outside, and she turned to listen.

'Horses,' she said.

Into the courtyard cantered three army horses. Two were ridden by troopers in the uniform of the Aquae Sulis company. They dismounted neatly, throwing crisp salutes. The third horse carried a very tired little man, dark-skinned and rumpled. He slid off his mount, near to collapse as his feet hit the ground.

'Sir, *Frumentarius,* I come with an urgent message from Commander Marcellus Crispus.' Tertius managed to look both daunted and proud as he handed a sealed letter over. Quintus's mind snapped back to attention.

'Thank you, Tertius. Good to see you back.'

The message was concise. The Second Augusta was being mobilised. Marcellus had orders to bring his detachment to muster with the legion at Corinium in three days. From there they were to head east.

Marcellus proposed to ignore the orders.

Frumentarius Quintus Valerius, greetings.

I beg you to make haste to meet me on the road east from the Sabrina landing at Aust. I will brief you then. Time does not allow more now. Send whatever force you can northwards on the Fosse Way, but I urge you yourself to come by sea to save time. I have ordered a navy bireme to embark you at high tide at Cranford Bridge, for passage north up the Severn Sea. From the Aust landing you can ride on to strike my company's path on the road from Aquae Sulis.

On no account land on the west side of Sabrina. You must not risk meeting the Augusta before we join forces. You and I must stop this together. Only disaster can result for my deluded legionary comrades.

I look for you, Brother, by sunset on the second day from receiving this letter.

Marcellus Crispus

Quintus studied the letter, frowning. He nodded to Tertius to follow him into a quiet corner of the stable.

'Tell me what you know.'

The little man swallowed. 'Not much more than is written there. The legate of the Augusta is rumoured to be ill, hasn't been seen outside his quarters in weeks. Centurion Crispus no longer trusts some of his brother officers in the Augusta. He fears they may have been coerced or bribed to raise revolt.'

'Bribed with Vebriacum silver?'

Tertius said nothing. He looked down at the dirt floor, and wriggled his sandals in the dust.

'Right. You don't trust me either. Although I have saved your life, Tertius, perhaps twice. As you have saved mine. Are we not now brothers?'

More silence. Tertius looked up at the Roman with unhappy eyes.

'At least tell me where Marcellus believes the legion is posted to.'

'He fears they will be marched to Londinium.'

So this was it. The coup had begun. Only two men in the province had the authority to command the legate of the Augusta to mobilise his legion. One was his old comrade, the Governor Gaius Trebonius. The other was the Provincial Procurator, Aradius Rufinus.

Tertius cleared his throat.

'Centurion Crispus wonders whether the Druidess Fulminata has gone to raise the Dobunni tribe at their capital in Corinium.'

'What! Did he not receive my message to arrest her?'

More unhappy circling of feet in the dust.

'Yes, but the men he sent to intercept were... amenable to her persuasions. Instead of bringing her back to Aquae Sulis, they escorted her to the Dobunni capital. Marcellus was very angry, saying they are deserters. But they might believe themselves to be acting under legionary orders, as part of a plan to unite the rebelling tribesmen with the Isca soldiers.'

By Mithras! Quintus was very glad they still had Caesulanus. At least here was one source of information. The time had come to press harder for the truth.

Quintus looked around for Tiro. He wasn't to be seen, but it was a good bet he'd be in the kitchen, just about the only cleanish intact room left in the villa and where he'd find Britta and Gwenn, no doubt, as well as food and warmth. He sent Tertius with Aurelia to the kitchen, and went himself to find the Sorios. The short day was beginning to wane. Before leaving, Quintus wanted to be sure that their promises of help would be honoured.

Julia found him first. She glanced at his arm. He scowled, then feeling ashamed of himself raised a fleeting smile of greeting. She smiled back, but after a hesitation that said everything. He made an effort.

'What help do you lack here? I'll speak to Sorio.'

'No need. Our neighbour has already arranged to send over a construction gang from his own estate at Bawdrip. We should at least have a roof over our heads soon. I will arrange the funeral for tomorrow, and then take Aurelia home with me to Aquae Sulis until probate has been settled and her future is clearer. Britta and I will take care of Aurelia. Don't be concerned for her, Quintus. I know my brother's wishes. Aurelia is the sole beneficiary of the estate, and under my guardianship till she comes of age.'

'Claudia?'

Julia screwed up her face. 'My brother's will makes provision for her, but Bo Gwelt is no longer her home. I think we will let Claudia go back to Iscalis and live the quiet life of a widow in Bulbo's villa.'

Quintus made no objection; his mind was already elsewhere. Julia might feel he should be consulted about their daughter, but he knew himself to be unworthy of the vibrant little creature who made him yearn for home and peace. He looked away. There was one final thing to be said, and he found it hard to say.

'I know you will do what you have always done for our daughter. You will think of her best interests, love her, and fight for her future happiness. For what it's worth, I thank you.'

It was a goodbye, of sorts. Quintus knew what was coming at the end of his road: the final act of his soldier's life that would settle all. If he lived, he would think then about the future. But he saw little need to plan ahead. A whole trained experienced legion, quite possibly two, against the few men he might scrape together?

Julia was watching him again. To his surprise she came close, sliding her arms around him, still watching. She lifted her face a little. Her clear blue eyes looked into his. He smelt roses, and saw the flash of the gold owlet necklace as he bent to kiss her mouth.

Something inside him tore, began to break free.

A throat was cleared nearby, and Sorio *pater* spoke. 'You sent for me, Frumentarius?'

'How could he have escaped?'

Tiro had been dragged away from his tete-a-tete with Britta. There was no sign of the prisoner, Caesulanus, and no horse where Tiro had left him the previous night.

'To be honest, boss, I just plain forgot him, what with the fire and everything.'

'You moron! You useless British moron!'

Tiro looked upset.

'I apologise, sir. I neglected my duty. I understand you have to punish me, but if there is anything I can do to make up for this, I will.'

Quintus uncurled furious fists. His burned forearm was awash with fresh pain. He drew a deep breath, and then another. It wasn't Tiro's fault. They had all been caught up in the disaster of the fire. Tiro had willingly put himself at risk to help rescue Aurelia. Quintus of all people could appreciate how much fear Tiro had felt in the tunnels of the hypocaust. And gone in anyway. That took guts and commitment.

'Right. You *will* be punished. You're coming with me now to undo your omission. Thanks to Marcellus we know where Caesulanus is heading. We may just get there before him.'

'Where, sir?'

'Maybe the biggest battle of our lives, Tiro.'

Reading the Investigator's set face, Tiro guessed their chances of coming back alive were not good. He cursed the gods. It seemed unfair to find the sort of girl he'd always looked for, only to lose her now. Just as he'd begun to hope she might feel the same. The words she'd whispered to him a few minutes ago might be the last he would ever hear from her.

Chapter Twenty-two

Tiro was grateful for the full moon and lack of clouds that night, as they rode west along the low ridge of the Poldens. It was a silent night, with only their own hoofbeats and the occasional fox bark to punctuate the quiet. Tiro stretched, easing sore muscles in his back. The healing grazes on his elbows and knees were beginning to itch. He felt thoroughly miserable. Why had he spent his whole life so far making a mess of everything, chasing booze, fun and easy sex? And now, when at last he knew what kind of life he really wanted and maybe had a chance to achieve it, *now* it seemed likely he would die first.

At least the scar on his forehead had stopped hurting. He took cheer from that and thought about their next steps. They were to take fast ship at the little port of Crandon Bridge, on the estuary of the Pedrida river. He didn't need to know more. He'd just go with the flow and throw himself into whatever adventure awaited.

Ahead of him the Sorio boy led the way, sitting easy on his horse with a light spear in one hand. Nice bit of horseflesh he's got there, thought Tiro, distracted by the horse's strong lines and well-pricked ears. Drusus hadn't needed to be asked twice to be their guide tonight. He seemed keen to shed the lingering image of stooge to Lucius.

Tiro heard the soft regular footfalls of the chestnut bringing up the rear. As so often the boss was silent, keeping himself to himself. Tiro reckoned Quintus had had words with his lady, too, but there was no knowing the upshot there. And what about young Aurelia? Her true parentage couldn't be denied; soon as you saw her with the boss, you knew. Poor little lass. Her world had turned upside down, and now her new father was leaving too. But perhaps Aurelia didn't yet know who Quintus was, wouldn't know until the Imperial Investigator came back from this mission. That made Tiro sit upright. He'd make damn sure Aurelia got her real father back and in one piece. He'd made that promise in a quiet moment to Britta, and he'd keep it even if all the Furies came after them.

They broke out from the tree-cover into bright moonlight. Drusus drew rein. They were near the western end of the hills, looking across the bronze-brown Severn Sea towards the country of the Silures. The boy raised his spear, pointing to the left. Tiro saw that a narrow well-made bridle path zigzagged down to a small town on the river bank. The Pedrida looped its way across country from the east, widening and turning muddy as it reached the little port. Decurion Sorio had explained that the silt washed along by Sabrina was carried upstream into the Pedrida by vast tides.

'You won't believe the tides are round about here, Frumentarius. And we get tidal bores, many times the height of a man. You can't outpace the water if you're caught out on the sands. Very dangerous the Summer Country waters are, especially when it's full moon in spring.'

Tiro doubted Quintus believed the Decurion. Everyone thinks their own patch is special, after all. But Tiro had seen the difference between high and low tides in the Tamesis, and knew how dangerous tidal waters could be. He edged up to Drusus to peer down over the moonlit settlement. It was a gaggle of storehouses and a few small cottages huddled together between the slope under them, and the sombre silty riverbank. Small merchant ships were tied side-on to the quay, their mainsails furled away. One or two round hide-covered coracles were drawn up downstream.

Tiro shuddered. He had never learned to swim properly, and had an aversion to the sea. The only waters he enjoyed were the steaming ones in town baths. He didn't even like water to drink, preferring beer at any time of day. And there was no sign of the fast naval galley Marcellus mentioned.

'When is high tide, Drusus?' Quintus asked.

' Around an hour before sunrise.'

'Good. Your father tells me the crossing upriver to Aust should take no more than eight hours with a fast-rowing crew, so we should disembark before dark tomorrow. I gather the waters can be challenging.'

Tiro spat over his shoulder for luck, catching the cynical look on his superior's face.

'Time enough for Tiro to make his offerings to the goddess of the river.' Drusus helpfully pointed to a worn stone marker overlooking the muddy foreshore. Tiro had every intention of paying his respects to the ancient and important goddess Sabrina before entering her watery domain. His musings were interrupted by Drusus.

'That's odd. There's a horse coming up. She seems to be riderless.'

An old mare shambled up the path, turning onto the wider brow of the hill with a faint whinny of greeting to the other horses. She stooped to graze, and Tiro recognised with a shock the old nag they had requisitioned in Lindinis.

'Sir! That's the horse Caesulanus was tied to.'

Quintus pulled his chestnut round and began to descend the steep path in haste. Tiro blessed Luna for her timely gift of brilliant light as he followed. Drusus, being young and heedless, kicked his boots into his grey's flanks and managed to bypass both of them, galloping headlong downhill.

'Young fool,' Quintus said, but he and Tiro kept pace with Drusus. Miraculously they all arrived at the bottom intact. The moon was still high over the Severn Sea and now they could make out a figure stumbling along the beach. Caesulanus was making for the coracles pulled up beyond the high tide mark. Large pools opened under his feet, making a sucking noise loud enough to be heard over their hoofbeats. They cantered after him, gaining quickly. The man swerved away, heading directly for the water. Perhaps he thought he could get away by swimming.

Drusus pulled his horse up sharply, and yelled back to them. 'We can't ride any further. These are shivering sands. We'll all be sucked under if we go further on horseback.' He flung himself off his horse. The others copied him. Quintus reached for the boy's spear. Caesulanus turned his head to look and his very next step slid him knee-deep into the treacherous mud. He seemed to pause, swinging his body to and fro in a vain effort to free his legs. Each movement sucked him further under the silt, now a watery black under the shining eye of Luna. He froze as they cautiously approached, Quintus testing each step with the spear.

'Get me out of this stinking mud, and I'll tell you whatever you want to know.'

The trapped man's voice shook. Even that small movement made his body sink deeper. They were close now, Tiro not far from the prisoner. He could see the whites of his eyes, and the shallow rapid breaths betraying his panic. With every breath Caesulanus was sinking further.

Afterwards, Tiro had leisure to wonder at his own recklessness. Number one, he couldn't swim. Number two, he knew as well as any man how dangerous estuary silt can be. Number three, the dark brackish mud was freezing cold. Number four, he maybe had a better life come back to, with a decent job, and this was no time to act the hero. He stopped counting after number four.

An image he had seen as a mudlarking child on the slippery banks of the Tamesis thrust into his mind. He had been watching a fisherman with a mud-horse, catching shellfish and spreading the loaded nets carefully into the wooden sledge.

'See this 'ere mud horse, lad? It makes it safe for me to go out after the fish without getting stuck in the filthy mud. Spreads the weight, like.' And Tiro had seen the point, even as a child. The wider the load was spread out on the sledge, the safer the operation would be.

He flung himself flat onto the cold stinking mud, calling back to Quintus, 'I'll get him, sir.'

He began to crawl, keeping his weight as spread out across the mud as he could. It was terrifying and disgusting in equal measure. Had he been able to look up he would have immediately retreated. Drusus told him later that even as he wriggled his way onwards, Caesulanus had already sunk up to his neck. Tiro could hear the man blubbering, swearing and praying to Neptune. But he couldn't see what Drusus had already spotted out to sea. He couldn't hear the lad's screams of warning over the sucking noise of the wet mud, either. At last he lifted his head to check direction. Only a couple of yards now from the drowning man. Then he heard Drusus's desperate shouts.

'The bore — Tiro, the bore's coming in from the sea. You have to come back. Leave him, come back!'

Tiro didn't like the sound of this at all. Craning his neck almost to breaking point to lift his head, he saw a dark line approaching on the river, silvered where the moon glanced off the leading edge. It swept in from the Severn Sea at horrible speed, racing up the river and growing taller all the time. Tiro tried to turn. His leading arm sank into the mud. He thought he would die of panic. He couldn't draw breath. He remembered the awful choking sensation of being trapped in the dark in the hypocaust, expecting to suffocate at every moment. This was like that, but worse. He felt the air squeezing out of his chest, and waited for the cold slimy mud to crawl down his throat.

A calm voice, clear and commanding, broke through.

'Don't try to turn. Reach your right hand back towards me, carefully. As far behind as you can. Extend it fully. You're within touching distance of Drusus's spear. We'll pull you out. Just lie completely flat and still, let us do the work.' The broad iron head of the boy's spear was pushed into his open hand. Tiro closed his freezing hand round it. He wriggled over to grab the shaft with his other hand. At once he felt a steady pull, gradually swivelling him round to face the shore. With gathering power Quintus and Drusus heaved on the spearshaft. Tiro was moving faster now and could help with some movement of his legs. The smell of the deadly sands was right up his nostrils and his eyes were watering with salty grit, blotting out vision. Drusus shouted, 'Too late, Sabrina has him!' Tiro shut his eyes, thought one last time of Britta, and waited for the tall wave to close over his head.

Before the bore reached him his feet abruptly steadied into firmer sand. He was washed waist-deep by rising silty water, but with feet down and firm he could release the spear. He stumbled onto the shore, and turned back to look across the estuary. He was dripping and shivering convulsively.

There was no-one there.

'Where's he gone, the prisoner?'

'To Hades. Without telling us anything.' Quintus sounded defeated, and turned away. Drusus had a lingering look of terror on his young face.

'The river took him! The Goddess Sabrina in her wrath rose in a massive wave and rolled over his head. He just disappeared. It was horrible.' The boy choked in apparent effort not to cry like a small child. Quintus was already climbing up the slippery river bank, back turned. Tiro pulled himself out of his stupor, cursing, and grabbed Drusus by the arm.

They trudged back to the port, cold and dispirited. They gathered the horses back together, retrieving their bags and cloaks. Caesulanus had been a villain all right, but Tiro had seldom witnessed a more disgusting death. He wrapped his dirty but welcome *birrus* round himself, and tried to steady himself.

It was probably only a few minutes' wait, but Tiro was numb with cold by the time Quintus called out, 'Here they are!' He heard the swift rhythmic beat of oars moving in disciplined momentum. A sleek double-banked naval ship swept along the river towards them, helped by the spring tide and buoyed up on the lingering bore. It raced past them, appearing to swivel on a *sestertius* as commands rang out along the open deck. The mainsail was swiftly gathered in, and the ship hove-to alongside the quay, settling into position as if it had always been there.

A dark bearded man in the uniform of a naval officer leapt lightly off the bow calling, 'Frumentarius Quintus Valerius?'

Tiro groaned. A ship meant more waves, more water. And more danger, from the description Decurion Sorio had given them of the passage up the Severn Sea.

No time to waste then. Tiro hurried over to the ancient pillar where a tiny spring washed the Goddess' stony feet. He reverently dropped a *denarius* he could ill-afford into the water, and prayed earnestly to the lady of the mighty western river for a safe passage. They bade farewell to Drusus, who grinned, saluted and leapt onto his horse with the ease of a boy who has lived all his life in the saddle. The last Tiro saw of him was a clod of mud flying from the grey's hoofs as the boy set him at a canter back up the hill.

Well before dusk the next day Tiro had to concede that the goddess Sabrina had heard him, and that the skilled sailors of the *classis britannica* knew their business. A friendly marine took him under his wing on embarkation, and rustled up a change of clothes while Tiro's filthy clothes were rinsed and dried. Tiro kept well inside the cabin, praying. His marine winked at him, saying, 'No need to worry, army boy. Our flotilla is based nearby at Abona, and we spend all our time charting these waters. You're in safe hands.'

Wooden bowls of hot stew were passed out of the tiny kitchen. Warmed and fed, Tiro drifted off into a doze. Quintus spent long periods on deck, talking quietly to the bearded captain and looking north.

By the time the planked keel of the galley slid up the landing at Aust, Tiro was feeling rested and very grateful. It had indeed been a rough voyage, with shifting sandbanks and waters writhing in and out of the inlets along the shoreline. He helped the sailors disembark their horses, who had not enjoyed the passage. A few words from Tiro soothed them, impressing his marine. He saluted with a grin as they passed down the gangway.

The tiny port of Aust crouched under a low cliff, glowing stripes of pink sandstone and green limestone. Tiro felt in more than usual need of worship, but was disappointed to find there was no time to visit the little temple perched on the cliff. He had to concede that dusk was quickly sweeping up before them. They had some distance to go before night fell. A road built for the legion at Isca would lead them to an intersection with the highway heading north to Glevum, as long as they didn't miss the crossroads in the dark.

It was a cold night of empty landscape. Tiro hoped it stayed that way till they made rendezvous with Centurion Crispus. He was eager to see the redheaded officer and his troopers. *I just hope you know what you're doing, young Crispus.* He prayed to Mars, god of war, and then to Minerva, goddess of justice and righteous combat.

He feared they would need all the divine support they could get.

Chapter Twenty-three

Two broad roads swept north from Aquae Sulis, like the outspread wings of the Goddess Victory. Each headed to a major city: on the west to Glevum, the old fortress and colonia; on the east to Corinium, the civitas of the large Dobunni tribe. Quintus guessed the Second Augusta would approach the quicker way, direct from Glevum to Corinium on the Great West Road and so on to Londinium. No uprising in Britannia could be successful without taking the capital. That was why both the provincial heads were based there: the controller of military might, the Governor; and the man with the money, the Procurator.

Marcellus had orders to join the legion from Aquae Sulis. Quintus reasoned anyone looking for the reluctant cohort would do so along the direct eastern route to Corinium. So Quintus looked for the Aquae Sulis boys along the west road, where their little camp was masked by the substantial Cotswold Ridge.

The Augusta were impregnable while garrisoned in their fort at Isca. The Aquae Sulis vexillation would have to wait while the mother legion made its long way round the north of the Sabrina estuary, and then use surprise to bolster interception. If interception was indeed what Marcellus had in mind. It was difficult to believe that surprise could make any difference against such overwhelming numbers, but what else could they do?

It was a relief when Tiro's sharp eyes picked out the low smudge of campfires ahead in the dusk. The Aquae Sulis century was encamped, snug and well-organised, beyond the cleared margins of the access road from Aust. Quintus and Tiro were quickly ushered into Marcellus's tent in the centre of the camp.

'Brothers!' Marcellus rose from his portable desk, and embraced each of them. 'My *optio*, Decimus Senecio.' He nodded at a grizzled veteran, bandy-legged and scarred, who stood to rigid attention. 'Anything we discuss can be said in front of Decimus. He is my most loyal and experienced man.'

A slave entered the tent, bringing hot wine and bread with chunks of cheese, all gratefully accepted. Then with the tent flaps secured by an armed guard stationed beyond, they settled to confer. Quintus raised the subject of the Dobunni tribe.

'I understand from Tertius that Fulminata escaped arrest. No fault of yours, Brother,' he added hastily.

Marcellus looked angry. 'There will be a reckoning for that betrayal when I catch those two wastrels. I imagine they plan to scuttle back to the bosom of the legion in Isca.'

'Right. Let's assume she is still on her way to Corinium. She'll wait until the legion is close before stirring up the Dobunni, not wanting to lose impetus once she has roused the passions of the young men. The soldiers will join up with the tribesmen. If anything goes wrong, their cover would be that they mobilised to prevent a Dobunni rebellion. By the time the enlarged Augusta enter an unsuspecting Londinium, it will be too late to stop the insurrection.

'Marcellus, you know this country better than we do. How long for the Augusta to reach Corinium?'

The centurion glanced at his *optio*. The older man spoke slowly, a deep voice with a heavy local accent. 'Well, sir, I reckon that'd be all of three more days. See here, it will take a day or two at least to recall all the scouting parties and out-posted men back to Isca. Then they need to assemble and pack, ready to march—something the Augusta has not done for many years. It's a fair step then from Isca to Corinium.'

'Agreed,' said Marcellus. 'I think they will not get there for another few days, most likely on the fourth day from now.' He fell silent for a moment, sipping at his wine. The only sound was the faint crackle of coals burning in the brazier. A buffet of breeze made the tent walls wallow, presaging rain coming in from the west. Full dark had fallen, and pressed in behind the flickering oil lamps.

'So, here is our position. Apart from your company, Marcellus, there are just we two. That limits what we can realistically do. Fortunately the community leaders in Lindinis scuppered the attempt by Fulminata and her cronies to raise rebellion there. I have asked a Lindinis town councillor, Decurion Agrippa Sorio, to raise and arm the Durotriges to follow us in support. But it will take time to muster them, and time to march them to our aid. Neither are they trained or adequately equipped to fight. Is there any other help we can call on, anyone nearby we can rely on to remain loyal to the Emperor?'

Marcellus shook his head. 'No way of knowing, sir. My men are all with me to the end, of course. But they are only a century, though at least an over-sized one. With all my couriers and scouts now recalled, we are 105 men.'

'107, sir, counting me and the boss!'

Marcellus smiled faintly at Tiro, but the smile was tired and did not reach his eyes. 'I thought to call out the citizens of Aquae Sulis, who know and value our garrison, I believe. And — well, I wondered, Quintus, whether the two of us could appeal directly to the men of the Augusta legion? The officers are mostly bought and sold, but I would bet the ordinary troops—who always bear the brunt of any fighting—might be open to persuasion. They all worship the Principate, of course, and have sworn their lifelong loyalty to the Emperor. Perhaps they will disobey their officers' orders, and keep faith?'

Quintus shook his head at that. He feared Marcellus was allowing his sense of what was right to overcome reality. The men would follow the lead of their centurions. And the centurions, the backbone of any legion, would sniff the wind to see which way it was blowing, and vote in favour of the strongest-seeming leader. Right now, that person was whoever had planned this coup. There was only one chance of reinforcement left, a very remote one. There was another legion in Britannia Superior. The XX Valeria Victrix, based at Castra Deva in the far north-west. Could that legion be persuaded to stay loyal and march south to stop the rebellion? Could it be done in time?

Marcellus was doubtful.

'I know very little of the Deva legate, only that he is quite new in post. I believe he took over the Twentieth a bare few weeks before our Provincial Governor Trebonius arrived in

Londinium. His loyalties are not known to me. His appointment may well have been at the request of the new Governor.'

Quintus nodded. That was often how promotions and appointments happened. It was all about who you knew.

'Too late anyhow,' broke in the *optio*. 'No chance to alert the Valeria Victrix now. By the time we get a message up to Deva and they march all the way south to us, we'll be dead and buried. Or food for crows.'

It was a blunt but likely assessment.

'No point in even thinking about the third British legion at Eboracum. Separate province since Emperor Septimius Severus split Britannia, different Governor, even further away. They won't get involved in our internal disputes.'

Quintus sighed. For a moment the name of Eboracum took him back to the old days there: to pain and poppy juice; to nights battling drugged visions of the pleading eyes of Flavius; to the smell of rosewater and sunbathed dusty city walls; to long fair hair ruffled by the summer breeze.

A disturbance came from outside the tent. The guard poked his head in.

'Sorry to disturb, sir,' he said to Marcellus. 'Message from our vexillation *medicus*, Anicius Piso.'

'Yes?'

'The surgeon was summoned to attend the Legate of the Second Augusta in Isca.'

Marcellus wrinkled his brow. 'Yes, we know this. The Legate has been ill for some time.'

'The surgeon reports the Legate has died, sir. He thought you should know.'

'Is Piso there still?'

'On his way back to Aquae Sulis, probably arrived by now, sir. His courier said something about needing to be back at the hospital urgently.'

Marcellus waved the man away, and raised a concerned face to Quintus.

'So we now know for sure our legion's general had no hand in this plot. I thought it unlikely. He was always a man of honour, but fast losing any ability to command in recent weeks.

Someone else of standing in the legion is behind this.

'What should we do now, Frumentarius? My men are loyal and well-trained, but is it my duty now to lead them into a deathtrap?'

Three pairs of eyes fixed themselves on Quintus. Marcellus looked worried, and upset at the loss of his general; Senecio resigned to obey; Tiro alert and keen.

'Well, it's just us and the Aquae Sulis men until Sorio joins us. Let's use what we have to best advantage. Marcellus, I suggest sending scouts out along the three main roads. A pair to Corinium to assess the Dobunni mood. One man to report back to us, the other to carry on towards Deva. He is to check along the road north out of Corinium and hopefully discover whether the Twentieth legion has been mobilised. We may not be able to raise the Valeria Victrix ourselves, but we have to know whether anyone else already has.

'We should also keep an eye on the progress of the Second Augusta from Isca. And finally, I want to know if there is any movement of troops on the east road. But warn your scouts to be very wary. It is highly likely our opponents will be watching the same routes.

'We should keep our century hidden here meanwhile. Once we know the Augusta is nearing Corinium we'll move to intercept and do whatever we can to upset their plans at that point. Though I fear it will be little enough.'

Marcellus and his *optio* left to issue orders to the scouts. Tiro looked at Quintus.

'Sir?'

'Mmm?'

'I realise you may not want to share all your thoughts with me. But do you know yet who might be behind the plot? We know how the Vebriacum silver was being used to bribe the Augusta's officers, but it can't be the legion's own commander issuing the orders, can it?'

This was the question foremost in Quintus's mind for some time. He didn't like the only answer he had. Now Tiro was asking, and he could no longer avoid answering.

Tiro spoke again.

'Just now you asked Marcellus to post scouts on the road east. Are you expecting to see troops arrive from Londinium before any come the other way from Isca?'

'Yes.'

'Who is coming from Londinium? Is this the real threat? Has this person got control of the Twentieth Valeria Victrix as well?'

Quintus looked thoughtfully at his *stator*. Tiro swallowed, and continued.

'I may have it all wrong, sir, not being a thinker like you. But if what I've said is right, it can only be one of two men.'

Still Quintus was silent. Tiro looked really unhappy. What he was suggesting amounted to sedition. Quintus was aware that Tiro had his faults. He was too prone to drink, impulsive, forgetful, disinclined to obey unless he agreed with a course of action. But he was also resourceful, courageous, and, Quintus believed, loyal. Quintus smiled wryly. The time they had travelled together was short in count of weeks, but they had both moved a long way from their initial distrust and dislike. It had taken the imminent prospect of death and defeat to make him understand this, as with so much else in his life.

'You're quite right, Tiro. I *do* have an idea who we might be dealing with. But even here there may be unwanted ears. So I suggest you think about a few things.

'First, where we have seen white wax tablets?

'Second, why didn't Claudius Bulbo want to visit Southwark?

'Third - and I say this with great reluctance - why were we two chosen for this mission?'

Tiro looked even more puzzled.

Quintus stood slowly, feeling drained. What wouldn't he give to rest now, to sleep deeply and to wake with no need to think more of this? He stood lost in his dark thoughts, twisting the bronze owl ring round his finger. He realised Tiro was watching, and mentally shook himself. There was still his duty to be done.

He alone knew who he was up against. He thought briefly of the people he would never see again: his family so far away in Rome; Julia; Aurelia. The best outcome he could hope for was a good death.

He reached out to grip Tiro by the shoulder.

'Come on, let's get ourselves a tent and see to the horses.'

The next two days crept snail-like for Tiro, while the century remained quietly encamped waiting for the scouts' return. He felt prickly with inaction. His various hurts had eased by now, though he noticed that Quintus still held his left arm hanging straight and avoided making contact with it. Julia had given him more honey and each evening the camp medical orderly replaced the dressings. Tiro caught one glimpse, and saw the arm from wrist to well above elbow a mass of angry red blisters, some of them oozing yellow. He looked away quickly. While he could contemplate his own wounds with equanimity, his stomach for other people's injuries was not as strong.

So he wandered off to look around the camp for diversion, finding it in a scratch fight competition set up by the *optio*. Tiro grinned, and pushed his way to the front of the onlookers. Anyone not engaged in their duties—and Decimus Senecio was very good at keeping his men busy—was gathered in a ring around a pair of men. The crowd was cheering, casting insults, and placing bets. Tiro looked on with interest, and rolled up his sleeves. The combatants were well-matched, being of a height and not dissimilar weights. The dark-haired trooper sweeping his fringe out of his eyes was older and more experienced, Tiro judged, but his younger opponent made up with a willingness to keep wading in. They were both using standard army boxing techniques, panting and sweating as they circled each other to trade blows. Eventually the older man landed a punch full in the eye of the younger. His eyelid immediately ballooned, and the *optio* raised and dropped his arm to signal the end of the bout. Exercise and keeping the blood for battle circulating was one thing. Rendering men unfit to fight another.

Tiro stepped forward. 'I issue challenge to any who will meet me.' The little crowd cheered. He heard whispers of "Governor's Man" and "Londoner" passing from man to man. Right, if they wanted to find out how a city boy fought, they were on. He looked round, wondering who would take up his challenge. A much louder cheer rang out when a tall dark man stepped confidently into the ragged ring. Tiro swallowed. The man had huge bulging muscles, biceps gleaming as if oiled and a torso so sculpted he could have been an ebony statue. Tiro wondered whether he was the cohort's specialist blacksmith. His upper body development was the most impressive he'd seen in a long time.

'Messalinus! Messalinus!' the crowd bellowed. The African grinned, showing perfect white teeth, and darted in like a cobra to grab and throw Tiro. *Oh yes,* thought Tiro, *now we'll have some fun.* He fleetingly regretted not being able to bet on himself, then brought all his attention to bear. Messalinus was swift, skilled and astonishingly strong. Deserving of his opponent's full regard. Just how Tiro liked it.

It was all over in five minutes, but not before Tiro had a bleeding eyebrow and Messalinus was stretched out in the dirt, knocked senseless by one of the shorter man's crafty moves. Someone threw Tiro a rag, and he mopped the blood off his face to see Quintus and Marcellus applauding.

'Just won five sesterces on you, Tiro.' Quintus slapped him on the back as they walked back to the command tent. Tiro was insulted, and said so. The bout had been worth more than that. Quintus actually laughed out loud. Some good news must have come to lift the *frumentarius*'s mood.

Inside the tent the slave poured watered wine and they sat down round the jug. Senecio bustled in, and Quintus nodded at Marcellus, who waved a hand in deferral back. Quintus looked round at all of them.

'Right. The scouts should be back soon with their reports. Let's start making our plans.' Outside the first rain for many days began to patter on the leather roof of the tent. Tiro drew a slow breath, and leaned forward to listen.

Chapter Twenty-four

Julia dozed fitfully. Her thoughts jostled, trying to make sense of the senseless. She grieved for Velvinna, hoping her friend had not suffered. Her heart jolted faster as she pictured the witch Fulminata, pretending coy gratitude as she entered Velvinna's little house, leaving poison in her wake. The stomach-churning image of Antoninus Labienus, stalking the innocent boy Catus and killing him with a single barbaric blow. And now Marcus, struck down too—

She was suddenly roused by Britta calling.

'Mistress, come quickly! It's the man from the mines, Tiro's friend. He's lying here bleeding on our doorstep!' Julia tumbled out of bed, thrusting her feet into sandals and flinging a shawl around her shoulders. She grabbed her nightlamp, and made her way downstairs as quietly as she could. She was trying not to disturb Aurelia, who had been unusually quiet the whole way back to Aquae Sulis. She'd refused any food at the funeral feast. Only once they had arrived home had she finally given in and sipped a cup of hot milk and honey pressed on her by the worried Senovara.

By the smoking light of wall lamps Julia saw that most of her household was in the atrium. Not including Aurelia, thank the Lady. She glanced at Tertius lying unconscious on the tiled floor, and called to a maid to fetch a blanket. She knelt down by the little man.

'Who found him?'

'Me, Lady Julia. I opened the door when I heard a faint knocking. The man fell in, and collapsed as you see him.' It was Senovara, looking shaken.

'All right. Britta, take Rufus and a lantern, get to the hospital and bring Anicius Piso back with you. Fast as you can!'

Britta turned to find Rufus already coming in from his bedspace above the stable. The two left at a run, Rufus holding the lantern, Britta catching her plaid throw around her as she struggled to keep pace with the young groom.

Julia crouched low over Tertius, and pressed a finger into the skin beneath his jaw. His pulse was thready, very faint. She lifted up his outer garments and tunic, and discovered why. There were several bleeding slashes on his arms, but the real problem was a deep stab below his ribcage. Blood was pulsing from the wound. Not the bright red arterial colour that would bring quick death. This was a welling, purplish flow of blood, not fast but thick and unstoppable. Julia guessed the major vein in his liver had been severed. Tertius was dying.

Julia prayed briefly, while she leaned hard on his abdomen, pressing both hands into the wound to try to slow the bleeding. *Lady, I beg you, please preserve this man. There have been so many deaths already. Don't let this brave innocent man die too!*

She sent to Senovara to get cloths, and balled them up to thrust into the bleeding. It slowed somewhat, and she saw the man's eyes flicker.

'Senovara, tell me what happened.'

'It were so quick, mistress, and I was fast asleep.'

'Yes, never mind, you heard the knocking, opened the door. What then?'

'I found this man swaying on the doorstep. He was trying to say something. And then I saw a woman, just out of the corner of my eye, like.'

'Saw who?'

'I dunno, mistress. Just a flash really, someone running down the street. Wouldn't have seen her at all, if she hadn't stopped by a street lamp and looked back.'

'Well? For goodness sake, what did you see? Did you know her?'

'No mistress, though I would know her again.'

Julia, still pressing on the bloody heap of cloth as hard as she could, found her teeth gritting.

'What — did — you — see?'

'Well, mistress, she was youngish, quite tall I think. With eyes!' Senovara paused as if in triumph, then seemed to realise this wasn't enough. 'Black eyes, like sloes. Creepy-like, the way she looked at me.'

'Anything else?'

'Oh yes, mistress. Then there was the hair.'

Julia decided to cut short the agony. 'Long, red, curling?'

Senovara gawped. 'You must have seen her too, mistress! Exactly right. She looked at me, or mayhap at him, the man here lying at our door. Then she ran away.'

The body under her hands stirred, and she looked down to find Tertius awake and looking at her.

'Shush, Tertius, don't try to speak. I have sent for the surgeon. We'll get you to the hospital and you'll be fine.' She pulled the blanket across his legs and lower body, knowing it was too little, too late.

His face was very pale, the olive skin whitened by blood loss. She shifted one hand to his wrist, checking his pulse again. The hand was cold and clammy. If Anicius didn't get here soon, Tertius would die on her doorstep.

He seemed to read her thoughts. 'Tell the *frumentarius* —I was faithful. Trust—me. Help is coming.' His voice was almost too faint to hear. His eyes fluttered again, and he groaned. More blood welled up out of her makeshift compress. She knew he was nearly gone. She lowered her head so she could hear him better.

'Enica—'

'Don't worry about Enica. I will make sure she is looked after and has a happy home. Tertius, who did this to you?'

He seemed to be listening to someone else. He suddenly smiled, radiantly.

'Tell Enica not be sad. Catus —is waiting for me.'

Then he turned his head with eyes closed, and she thought he was gone. Very faintly she heard, 'Tell him to watch the — Londinium road.'

There was no more.

She stood, straightening her stiff back, unaware of the tears rolling silently down her face or the bloody clout clutched in her hands. A horse clattered up the street from the bridge, and Medicus Piso threw himself off and came in to kneel by Tertius. Two orderlies and Rufus ran up behind, Britta following more slowly. Julia sobbed aloud, not hearing herself. The surgeon checked the Syrian's body for breath and pulse, then stood slowly. He looked at Julia with affectionate concern, and put an arm round her in a respectful embrace.

'I'm so sorry, Lady Julia. I supposed that Tertius had left Aquae Sulis with Marcellus and the cohort. I had no idea he had stayed alone in the city. Now I wonder why.'

Julia let herself weep a little on Piso's shoulder. She lifted her head, trying to say something to the servants, to summon some vestige of control. Britta shook her head.

'Julia, my lady, you must rest now. If you want to avenge our friends and your brother, you need to be strong. Let me look after you, just this once. Tell me which herbs will help you. I'll fetch you some in warm milk. Then you *must* sleep. I'll speak to Surgeon Piso, settle the servants, and check on Aurelia. The morning is soon enough to decide what's next to do.'

Julia surrendered, letting Britta lead her up the stairs to her bedchamber and pull back the covers so Julia could climb into bed.

The Aquae Sulis baths were open to women from noon. Julia and Britta waited in the queue outside the Great Bath, both veiled and wearing the undyed tunics of working countrywomen. They watched carefully as the men emptied out after their morning of exercise, gossip and drinking. Soon Julia spotted a young auburn-haired woman swaying seductively along the departing line, catching the eye of every passing male. She nudged Britta.

'There she is!'

'Wish me luck,' muttered Britta. She left Julia, removing her head scarf and bustling off as if on a different trajectory. As she neared the departing bathers, she caught the young woman with an apparently inadvertent arm swing.

'Many pardons, my lady!'

The girl swung round bridling. Then she smiled, apparently mollified by the respectful form of address.

'Would you be going into the baths, my lady? I see you are quite a favourite with the local people. So beautiful and graceful you are, it's no wonder. I wonder—' Britta said all this in a slow-drawling country voice, with downcast eyes, '—you see,

I'm a visitor here, and feeling shy about going alone into these famous baths. I'm sure to get lost and make a fool of myself. May I come in with you, just till I find my way around? I am happy to pay for both of us, if you would let me come with you.'

Fulminata's innate vanity needed little encouragement. She apparently decided the country bumpkin was comely enough to be an asset, and grateful enough to be a generous companion. There would still be young Dobunni tribesmen around, practising their martial skills in the exercise yard outside.

'What's your name?'

'Veronica, my lady.'

'Well, Veronica, you can call me Fulminata. Come on, I'll show you the baths.'

Three hours later, Britta emerged, cleaner, poorer and having achieved her objective. She took a careful route home.

Julia was waiting impatiently. The two women changed into the long white hooded robes of the Sisterhood, and set off again into the city as the short spring afternoon faded. Britta paused to drop donatives of respect at the main altar to Sulis Minerva, while Julia made her way past the Sacred Spring. She slipped inside a hidden door and joined the elder Sisters of the Wise Women, who were gathered already in this holy and ancient temple. The place had been sacred to Sulis since long before Rome brought her twin goddess Minerva. Inside the room was tiered with steeply descending banks of wooden benches. Some dozen of the Sisterhood, the most senior healers, judges and teachers of the Aquae Sulis community were seated on wooden banks and chatting quietly when Britta entered a few minutes later. She was accompanied by a new supplicant for membership.

Fulminata looked smug. Britta had been both obsequious and disarming when she confided to her new friend that she was visiting the local Wise Women. She was sure they would be delighted to welcome Fulminata. The girl had the audacity to walk into the centre of the temple's circular space and fling off her hood with a show of confident beauty. She looked round with practised poise.

A bell, high and silvered in tone, struck once. Silence fell on the group. Julia stood, still hooded, holding out her arm to support a very old woman. The Sisters at once rose, and bowed their heads in respect. Fulminata turned to look. Unease crossed her face. Still she held her head in the same arrogant pose.

'Be seated, my Sisters.' The old woman had a surprisingly deep and rich voice. Julia led her to an ornate wooden chair at the highest level of the banked room. She herself sat on the tier below her, listening while the Elder Sister continued. 'Sisters, we are gathered in judgement today. One is here who has broken our most sacred laws, and deeply offended the Goddess.' The Sisters all raised their left arms to pointed accusation at the actress.

'Veronica!' Fulminata screeched, glaring at her supposed sponsor. 'What is going on here?'

The old woman stood. 'You will be silent, Fulminata. You are here under accusation by our Sister Julia. You are accused of murder. One of your victims was our beloved Sister Velvinna. Thus your judgement and punishment fall into our jurisdiction.'

Fulminata shouted, 'You have no authority, no witnesses and no evidence! I have powerful friends in the Roman authority. I reject your jurisdiction utterly –'

A muscular Wise Woman jumped up from the front bank and slapped Fulminata hard across the face. The actress wailed and subsided into silence, rubbing her flaming cheek.

The old woman went on. 'We have prayed together to the Goddess Sulis, and heard the evidence from our Sister Julia. As a trained healer and senior member of our sacred order, her word is her bond. Her witness has been corroborated by others who saw your attempts at sedition. Fulminata, you have committed the most heinous crimes for which there is one punishment only. In avenging our beloved Sister Velvinna, we sentence you to banishment. There will be no rest, no succour, no friendship for you henceforth, wherever the circles of Wise Women hold sway across Britannia and elsewhere.'

The old woman threw her arms wide. 'Sisters, do you concur?'

The Sisters erupted, standing to roar their approval. Julia allowed herself a quick bitter smile as she made her way down into the central circle. The raging Fulminata cast her a look of hate, but as two Sisters had her pinioned by the arms, there was little she could do.

'You're too late,' she yelled. 'None of you will survive what is to come.'

'Silence her,' said the Elder, and the guards gagged Fulminata.

Julia spoke. 'Sisters, I thank you for your trust. This woman has taken innocent lives, and was actively planning to raise rebellion in our town and beyond.

'It is not our way to punish with death. Nevertheless, the death sentence would have been the right of Velvinna's family under Roman law, had she any living relatives. As Velvinna's lifelong friend and pupil, I ask the Sisters to avenge our friend. Brand this woman so that all who see her henceforth will know she is under order of banishment.'

Fulminata tried to struggle, but was held firm. A brazier with a slender branding iron tipped into the coals was brought into the circle. Julia held out a cup to Fulminata, loosening the gag.

'The Sisterhood of Wise Women is not needlessly cruel. Here is pain relief for you. Drink it.'

The prisoner sneered, and tossed her bright red mane. 'And let you accomplish with poison what your weaker sisters will not command?' She lashed out to knock away the cup, sending the white liquid spilling.

'No,' snapped Julia. 'I leave that kind of wickedness to you, Fulminata. May the Goddess Sulis Minerva curse you all your life.'

She gave way to the punishment detail, three sombre-looking Sisters whose masked faces stood out black against their white robes. Julia walked back to her seat, not looking back as the actress was forced onto her knees, nor flinching when Fulminata screamed. The smell of scorching flesh made Julia's stomach churn, but still she did not look. Not till she was seated next to Britta, and the Elder Wise Woman had reached down to rest her feather-light old hand on Julia's shoulder, did she force herself to look at the new-blazed crimson of the owl brand on Fulminata's cheek. The prisoner was led away to be cast out beyond the sacred precinct.

Then Julia drew her hood up, and wept silently for Velvinna and Tertius and Catus. And for Quintus and herself.

Chapter Twenty-five

'Sir?'

Quintus turned round quickly, and Marcellus looked up with a frown. They were both peering at the floor where lines drawn and smudged out in the dirt marked their attempts to plan anything less than annihilation from the upcoming confrontation with the Second Augusta. Tiro and Decimus Senecio were seated nearby. The older *optio* looked tired.

A young guard stood in the tent opening, acne-scarred cheeks blazing with embarrassment. He swallowed at the sight of four senior officers eyeballing him.

'Yes?'

'Umm, sir, scouts are back.'

'Well, show them in, man. What are you waiting for?'

'Yes, sir. Sir, there's a lady too, just arrived. Says she brings important messages for the Frumentarius. And you too, sir.'

'Name?'

The guard looked puzzled. 'Plautus, sir.'

'Not you, moron. The lady.'

'Oh. Lady, err… Julia. Julia something.'

Marcellus looked at Quintus. 'Well, Brother, as we both know a Lady Julia Something, I think we should admit her, don't you?'

Quintus made no reply. His dark eyebrows drew together. He stalked over to the open tent flaps in two steps. Thrusting the guard out, he pulled Julia inside. He was horrified to see her, and furious at the risk she had taken. He gathered her into his arms, crushing her cheek against his *hasta* badge. They stood glued together for a brief moment, both breathing hard, while Marcellus tried to pretend he was somewhere else. Senecio frowned, and Tiro frankly grinned. Then Quintus pushed Julia away.

'What are you doing here, Julia? Are you completely mad?'

She stiffened, straightening the fold of jade-green *palla* he had knocked off her shoulder.

'I'll see to the scouts outside,' Marcellus murmured, wagging a beckoning finger at Senecio and Tiro. The tent flaps fell back into place behind them with the finality of a door slamming.

'I'm sorry...' Quintus began.

'So I see! Sorry you ever came back to Britannia, sorry you had to see me again, sorry to discover you have an inconvenient daughter.'

Quintus had never before known that anger and desire were such close bedfellows. What she said was true. He *was* sorry to be in this predicament. He wished desperately that he could return to the easier numbed times before he had sailed back up Tamesis.

And yet she was still here, the impossible wonderful infuriating Julia. The broken thing inside him washed around, making him feel seasick in a way sea crossings never had. He tried to back away, and found instead he had stepped in closer to her. The familiar scent of rosewater swept aside whatever he had intended. He roughly pushed past her. She turned on her heel to stare, a look of intense hurt forming on her face. He reached for the leather door flap ties, fastened them into a ruthless knot, and came back to her. He took her hands, and looked intently into her face. They were suddenly very close. He could feel her warmth, despite the chill of the little tent.

For a moment of madness, he considered removing her *tunica.* She was saying his name, and the madness continued long enough for him to know that his Julia, the Julia of Eboracum, had not gone away after all. He reached his hand around the back of her neck, and his fingers snagged on the necklet of owls. He paused. Yes, that young girl who had trusted him once might still be here, but so was the mature beautiful woman she had become. 'Not here, Julia, not now,' he whispered. She pulled back to look at him, and nodded.

The broken thing inside him dissolved and floated away. He held her still for one more moment.

' I can hear Tiro breathing outside,' she said.

'Sir?' It was definitely Tiro.

'Yes, yes, come in.'

'I'll just fetch the Commander and the Optio, then.'

At least he'd been that tactful.

Marcellus was full of news, and after a brief welcoming smile for Julia got straight down to business. 'Shall I begin with the scouts' reports, Frumentarius, before we come to Lady Julia's business?'

Quintus nodded.

Marcellus began. 'The men of the Summer Country are coming to our aid, and the good news is they'll be here by tomorrow. Decurion Sorio has them in charge, and he's found them an assortment of weapons. The scout reports that there's a goodly mix of retired soldiers among them. It seems Imperial soldiering is a tradition among the Durotriges.' He paused.

'And?'

'Well, we could have done with more of them. Perhaps Fulminata did more harm than we guessed. There are some well-equipped young noblemen, but for the most part the company is formed of older soldiers and farmworkers of all ages, a couple of hundred in all.

'Of the two scouts we sent north,' Marcellus continued, 'there's no word yet from one of them. That may mean he hasn't yet met up with the Twentieth Valeria Victrix. The other reports no troops on the road as far north as the salt baths at Salinae. '

'Or it could mean the Victrix isn't bloody-well coming!' burst in the *optio*. 'Or that they're in league with our enemies and taking their time on the road. I'm sure they'll arrive in time to mop up any little bits of us left by our treacherous mates in the Augusta.'

Quintus wasn't surprised that Senecio sounded so bitter. The *optio* was a career soldier who had undoubtedly done a good solid job for many years. He would have been looking forward to a wife, a family and nice bit of land for his retirement. Not the horror of fighting his old comrades to the death.

'And no significant movement reported on the Londinium road, either,' finished Marcellus.

Tiro had been rubbing his bristly chin for some time, a sign of anxious thought. He jumped up.

'I'm sorry, sir,' he said, turning hastily to Quintus. 'I for one

194

can't go on not knowing. Just who *is* this enemy? Who's leading those filthy traitors of the Augusta, bribing them with the Emperor's silver? Just who is this traitor who fancies making himself the Emperor of Britannia?'

Marcellus looked steadily at Quintus. The same question was in his eyes. Senecio stared down at his folded hands, grim and intent.

Quintus sighed. 'All right. Maybe the time has come to share my reasoning. I hope you can find fault with it. I pray to all-powerful Jupiter and Mithras the Sun God that I'm wrong.

'Tiro, I told you last time you asked to think of three questions. Where did we see white wax tablets? Why didn't Claudius Bulbo want to cross the bridge south of Tamesis? Why did the Governor ask for you and me in particular for this mission?

'Let's go back to the beginning. Before you and I first met, Tiro, the Governor tacitly admitted to me that he was at loggerheads with the Procurator. The top two men of the British government, fighting for overall power. And later you heard the Procurator's men badmouthing me as the "Governor's Man". Let's take that last accusation first. I am on the staff of *frumentarii* detached from their legions. Our sole task is to protect the interests of the Emperor and the Imperial Estate. None of us are ever formally attached to a Governor while on missions. We merely keep provincial governments informed, and expected to be resourced by them. '

Marcellus interrupted. 'Have you no previous experience in Britannia then, Frumentarius?'

'Only as a raw young officer in the army brought here by Emperor Septimius Severus to invade Caledonia. I have not once set foot here since I was invalided home to Italy at the end of that campaign, many years ago.'

Tiro frowned. 'Surely, sir you were a comrade-in-arms and close friend of Gaius Trebonius? I heard he asked for you by name.'

'Oh, yes,' Quintus murmured, 'Gaius asked for me. He saved my life in Caledonia. Since my return to Rome and transfer out of the Praetorian Guard, I have remained a centurion in the frumentariate. While he rose to become a Provincial Governor with two legions at his command. My career as an Imperial Investigator has all been spent in the eastern Empire. I don't speak a word of the British tongue, I don't know the country, I don't know the politics, I have no network of informers here. So why choose me?'

They were silent. Probably wondering what sort of friendship this was.

'Next: Claudius Bulbo. According to Drusus Sorio, he didn't want to cross the river to Southwark because he was frightened of being mugged in the stews of Southwark. And that may well be true. But think about it: the two rivals, the Governor and the Procurator, both have impressive palaces in Londinium, both have large staffs, both have the authority to investigate frauds affecting an Imperial estate. But only one of them is based south of the river.'

'The Procurator, Aradius Rufinus! I never trusted that pale slimy man!'

'You're missing my point, Tiro. Bulbo refused to go to Southwark with Lucius because he didn't *need* to go there. Lucius claimed they met Fulminata "at a meeting of important people in a big fancy building" where the appearance of tribal rebellions was being planned. As we now know, that meeting took place *north* of the river.

'Now, let's turn to the wax tablets. Julia, you raise bees and know about wax production. What did you tell me about the use of white wax for letter tablets?'

'That it's rare because it's difficult to produce. Compared to yellow wax, which does all the same jobs and is much cheaper and easier to get hold of.'

'So most people, most of the time, would use yellow wax in writing tablets?'

'Yes, of course. Only people wanting to impress the recipient with their high status, those with money to throw around, would use white wax for correspondence.'

'So, does it strike anyone that it would be quite some coincidence if –'

Tiro broke in, ' – two white wax letter tablets, written in

Londinium around the same time, and both connected with our investigation, *weren't* from the same sender.'

'Correct. And on whose desk did we see the first one?'

'The Commander of the Londinium garrison, who was instructed in that letter to assign me to you as your *stator*.'

Quintus looked at the others, letting that sink in. 'The second tablet was handed to us by Tertius. It was sent last winter to Bulbo, asking him to bring samples of newly-minted silver coins to a meeting in Londinium. Samples of the same coins I later found to have been shipped to Isca of the Legion, the base of the Second Augusta.

'If I'm right — and Mithras preserve all of us if I am — the sender of the first letter was my generous friend Gaius Trebonius, who knew I needed a replacement for my previous *stator*. That gave Governor Trebonius the chance to choose for me a man recently reduced to the ranks for drunkenness, who he hoped would be unreliable, resentful and truculent.'

'And illiterate,' muttered Tiro.

'I suspect Trebonius believed me to be a broken man when he requested me from the Frumentariate. Not without reason. He hoped to further stymie my mission by assigning me Tiro. How very wrong he turned out to be — with regard to Tiro at any rate. I could not have found myself a better assistant if I had scoured the Empire.'

Tiro looked away, his neck reddening.

Quintus went on, 'The second letter gave us the evidence that Bulbo's meeting of important people, held in an impressive building *not* on the south bank, was instigated by the same man. Gaius Trebonius, whose Governor's palace is on the *north* bank of Tamesis.'

Marcellus broke in, 'And who also happens to have been the previous Legate of the Second Augusta. And he had the means to provide the flow of silver denarii I saw at the Tribune's birthday party. It's all so obvious now. Trebonius was quite the war hero. Always a very popular Legate, spent a lot of time socialising with the men. If anyone could suborn the legion's loyalty away from a distant and untried young Emperor, he was the man to do it.'

Quintus nodded. 'We have Tertius to thank for these revelations. He's the bravest among us, with the most to lose as a whistleblower.'

Julia drew a sharp breath and spoke, low and unhappy.

'Quintus, that's why I'm here. I came to tell you. Tertius has been killed.'

There was a moment of silent shock. Only Senecio among them had not known Tertius. They sat numbly while Julia told of the murderous attack by Fulminata, and how she had been caught by Britta and punished by the Sisterhood. 'So at least the threat to Aquae Sulis and Corinium is now negated. No tribesman will even look at a murderer who's been judged, marked and cast out by the Wise Women, let alone listen to or give assistance to her.

'There's something else. Tertius gave me a message for you, Quintus. Only a fragment, but it seemed to matter very much to him.' Quintus saw her lips quiver, and knew her to be on the brink of tears. He touched her arm, the lightest of caresses. Her mouth trembled.

'Even in great pain, and knowing he was dying, he managed to say: "Tell your man that help is on the way. Watch the Londinium road."' Julia turned her tear-marked face away.

The three men looked to Quintus.

'From Londinium? Who could send help in time from there? I sent word to the Castra in Rome, but that report must still be a long way from reaching my Commander there. Copies of all my reports also went to Trebonius, damn him. He knew all my thinking. At least until I began to suspect that he himself might be the usurper.'

'Could it be the Londinium garrison?' Marcellus wondered aloud. 'If Trebonius has bribed the mighty Augusta, he may not worry too much about the loyalty of the Londinium boys.'

Tiro groaned. 'He won't worry about their loyalty at all. The numbers there have been reduced to a tiny garrison in recent decades. Just rattling around in a corner of that huge old fort. We couldn't hope to hold back the Augusta with such small numbers, even if they could get here in time.'

'There's the men of the Summer Country, don't forget them,'

said Senecio, a Summer Country man himself and proud of it. 'Our boys'll make holes in they traitors.'

Quintus was still pondering Tertius's final message. But the last words of a dying man could simply be ravings, and he couldn't rely on wishful thinking. Plus there was still the dreadful possibility that Trebonius had got to the XX Valeria Victrix first. If they did come marching down that north road from Deva, there was no saying whose side they'd be on.

He turned to the young centurion. 'Marcellus, you suggested to me that we could appeal to the loyalty of the men of the Augusta. It is always possible that the shortfall in the bribe caused by Lucius's theft might have an effect, and make some of the legionaries think again. Now, I know as well as you do that we're in a bad position right now, with little might to throw against a full legion of five thousand trained soldiers. Any extra swords we can muster will help, but if help is coming, it's not here yet. As I see it, we have two choices. We could just surrender to Trebonius when the legion arrives at Corinium Dubonnorum. It might save a lot of lives.'

There was another shocked silence. Quintus waited, a grim smile on his face.

'Begging your pardon, sir,' said Senecio. 'But that's not even funny. I think I can speak for all of us. Let's hear your other option.'

'Right. Unless anyone has any better ideas, I propose that we use any and every tactic to delay a pitched battle with Trebonius and his legion. The Summer countrymen are on their way, and that's one advantage our enemy doesn't know about. If Tertius was right, and there *is* more help coming from the east, we must do everything possible to keep that road open. Here's what we might do ...'

Chapter Twenty-six

Tiro was feeling surprisingly upbeat.

The previous day Marcellus had sent his best scout west towards Glevum to watch in secret for the approaching legion. At dawn the scout brought word back that Trebonius and his large force had left the colonia, and were marching east along Ermin Street on the final leg to Corinium. By then Marcellus had moved his company out of camp and cross-country to cautiously circle round to the south side of Corinium. Quintus reckoned Trebonius would assume the non-responsive Aquae Sulis detachment was cowering in its little riverside fort, keeping a low profile till the revolt was over.

Tiro joined Decimus and the lads to eat his evening meal. Marcellus and Quintus were deep into discussing tactics. Tiro was quite content to be told what to do once they'd worked out a plan. The lads were in a good humour, and Tiro was offered beer by men who had won bets on him at the pancratium competition. He reluctantly turned down a third beer, remembering he would need to be at his sharpest the following day.

So this morning he was feeling quite chipper. He was cantering along the muddy road with three troopers when they saw what could only be the Durotriges approaching them. A compact force of a few hundred, kept in reasonable order by some robust middle-aged men with various mismatching bits of old uniform and kit. The main body, mostly farmers and tradesmen, were carrying a variety of weapons. Old spears, axes, an assortment of swords — both short gladii and the more popular longer spathas — hoes and spades, even what looked to be sharpened billhooks. One broad-shouldered man carried an enormous hammer. Probably the town smith. Tiro arranged his face into a confident welcome as the leading horseman saw him, and spurred ahead.

'Decurion Sorio, you've made good time.'

The councillor was dressed in an old mail shirt and leather

breeches, with his toga swathed about him. It looked an uncomfortable turnout, but no doubt imposing to his men. His sword at least was high quality, burnished to a gleam, and very much on display. The eager Drusus was by his side. He and Tiro greeted each other warmly.

'This way, sir,' said Tiro, wheeling his horse round. 'We have food and campfires waiting for your men.' A ragged cheer greeted this, and the footsore Durotriges picked up their pace. Tiro held his horse to one side while they passed, noting with pleasure that there were no stragglers and everyone kept in line, more or less.

Not everyone. There *was* a straggler, a horseman clearly reluctant to ride with the others, so shy he was keeping to the shade of the dripping trees along the verge. Tiro's hackles immediately rose. Was he a spy for Trebonius? Tiro spurred to the rear, and caught up with the rider just as he realised he'd been spotted and tried to turn away. *Little bloke, skinny as a rake, oddly long hooded robe and not even armed.* Tiro accosted him, knocked him sideways and nearly out of his saddle.

Tiro discovered he had captured Aurelia. The girl cocked her little face up at him.

'Hello, Tiro.'

Tiro suddenly found out what it must feel like to be a father. He looked sternly at the grinning Aurelia.

'Oh no. *You are not here.* You're in Aquae Sulis with Britta.'

She dimpled at him. 'I couldn't stay at home. I thought about it, but when Aunt Julia explained that she *had* to leave with an urgent message for Quintus, even though she most wanted to be with me, and then Britta said you were here helping Centurion Marcellus, I just had to come. Aunt Julia said how proud she was of me being brave and staying at home where she needed my help. But coming here to fight is even braver, isn't it? Don't worry, I've been sensible. I left a note for Britta, and specially asked her to look after Cerberus.'

'How did you know where we were?'

'Oh, I just listened at the door when Julia told Britta where she was going. What with poor Tertius dying, and Anicius and the Sisters coming and going, no-one was taking any notice of me.'

'Well, you've put me in a right hole, my girl. We're expecting serious bother round here soon enough. It's not safe. You'll have to go back to Aquae Sulis straight away.'

Tiro expected tears and resistance. He didn't know how to deal with a teasing face and wheedling tone.

'But, Tiro if it isn't safe for me to be round here, surely it isn't safe for me to go home through this dangerous countryside on my own, either.'

Curse the girl. She has me there.

He scratched his chin, thinking.

'See here, miss, you want to come with us? Then you keep completely quiet, pull your hood well down, keep alongside of me. And do exactly what I tell you. Any trouble, I'll tell your mother and your—'

'My what?'

Oh Gods, Tiro, now you've done it!

He held Milo's reins steady in his hand and held the girl's gaze. 'I will make a deal with you, Aurelia. Here's what I'll do. I will ask your aunt to tell you what you need to know, when this is all over. On one condition.'

'Yes, yes of course.' She spoke so quickly she nearly swallowed the words. *I wonder… I think she may already know. I wish Britta was here. She'd be able to handle this. What am I supposed to do?*

'You must promise me, by the most solemn oath you know, that you will do exactly what I say, when I say it, no ifs or buts.'

The girl reached for the bronze owl brooch pinned on the shoulder of her cloak, and rubbed it. 'Yes, Tiro. I swear by the Goddess Sulis Minerva, she of the wise owl, that I will do exactly as you say. And then you will tell me what you meant by "your mother and your…"'

'Only when we've got this sorted.'

'All right, then.'

Corinium was a fine town, Tiro had to concede. A proper city really, not far off the size of Londinium. A mighty wall bounded it, pierced by four cardinal gates. The north-east boundary was paralleled by the River Churn, bridged just outside the towered north gate. Not far beyond the south gatehouse was their destination, a large handsome amphitheatre.

Tiro took Agrippa Sorio into his confidence. The round-bellied decurion was taken aback at first. 'The little minx. She needs a good sorting out.' Then his expression softened. 'I feel sorry for the poor thing all the same, just lost her father, Bo Gwelt all burnt down. I suppose I can see why she's followed her aunt here. You're right, Tiro, we can't send her away now, wouldn't be safe at all.'

He thought for a moment, then laughed and nodded.

'Let me have care of her. You've got your own duties. I'll engage to keep the girl safe. I have acquaintance here in Corinium, and I'll find a suitable billet for her. Are you sure you shouldn't tell her aunt, though?'

Tiro was at a complete loss. All these secrets, none of them his to tell. On the one hand, Sorio was perfectly right that Julia should know her recalcitrant daughter had disobeyed her and turned up here. As should Quintus. But Sorio had no notion of their true relationships to Aurelia. Tiro simply didn't feel up to negotiating his way through that on the verge of a major battle. Knowing himself to be a bad liar, he took refuge in a partial truth.

'Lady Julia has business in Corinium, delicate negotiations with the town council from what I can tell. It would be best to keep Aurelia with you for now, and as you suggest find her somewhere safe to stay.'

Sorio soon had Aurelia riding with him, entertaining her with tall tales of his long-ago military service. By the time they entered the amphitheatre, Drusus, usually inclined to be shy round Aurelia, had joined in and was telling her jokes and sharing his slight knowledge of classical battles with her. Tiro sighed, sagging slightly as he dismounted and secured the tall gates behind them.

The men had set up their *contubernium* tents on the steeply-tiered sides of the amphitheatre as best they could. It was a vast auditorium, fortunately, and there was plenty of room for them all. Plus picketing for the horses and space in the centre for the command tent. One side had been left spare for the Summer Country men, and the troopers good-naturedly helped the tribesmen settle in. Tiro left Aurelia with Sorio and went to the Principia tent to report to Quintus.

'Durotriges all present and settled, sir. Being fed and watered right now.'

'Good.' Quintus lifted his head as the tent flaps opened, and Julia came in, lifting her hood away from her head.

'Sorted?'

'Yes. The Sisterhood of Aquae Sulis had sent word. I spoke to the Elder Wise Women of the Corinium Sisterhood. They have liaised with the Town Council to get the word out to all the city families this evening. That should ensure people obey the curfew, the shops are boarded up, and the gates opened and shut precisely as we instruct. There's more food for us and fodder for the horses being delivered, and tents for the men of Lindinis. The Elder Sister said the townsmen wanted to raise arms and stand with us, but I persuaded her that we had help coming. I told her we don't wish any harm come to this city. I'll go now and make final arrangements with Sorio and our people for tomorrow.'

Tiro thought she looked anxious as she left. Quintus grunted by way of response, and Tiro's heart sank a little.

Marcellus arrived, splashed with mud and looking weary. Quintus passed him a cup of wine wordlessly, and the centurion tossed it down in a single swallow. He wiped the back of his hand across his mouth.

'It's all confirmed,' he said to Quintus. 'Scouts saw the Augusta legion camping for the night about five miles away. They mixed in with a couple of pickets. Word is they still expect to pick up more recruits here. So the legion will march right into the city through the Glevum gate tomorrow, pausing in the forum to add in whatever Corinium men they can add to their ranks. They'll leave through the Verulamium gate.'

'And no sense that they expect any resistance?'

'No, Brother. We are a well-kept secret still.'

'Till dawn tomorrow, then.'

'Indeed.'

Quintus smiled at his fellow officer. It was a rare sight, that smile, and Tiro was more pleased to see it than he would have thought possible. Their very slim chances rested largely on Quintus, and Tiro hoped the *frumentarius* would have it in him to lead their little army with spirit when the time came. Or just as likely, he thought gloomily, the Roman would sink back into his usual silent moroseness. And then they'd all make a swift passage to Hades tomorrow.

At dusk Marcellus and Tiro set off on their final camp rounds. Tiro lingered to chat to the Durotriges, as Marcellus went to speak to his section leaders and check the horse lines.

Sorio nodded in greeting. 'She's fine, she's in the tent there. She's been to look after her pony. Drusus has wagered her a game of *latrunculi,* and I think he's being badly beaten. I just hope he hasn't gambled away all my fortune.' Tiro glanced into the tent, where two young faces were intent on the game. Aurelia looked up when he said, 'Remember your promise, young lady.'

She nodded. 'I shall be a model of obedience.'

'Good. Decurion Sorio has arranged for you to be billeted with a local family first thing in the morning. Be dressed and ready with Milo before dawn.'

She grimaced, and for a moment he feared she would renege on their pact. Then she smiled brilliantly and nodded. 'Whatever you say, Tiro.'

Well, that was easy. Too easy? By Jupiter, I'll be glad when tomorrow is over, and Quintus and Julia can sort their daughter out for themselves.

As he approached the command tent he heard raised voices, and flinched. The last thing he wanted was to wander into the middle of another row between the *frumentarius* and his lady. He was relieved to see Julia leaving the tent. She stopped, looked at him.

'Um, good evening, my lady,' She ignored his greeting.

'Did you know what he's going to do? Afterwards, I mean?'

Tiro felt horribly uncertain. He cast about for some response, but she rushed on.

'If he survives — which of course he won't because he's got

this lunatic sense of responsibility, and he doesn't value himself, or me, or Aurelia, or — or anyone — '

Tiro, feeling useless, stood like a block.

'—so, even if he does come out of this in one piece, do you know what he has planned?' This time Julia paused, and seemed to want a reply. Tiro longed to run away. *I'm completely out of my depth with this. Women! Gods, what I'd give for Britta to be here instead of me.*

'He's going to scuttle back to Rome, that's what!' She almost spat this out. Tiro saw uneasily that her eyes were wet, her beautiful complexion reddening into splotches and — oh Gods, was she about to start wailing? But Julia dragged a breath in, and composed herself. 'Tiro, your boss is a coward, a cold-hearted bastard, lacking all self-worth and determined to sacrifice himself and everyone who loves him.'

Even to Tiro, these varied epithets didn't hang together well. But he could see why she might be upset. Come to think, this cosy homecoming plan of the boss would drop him, Tiro, right in the shit too. He was distracted for a moment, trying to work out what the disappearance of Quintus, either into the arms of the Departed, or even worse back to Rome, would mean for Tiro himself. Return to gaol, he supposed. Or a lifetime of scrubbing out the Londinium garrison latrines.

He was jolted out of his introspection by a glare from Julia.

'You fool!' She pushed past, nearly knocking him over. She stalked past Marcellus, too, who raised his eyebrows.

'Don't ask, sir,' muttered Tiro, leaving in his turn. No way was he going into that tent. Marcellus could deal with the *frumentarius* tonight. Tiro headed off to eat with the troopers, promising himself he would avoid his infuriating Italian boss till morning. Maybe things would blow over by then.

It was a short and anxious night. Tiro woke in the dark with sticky eyelids, feeling cold and unrested. He was roused by the watchmen, silently stirring everyone two hours before dawn. After a scratch breakfast of cold bannocks and water, the men moved into pre-arranged groups. Tiro went to check that Aurelia and Milo had left with Drusus for their billet. Agrippa

Sorio silently grasped his arm in greeting, and pointed towards the gate out of the amphitheatre, now filled with a steady stream of men moving quietly towards the town. 'They've both gone,' he whispered. 'I told Drusus to stay with Aurelia, make sure she was safe with her host family and does as you told her.' He didn't sound convinced, but Tiro found a faint grin from somewhere and plastered it on. 'Time to move our men out?'

'Yes, Decurion. Straight in through the gate and on to the forum.'

'Right you are. Just like old times, eh?'

They saluted each other, and Sorio moved off at the head of the Durotriges. It was a simple desperate plan, but after last night Tiro wondered whether Julia would play her part. He joined the other senior officers for the final briefing in the Principia. Marcellus's specialists had left the amphitheatre at dusk the previous day. Their work was done now. Their messenger confirmed as much to Marcellus, adding they were standing by as commanded, waiting for the signal. The centurion glanced at Quintus, saying, 'I think all is in place then, Brother. The horses have been mustered, as you ordered. The final scouts have left. Time to move out.'

'Yes indeed.'

Tiro thought that if he'd had a bad night, the Imperial Investigator's must have been infinitely worse. He looked ashen despite his olive skin, and his face was rigid. That slight but welcome smile of yesterday was long gone. Tiro sighed, and Quintus snapped his head round to stare.

'Something to say, Stator?'

'No sir.' Tiro saw that the bandage just visible from Quintus's left tunic sleeve was clean and white. Julia had dressed his burns before leaving in high dudgeon. The boss's gladius was sheathed, and Tiro wished he'd gone back last night to offer to sharpen and polish it. Too late now. Too late for anything, including regrets, fear, and wishes. All that was left was Fate, and a soldier's death. He checked his own belt with his long dagger. Marcellus looked at Quintus and nodded. It seemed he had ceded command authority for today to the *frumentarius*.

'Right. Marcellus, Senecio, you know where to lead your

men. Deploy your men well before the road junction, and don't allow yourselves to be seen. Make sure you're masked by the trees, but close enough to hear me speak.' The young centurion and his grim-faced *optio* both nodded.

'Silence is essential. Trebonius may have spies even here. Any stray townspeople you come across must be directed swiftly to safety behind locked doors.

'Tiro?'

'Sir?'

Quintus held out his hand, and Tiro grasped it.

Quintus spoke softly. 'Look after her, if—just look after both of them. Right, let's go.'

Quintus took his share of the men first, a few mounted archers. They headed south, making their way in single file round outside the walled city. Marcellus left next, leading fully half their detachment silently in the tracks of the first party. Senecio and his troopers followed. All were intent on keeping as closely as they could to the trail set by the initial party, to mask their numbers. All were silent.

Tiro raised his arm in salute and set off on foot at a jog, entering the city through the Aquae Sulis gate. The adjacent streets were deserted and silent. All the houses and shops, mostly wood-framed with a few newer houses of pale limestone, had closed shutters. He knew water buckets had been placed inside every front door. He devoutly prayed they would not be needed.

Like the amphitheatre, the forum was large, and the few hundred Durotriges gathered in front of the imposing basilica looked a small group indeed. He was relieved to spot Julia on the colonnade. She was talking to Agrippa Sorio, and like him looked the part of the senior tribal noble. She came down into the square, joining three older woman, all in long white robes. They left the forum and turned towards the Glevum Gate.

After that it was a waiting game. The Durotriges, looking apprehensive but proud of their role in proceedings, chatted quietly as the slow dawn crept up the outside of the town wall. The first fingers of sunlight reached the battlements, and hesitated a moment before slanting down across the forum towards the open portico. Thanks to Goddess Aurora, it was a bright morning after all the rain of recent days. The puddles on the street shone silver.

They stiffened at the unmistakeable sound of five thousand feet marching in rhythm, approaching the city gate along Ermin Street from the west. The noise grew as the legion approached, the sound amplified and echoing off the temples and houses lining the main street.

Here it was, then. Tiro knew that Julia and the Sisters of the Corinium Wise Women would be standing at the north gate, welcoming the legion and its leader to Corinium. Soon enough the legion began to file into the big square. They were an imposing sight, a mass of disciplined men all swinging along together, shiny helmets, bright uniforms, their shields bearing the sea-goat Capricornus insignia of the Legio Second Augusta. The legion's bare-headed *aquilifer* carried a small round shield strapped to his left arm and bore the eagle standard in both hands. Its upswept wings and cruel hooked beak were the ultimate symbol of Rome. Tiro felt the hairs rise on his arms at the sight. Next came a group of mounted senior officers, six young tribunes, wearing engraved helmets and bronze cuirasses. With them came the man Tiro looked to as the most significant in any legion: the camp prefect.

Tiro's eyes widened. Surely he knew this man, with his hard experienced face, his cuirass covered with bronze phalerae awards, swinging his red twisted vine stick? The years rolled back. Tiro saw the First Spear, the *primus pilus* of the Londinium cohort, Felix Antonius. The man who had taken him off the streets and trained him as a raw new recruit. The man who'd fostered the fighting talent in the stocky Londoner and helped him reach champion status in the army pancratium competitions. The man who had beaten him too many times after he'd got drunk. Who nevertheless believed in him, and encouraged Tiro to keep pushing till he reached *optio* status. The man who had been like a father, harsh but fair, and who had looked away with disappointed eyes when Tiro was disgraced and thrown out of the cohort.

209

Here was his hero, Felix Antonius, third in command of the venerable Augusta, marching immediately in front of the usurper Gaius Trebonius.

Chapter Twenty-seven

Julia lingered at the back of the basilica colonnade. Having Sisters nearby should feel more comforting than it did. She had explained the plan to the Corinium Sisterhood, who had whole-heartedly endorsed it. Their interests were in saving their town, and so were hers, along with saving the people she loved. But their success so far in persuading the legion they were among friends was not enough to stop her heart thumping under her breastbone. She told herself there *would* be another day. And at least Aurelia was safe at home. The thudding inside her chest continued, and she began to feel light-headed. Maybe today would be all there was, for her and Quintus. For all of them.

Pay attention, Julia! she told herself fiercely. *The Lady Minerva despises the feeble of spirit.* She forced her back straight and head upright, watching carefully now as the Second Augusta turned out of the high street and swept through the colonnade into the large forum square. The soldiers turned on command and lined up in their centuries to face their senior officers. It was an impressive and quelling sight. Tiro was near her, and as the tribunes and the camp prefect of the Augusta dismounted to await their commander, she sensed him stiffen. He was staring at the prefect, a man of obvious experience with a chest full of gallantry awards. A sudden cheer on cue from the Durotriges, masquerading as Dobunni volunteers, switched her attention back. Decurion Sorio and his primed friends were discreetly orchestrating the cheering. At his signal, the Durotriges began to chant: 'Gaius Trebonius! The British Emperor! Gaius Trebonius! Our Governor for Emperor!' Governor Gaius Trebonius stood with legs wide apart, arms raised, seeming to bask in the crowd's loud approval. The soldiers in front called out too, and a few started to bang their javelins against their shields. The crash of the spears on wood was picked up and sent back in waves until it seemed every soldier was yelling in time, and every tribesman was calling, 'Our British Emperor, Trebonius for Emperor!' After a while

Trebonius waved the noise down and moved forward to speak.

"Good people of Corinium Dubonnorum!' They cheered again, long and loud.

'Thank you for your warm welcome. Thank you for your support. Thank you for your loyalty.'

More cheering. Julia was proud of them. Amazing how two hundred or so Durotriges could sound like a whole nation. Trebonius clearly thought so. He took his time before starting his speech of sedition.

Julia had stopped listening. She signalled urgently to Tiro. He made his way to her side.

'There, behind Trebonius, moving up from the street,' she murmured. 'Am I wrong, or is that Antoninus Labienus, back from the dead?'

Tiro looked puzzled.

'Not sure. Better check.' He left before she could stop him, slinking forward through the crowd of enraptured men like a fox in a hayfield. She watched him with her heart in her mouth, then looked again at the Labienus look-alike. This time she was almost sure she'd been mistaken. The man standing alongside the Governor was a stranger, wasn't he? Still, there was something familiar about his height, his looks and the way he tossed his jade-green cloak back over his shoulder.

She was continuing to ponder, aware that Trebonius was still speaking, when her sleeve was tugged imperiously. Two young people stood behind her, one eager and impulsive, the other shy and anxious. Julia felt her stomach somersault. She motioned to Aurelia and Drusus Sorio to move with her out of the colonnade. She threaded her way as delicately as she could between her older white-robed Sisters. She wished she was invisible and was growing angrier every second. At last they were away from ears and eyes, and she grabbed them both by the shoulders and forced them to sit while she glared at them.

Drusus went white, pink, then white again, looking unhappy. Aurelia was her familiar nonchalant self.

'Aunt Julia, I know you told me to stay at home, but wait till I tell you who we've seen.'

Julia opened her mouth to deliver an undertoned rebuke, then shut her mouth again. Too late for reprimands. Aurelia saw her chance.

'It's Lucius Claudius.'

'Lucius?'

'Yep. Right up there with the Governor - Emperor - thingie. That man whose taking over the Empire with a single legion. Ha!'

Julia opened her mouth again, in disbelief. Aurelia plunged on.

'And who do you suppose is with him?'

Julia waited.

'Go on, Drusus, you tell Julia. It was you who worked it out.'

Drusus still looked miserable.

'I'm very sorry, Lady Julia. know I promised my father to keep Aurelia safe and hidden, but when Aurelia sneaked out of the house, I couldn't *not* follow her, could I? I mean, someone had to stop her getting into trouble, and I thought...'

'By the Goddess Minerva, Drusus, just spit it out. Tell me you've seen someone who looks like the man in the blue cloak, who died in the fight in Lindinis. Haven't you?'

The boy's unhappiness was replaced by chagrin. Julia felt sorry then. 'All right. Good guessing,' she said. 'Tiro and I agree with you, and Tiro has gone to look closer. Now I want you to return immediately to your billet. It's not safe here.'

Too late. Trumpets rang out, the brassy sound horribly loud in the enclosed forum. The Augusta was on the move again, marching eastwards out of the city. The fake Dobunni volunteer brought up the rear. The only place to hide Aurelia was in plain sight among the Wise Women. Julia laid her finger across her lips, looking as stern as she could, and they moved backwards to mingle in with the Sisterhood. Drusus gave a crooked grin and slipped away into the ranks of the Summer Country farmers. Julia hoped Agrippa Sorio, marching along some rows ahead, wouldn't turn to see his disobedient son in the rear. The tribesmen were now passing low hand signals along their ranks, twitching out their swords and readying axes and sharpened tools. Once they were out through the gate, and it was slammed and bolted behind with the legion crossing the bridge ahead of them, those tools and weapons would be pressed into bloody use.

Tiro was even more alarmed by the raucous trumpet call than Julia had been. It caught him too soon, as he was still scurrying past the front ranks of the first century of the Augusta. He was not uniformed. He had no shield, no sword, and nowhere to hide. As soon as the men near him looked around he would be caught. All he could do was keep pace and hope his matching movements would disguise him till they had passed the city gate. Then he would have to trust to his legs and the Goddess Fortuna, and run as fast as he could to the nearest ditch.

A gravelly voice spoke in his ear.

'Optio Tiro, as I live and breathe. A long way from home, ain't you?'

Tiro could not stop the salute that sprang automatically from him.

'Sir, I mean Prefect. Yes sir.' He darted an upward glance. Marching by his side, staring ahead in perfect disciplined step-time with the legion, was his old training officer Felix Antonius, red-crested helmet and all. Not a twitch of his battered face, not a movement out of place of his horny hands. Tiro swallowed, and waited for his doom to fall.

'At the next street corner, Tiro, you will fall out of line and disappear back out of my life. I don't know what you're doing here, and I hope never to see you again. But with my luck, I fear I might. Understood?'

'Yessir. But -'

'No buts, no questions. Maybe I've made bad choices, but I always believed loyalty to be the soldier's ultimate virtue. Now fuck off, and never let me see you on the opposite side again.'

Within three more paces, the legion began to cross the Main Street. Tiro slid away into a doorway, where he tried his best to look like a door until the legion had passed. Then he moved out, still shaking, and joined the Durotriges. He wriggled his way forward to join Agrippa Sorio.

'Minor detour,' he told the surprised decurion.

The huge towngates swung apart and the leading ranks of the Augusta marched out in tight order under the towered battlements, through the gate and across the river onto Akeman Street. It seemed to take them forever to pass over the bridge, under which Quintus had left his small band with bows slung, crouching between the vast stone piers just above the waterline. Their job would come soon.

The men of the Aquae Sulis garrison were split into two halves, mounted and hidden among the woods that lined the road beyond the river. Mercifully there was no cemetery on this side of Corinium to cause the removal of trees.

Quintus and Marcellus with their men were bunched amongst oaks on the north-west verge. Decimus Senecio had command of the rest, waiting silently in the woods on the other side. Not far beyond their hiding places the road forked. The left fork headed north to merge with the Fosse Way. If Trebonius had summoned the Twentieth Valeria Victrix, this was the way the northern legion would come. At least, thought Quintus, he'd see the enemy coming and be able to choose the timing to charge. The righthand fork was a continuation of Akeman Street, linking Corinium on to Verulamium and Londinium. This was the road Tertius had told him to watch, though he had no hope of a miracle from that direction.

Quintus didn't expect any divine rescue. Which was just as well, given the lack of any sizeable military force in Londinium. That warning had been merely a dying fantasy of Tertius.

As the Augusta legion emerged Quintus could distinguish Gaius Trebonius at their head. He had been dreading this encounter for some time. His ultimate fear was that he would be unable to act, frozen by trauma into indecision. His mood was sour. During the long wait after dawn, while the horses breathed warm mist into the dark and the only sound was the dull shuffle of their rag-bound hoofs, his mind jumped back to his last encounter with Julia. She had been so angry when he outlined his tactics for this morning. But what else did she expect him to do? They were desperately outnumbered, and he had a whole city to protect.

'Why not let the tribe fight for you?' she said. 'It's their country too, my country. Why should you be the one to make these decisions? Even Marcellus has a better right; at least he's British! What is this maggot in your head — the drive to sacrifice yourself? You're no good to anyone dead.'

And then when he said that he hoped it wouldn't be a senseless sacrifice, and that he did plan to survive beyond the encounter with Trebonius so he could live to report to his commander in Rome, she became almost apoplectic.

'You bastard! So that was all it was between us, again. A passing lust like before. No wonder you have nightmares. How do you live with yourself, Quintus?'

When he held his hand out to placate her, to try to explain, she pushed past him saying, 'Just go back to Rome, Quintus. And this time, stay there.'

Hurtful though that look on her face had been, Quintus now found his inner eye dwelling on a different face during the chilly wait in the woods. Now he saw Flavius. Not on his knees in the freezing Caledonian bog, eyes dulled and dying. This was a younger Flavius, the year before he joined the Praetorians. Quintus had been home on leave, and they had gone hunting in the Tiburtine Hills above the vast palace built by Emperor Hadrian. Flavius had ridden ahead. Always impetuous, he'd speared a boar which refused to die. It turned at bay instead and charged the boy, whose terrified horse promptly threw him. Flavius had landed on all fours and remained there, frozen, with the squealing boar turning to charge him again. Quintus was already spurring his horse into the clearing and took immediate aim at the boar. His spear had skewered the bleeding animal and anchored it to the ground where it died, still emitting angry screams. Flavius had suddenly laughed with release and joy and rushed to Quintus, reaching up to grab his arm.

It was this laughing boy Quintus saw now, the Flavius who knew his big brother would always be there for him. Now Quintus finally saw that this was the same look Flavius had given him on the battlefield.

Forgive me, Flavius. You didn't doubt me, even then. You were sending a final message of love, not despair. You never stopped believing in me. But do I believe in myself? Is that what

216

Julia meant?

The noise of hooves and marching hobnails alerted him. He signalled to Marcellus, who passed the *Wait!* command to his own party, and on to Senecio. All remained still under the trees, while the legion spilled out through the gateway behind Trebonius and clattered across the bridge. The smaller party of tribesmen followed them. The din made by dozens of horses and five thousand pairs of boots on the wooden superstructure was more than enough to cover any noise made by the small party of archers, scrambling out from under the bridge. With the Durotriges in front to mask them they slipped in through the gates and slammed them shut. There came the sound of wood dragged across metal as the gates were locked and barred from the inside.

The centurion in command of the rearguard of the Second Augusta turned in surprise, and looked up to see helmeted archers now positioned between the defensive crenellations above the gateway. Perfectly positioned to shoot. A further surprise came as he realised that the Dobunni allies immediately behind had raised their weapons and were looking much less friendly.

The advance party saw nothing of this. They were already strung out along the wet road. Trebonius, flanked by the green-cloaked man with Lucius riding behind, paused. Quintus rode out from the trees and took up position in the middle of the road. Trebonius flung up a hand to halt the column. He put on his grey-plumed helmet and gathered his horse's reins into his left hand. His piercing gaze raked the man blocking his route. A slow smile curled his hard mouth.

'Frumentarius Quintus Valerius. Well, well, about time. I do hope you and your... allies have come to join us.' He looked over the heads of his army, towards the tight band of tribesmen now doing their best to menace his rearguard. He laughed openly.

Quintus made no acknowledgement. He raised his right arm, and heard the Aquae Sulis men move smartly out from the woods to range across the road behind him.

'Oh, I see. Quite the little army. We appear to be surrounded.'

Gaius Trebonius grinned widely. The Augusta men exchanged smirks. Only one man didn't smile. He tossed his fine green cloak over his left shoulder, and reached for the handle of his sword. Trebonius's face changed. He adopted a sympathetic look, leaning forward a little to address Quintus alone. It was such a familiar pose of warm confidence and friendship. Quintus shuddered as he recognised it.

'Quintus, old comrade, how long have we known each other?' Trebonius waited a moment for a response that didn't come. He shrugged. 'Fourteen, fifteen years? Too long for good friends to mistrust each other.' Quintus said nothing, but touched the *hasta* badge on his baldric fleetingly. It was a tiny gesture, but those pale sharp eyes missed nothing.

'I see. It's your old Roman notion of duty, is it? The sense of obligation, that feeling of owing something to the family, eh? Duty to the Emperor - pah! Alexander Severus is a weak boy ruled by his mother. What kind of blind loyalty is willing to let the Empire sink into anarchy and civil war, when an experienced hand on the tiller could save Rome? And your family? Long since plunged into disgrace and penury. But sticking with an old comrade who has risen in the world through ability and vision — that's the true loyalty of a good Roman soldier.'

Still Quintus kept silent.

The Governor's voice took on a less patient tone. He moved restlessly in his saddle, and the plumes on his helmet crest dipped and swayed. 'When you came to Londinium seeking my help, I supported you. In return I asked you to report only to me. Even though I knew from the intercepted messages of that little Syrian worm at Vebriacum that he was plotting to betray me to Procurator Rufinus. Still, I trusted you. You owed me your life and your unquestioned loyalty. Now it's time to finally choose your side, Frumentarius Valerius. Whose man are you: Governor's Man, or boy Emperor's patsy?'

He paused. Quintus saw the arrogance, the sense of entitlement in his posture.

It was true that he owed this man his life. Quintus had been waiting fourteen years to repay his debt to Gaius Trebonius.

Now the time had come to make recompense. He owed Gaius. He owed Flavius, he owed his father, he owed Julia, he owed the Emperor. He thought about the direction his duty must take him to settle his debts to each of them. The image of his brother flashed before his eyes once more. Now he knew which course of action to take, to ensure Flavius had not died in vain. He moved his horse three paces forward, then twitched the reins to bring the chestnut to a precise stop.

'Sir, Governor Gaius Trebonius, my duty to the Emperor and to my men here does not allow me to betray the Empire. However, I understand that the men of the Second Augusta also feel loyalty to their old Legate. It would be a terrible waste of blood to settle our differences in battle and lose these men, if another way can be found.'

Trebonius looked interested, an eager expression that betrayed his hopes. Quintus began to think he would take his bait. He looked down at the road carefully, finding what he needed, and dismounted. One of his little company ran forward and took his horse's reins to lead it away. Quintus drew his gladius. He knew this might be the last time he did so. He saluted, bringing the blade upright before his face, and swung it away again.

'Gaius Trebonius, in my role as Imperial Investigator on commission from the Emperor and the Commander of the Castra Peregrina in Rome, I pronounce you traitor and criminal. I strip you of your office of Governor of Britannia Superior. I offer you one last chance to save your honour. Dismount and defend yourself against me, in single combat. Mithras, Lord of Light, I call on you to witness the righteousness of my actions and strengthen my hand.'

The Governor dropped all pretence at comradeship. He scowled. Quintus held his breath. Would Trebonius accept the single combat challenge from an inferior officer?

Quintus had no shield, so took up the defensive position as best he could, with knees flexed and sword angled up. Trebonius flung his reins to Lucius and dropped off his horse, drawing his own sword as he landed. Quintus saw he carried a *spatha*. The longer blade would give the Governor the advantage. So he did the only thing he could. He rushed Trebonius before he could take up a pose, forcing him to step back quickly. One more step back... There it was!

The road behind the Governor was cratered with muddy holes after the night's heavy rain. Trebonius's backstepping foot slid in a rut, he lost balance and fell. Quintus darted forward, thrusting. The man twisted like a cat and rolled onto his side. Quintus's gladius scored a deep line along the side of the other's gilded cuirass, and slashed across his arm. Whether out of vanity or lack of preparation, Trebonius was wearing only the sleeveless decorative breastplate by way of armour. His arms were not protected at all. He swore, rolling out of range again as beads of blood sprang up along the line of the sword cut. The wound was long and already bled steadily. Trebonius got to his feet, then slid again in the bloody slime. Quintus sprang forward. He did not see the man run out from behind the Governor's horse, a tall man who flung off his green cloak and stepped ahead of the bleeding Governor to threaten Quintus.

'You want a fight to the death, you bastard? I'll give you death all right. I am Cassius Labienus, the new Emperor's deputy. I accept your challenge as his champion. Mine is the right of vengeance. Vengeance for my brother Antoninus, who died at your hands.'

Quintus took stock. Unlike the short solid Governor, this man was tall with a long reach. He was fresh, and had a round shield as well as a *spatha*. He also had good reason to want Quintus dead.

Quintus took a deep breath, settling himself into this new fight. He blocked out all sights and sounds except the man in front of him. He was no longer aware of Trebonius being escorted aside, or the grizzled camp prefect watching closely, or the cheering rows of legionaries. He lost all sense of his own men gathered close, and even of the road under his feet. He called on his long experience and years of training. He knew not to watch the eyes, or the hands, or even the sword itself. He focused his gaze on his opponent's sternum. Any movement of the core of the body would betray where the next blow would come from, and allow a reflexive parry to be aimed where it should.

And all the time he was weighing up his situation. This man was fresh, tall and well-armoured. On the other hand, Quintus knew himself to be fast, with nimble footwork. His scarred leg might tire, but the short gladius suited his style of fighting. And, he hoped and prayed, he had the gods of Rome on his side, including Minerva the goddess of justice.

He took one more deep breath, rubbing his boots around in the damp gravel to centre his weight. He was ready to strike.

'Come and seek your vengeance, Labienus!'

Chapter Twenty-eight

Tiro looked round at the Durotriges, swords and axes in hand. They were ready to fight, but Tiro hoped desperately that they wouldn't need to. Apart from a handful of retired soldiers, they had no clue how to defend themselves against trained legionaries.

A better plan was needed. And being stuck here at the back of everything was not the place to deliver that better plan. *Off we go again, Tiro.* As he worked his way forward he recognised the young Sorio lad. He was standing at his father's shoulder, round shield slung on his back and sword out in a shaky hand. The boy looked round. Tiro put his fingers to his lips. No time to negotiate passage with Sorio senior. The boy nodded in understanding and pointed to the front, where Quintus was sitting on his chestnut in the pathway of the Augusta, making his crazy play for time. No sign of the support coming from the east.

Seems the Gods aren't going to oblige us with a Hercules or a Hector. So I'll have to do.

He prepared to heave his way through the ranks. But Drusus grabbed his arm. The boy unshouldered his shield and held it out. It was a generous offer, and Tiro thought for all of three seconds before accepting. The boy might yet need it himself, but to be frank if Drusus got engaged in fighting then it was already over, and Quintus and Tiro would be dead. He grinned at Drusus, holding his thumb up, and set off all the lighter for the heavy round burden.

Now Tiro's years of wrestling paid off handsomely. He ploughed low through the ranks packed together on the bridge, ignoring swearing and shoving. He made much better progress once off the bridge. Besides, the men ahead of him were so caught up by the sight of their new Emperor in a single combat challenge, even a Jovian thunderbolt wouldn't distract them.

But the man facing Quintus wasn't the Governor. It was a taller man, one who threw his cloak off with a familiar disdainful gesture. Quintus raised his sword to engage, and with that movement his sleeve moved up to reveal a white bandage. Tiro opened his mouth to shout a warning, and at the same time the tall bastard — Somebody Labienus? — stepped forward, halving the distance to his opponent. He brought his own left arm across his body, and then straightened it to hit out with the boss of his shield, buffeting Quintus hard on his burned arm. Quintus made no sound but his face went white, and he dropped his own left arm, turning away instinctively to protect it. Tiro saw immediately that this movement opened his right side to attack. He dropped his head and sprinted like an enraged bull through the soldiers in front, scattering them. Labienus heard him coming and whirled round, shield and sword up. Tiro fell into a skid, sliding along the wet ground. He was holding Drusus's shield aloft.

'Take it, sir!'

The *frumentarius* reacted immediately. Tiro was relieved to see that not even his injured arm slowed him much. He scooped up the shield while Labienus was wrong-footed. Using the weight of his swinging body, Quintus shoved in a blow with the little round shield, metal-edge uppermost. Labienus spun round, raising his sword in a hacking downward blow. Quintus had to leap desperately to avoid being sliced. The two men exchanged a series of sharp parries, neither making ground. Tiro could hear Gaius Trebonius screaming at his champion. 'Kill him! Kill the fool!' Quintus was beginning to drag his leg. Only a little, but Tiro could see it. No time for gentlemanly behaviour. *Let's fight dirty.*

At that moment Marcellus shouted to his bugler to wind the horn for attack. The Aquae Sulis vexillation surged forward, and a free-for-all began. The bulk of the legion couldn't see what was happening, but the front ranks charged at Marcellus and his men. Labienus glanced away, allowing Quintus to get closer. Quintus's sword traced a glittering path of movement that confounded the taller man, without quite allowing Quintus to penetrate his defence.

Satisfied that Quintus was holding his own, Tiro looked around for the nearest target. To his vast satisfaction he found

Lucius. Fighting lust rose in him, red hot. He reached Lucius before the boy even saw him, diving low to pull him down into the mud. Stabbing him would be too quick. Instead he smashed his fists into him, with great pleasure. He pulled Lucius bodily off the ground, ready to dash him back down and grind that pretty face to shreds. But the boy managed to rip himself away, leaving part of his torn tunic behind. To his regret Tiro saw Lucius run away, throwing his shield at Tiro. Tiro dodged and caught the shield up out of the mud.

'He didn't even swing his fucking sword,' grumbled Tiro, settling Lucius's shield on his arm and looking round for his next victim.

'Woah there,' said a familiar gravelly voice. 'Watch who you hit. Come to help an old mate, I have.' Prefect Felix Antonius grinned and stepped to Tiro's right side. They both turned and swung their shields in practised unison, catching two legionaries unaware and rendering them out of play, probably permanently. Tiro grinned too. He was beginning to have fun. Until he glanced towards Quintus, and realised the boss was now faced by two more men and still parrying with Labienus. The odds seemed a little unfair. With a signal to Antonius, Tiro extracted himself and plunged in to support the *frumentarius.* All about him was a frenzy of men, mostly slogging it out in pairs.

Tiro reached Quintus and popped up beside him, encouraged to see the Italian gaining ground. The point of Quintus's gladius whipped in and out, faster than anyone could cope with. One of his adversaries was down, slashed across the belly and wailing. Tiro took on the other, leaving Labienus to Quintus. Tiro thrust his shield forward and down, sweeping the legs from under his opponent. The man landed awkwardly on the ground with Tiro on top. Tiro smashed the shield into the man's face, then grabbed his dagger, reversed it in one smooth swift move and smacked the pommel into the exposed throat. There was a gurgle, then silence and Tiro let his opponent's head fall back, crooked and ghastly. He leapt to his feet to find another legionary coming at him. This time, not from the front. The bastard crunched his shield sideways into Tiro's ribs, and there

224

was a horribly loud crack. Tiro would have sworn except he couldn't breathe. *Shit, am I dead?* He had no time to ponder. Shrill trumpet blasts split the air, so close the din threatened to deafen him - once, twice, thrice. Sudden stillness fell over the maelstrom. Men paused in mid-blow, turning to see who was signalling so sharply. Tiro fought vainly to pull air into his lungs. Puffing and crouching over his ribs, he became aware that the battle had frozen. All eyes had turned to something approaching along the Verulamium road.

It was a litter, some invalid being carried along bang into the middle of the battle. Through his pain Tiro stared as the swaying litter came nearer. Now he could see that the purple-fringed drapes on either side were drawn back. The four litter-bearers stopped, lowering the litter with respectful care to allow the occupant to step out. Their passenger straightened up. He had a pale intelligent face, and obviously found it difficult to stand for long. He waited patiently, nonetheless, surveying the scene ahead of him.

A cohort of soldiers bearing a familiar standard marched up behind him, and one of the litter slaves hurried to bring a folding seat from an accompanying wagon. The man sat, passing a grateful smile to the slave. Tiro opened his mouth to say, 'It's my Londinium lads!' but Felix Antonius beat him to it. The camp prefect hustled through the silent crowd, and went down on one knee before the pale man.

'Your Honour,' he said, head bowed. The man placed one white hand on the wiry grey hair of the prefect.

'No need for apologies right now, Antonius,' he said in a soft voice. 'Time enough in duc course. For now, please tell me what is happening here.'

Quintus stepped forward, his left arm bleeding through the sleeve and held stiffly, his tunic covered in mud and blood. Tiro hoped little of the blood was his. But before either the prefect or the *frumentarius* could speak, Trebonius pushed himself forward, with two of his tribunes alongside.

'Procurator Rufinus, what a miracle! You've had yourself carried all the way from your counting house to grace my victory. I am happy to accept your surrender on the field.'

Tiro shuddered at the sneer in the man's voice. But he noted that some of the men of the Augusta legion were shuffling and looking uncomfortable. There was a slight but perceptible movement by some along the sides of the road, towards the trees and disappearance. They were stopped by the legionary centurions, more determined to hold their nerve. Tiro guessed they had most to lose if there was to be a reckoning. But he didn't think the London lads, tough town boys though they were, would be able to hold the field long against five thousand trained men.

The pale man didn't turn a hair. He looked placidly at Gaius Trebonius, addressing him in a cool clear voice.

'But I have come to require *your* surrender, Gaius Trebonius.'

The Governor laughed, loud and full-throated. His staff officers glanced around, as if wondering whether it was appropriate to join in his glee. One tribune did, until the mild glance of the Procurator turned his way. The tribune fell silent.

'Gaius, I know everything.'

'Do you, now, Aradius? And how is whatever you think you know going to stand up against my legion? Even with a few dozy garrison layabouts behind you, and the posse of disloyal farmers this *frumentarius* has dragged together.'

Trebonius nodded toward the Durotriges in the rear. Marcellus, standing next to Agrippa Sorio, drew himself up and his men stood a little taller.

'Also, I hate to tell you after you've been carried all this way in your litter that I've got another legion on the way. If I'm not mistaken, here it is now. You may want to consider a request for mercy to your new British Emperor right now.'

It was unmistakeable. The sound of thousands of booted feet, marching briskly in unison down the north road. The Twentieth Valeria Victrix legion had arrived at last. Tiro suddenly felt very sick. He retched. A really bad idea. He was so blinded by the pain of his broken ribs that he almost missed what came next. The pale man, Procurator Aradius Rufinus, waited calmly, merely summoning Quintus over to him with a wave of his hand. Quintus went, his bad arm hanging loose but holding his shield still. They exchanged a few low words. Tiro couldn't catch what was said, but noted that Quintus looked happier. Tiro began to feel a bit better. The Procurator turned back to his former colleague. His posture didn't change, but his voice hardened.

'The thing is, Gaius, the legate of the Twentieth Valeria Victrix had already decided where his loyalties lay. He put his legion at my disposal quite some time before your attempt to suborn him. So you see, there is little left for us to say to each other. I will now speak to the Second Augusta instead, whom you have led to this disaster.'

Tiro saw a panicky look of shock pass over the Governor's broad face. But the Procurator seemed not to notice. His voice, still even, was raised to a tone of authority. He addressed himself to the ranks of the Augusta, who were exchanging worried looks. 'Men of the Augusta, you have been lied to and misled by your former Legate, and now former Governor. I know most of you were staying loyal to your chain of command. A few, a very few, of your senior officers —' here his pellucid gaze swept across the Augusta, lingering on the tribunes, 'are more culpable, having accepted bribes provisioned by silver stolen from the Imperial estate at Vebriacum. That is a capital offence.'

Tiro silently applauded this tactic. *Clever, sir! That'll sort the blindly trusting sheep away from the plotting goats. No need to destroy a whole legion when you can simply take off its rotten head, eh?*

Rufinus paused to allow this to sink in.

'Enough blood has been spilt. If you immediately stand down and return to your base with new officers appointed by me, I will spare the legion decimation, break-up and obliteration. I will not punish the enlisted men if the rebellion ends right now. Those of your officers who took bribes — I know who they are — may have their inevitable sentences as traitors commuted to dismissal from the army if they co-operate with my investigation.'

The Procurator looked calmly at Trebonius and Labienus. Trebonius was red-faced now. He began yelling obscenities and drew his sword. Somehow the even voice of Rufinus rose above

Trebonius's protests, compelling in its certainty.

'You, the ringleaders of this deadly conspiracy, cannot expect the same mercy. It will be for the Emperor and the Senate of the People of Rome to determine your fates.'

Trebonius shouted, 'You'll die for this, Rufinus!' Quintus, his own blade drawn, immediately stepped between the furious former Governor and the man about to succeed him. Tiro himself felt so angry he knew he would have killed Trebonius on the spot. But Quintus was a Roman officer, and due process must be observed. He merely held the point of his gladius to Trebonius's throat. Tiro was impressed with his boss's control.

While Rufinus was speaking the Twentieth legion had moved in, led by their legate. Five thousand men proudly wearing the sign of the boar poured off the road from Deva, surrounding the men of Isca. A squad of four marched smartly up to the Procurator, saluted, and then at his signal pinioned ex-Governor Trebonius. His uniform and sword were stripped from him and he was manacled and left shivering in his tunic. Cassius Labienus was likewise arrested and put in irons, and both men were led away.

'Frumentarius, there is much I need to discuss with you,' the Procurator said to Quintus, with a slight smile as he got back into his litter. 'I know you need medical attention and rest, but I'd be very obliged if you would brief me later. I hope this will not be inconvenient? I shall be staying here in the city, and will send for you. Bring your *stator.*'

The pale man limped, and for the first time Tiro noticed that one foot was twisted and mis-shapen. He had seen children with similar deformities in Londinium, usually begging in the gutters and rarely surviving long. He wondered at this man who had overcome so much to rise to the top position in the Province. Quintus beckoned to Marcellus as Rufinus's slaves helped him up into the litter.

'Sir, if I may, I'd like to introduce my close colleague Centurion Marcellus Crispus, of the Aquae Sulis vexillation of the Second Legion. And my good friend, the Decurion Agrippa Sorio, of Lindinis, and leader into battle of our allies the northern Durotriges.'

Marcellus stepped forward and saluted smartly, his freckled face slightly red.

Rufinus turned his hazel eyes onto the centurion. 'You have my grateful thanks, Centurion. I never forget courage and loyalty. I will consider your future career path when time permits.' Rufinus smiled briefly, and turned to the Durotrigan. A broadly-beaming Sorio had pushed his way through the dispirited ranks of the dispersing Augusta, and had been hovering on the fringes of the conversation. Drusus, eyes bright, was with him. Through his gasps for breath, Tiro was delighted to hear the Procurator invite them to attend him later that evening. Quintus saluted as the slaves lifted the Procurator's litter and carried him through the ranks of the subdued Augusta, across the bridge and into the city. He raised his eyebrows at the sight of Tiro, curled over in pain.

'Hurt my fucking ribs, sir. Oh, sorry sir. I'll get that bastard Lucius though. When I catch the fucker. Sorry, sir.'

Quintus smiled wryly. 'I daresay Julia will have something that will help. Or Britta might.'

Tiro tried to grin. 'Are we heading to Aquae Sulis then, sir? Or will Lady Julia be going back to Bo Gwelt?'

'You will go wherever you can be healed fastest, Tiro. You're no use to me like that.' It was said drily, but again Tiro caught a hint of humour as well. Despite the pain of his bloody and blistered arm, Quintus had lost the grey look so frequently on his face these days. 'As for me, we'll see what our new Governor has to say.'

'Governor, sir? Aradius Rufinus, you mean?'

'Of course. I doubt very much the legate of the Valeria Victrix would have thrown his lot in with Rufinus so readily, had he not been assured by Rome there would be uncontested succession to the Governorship.'

Tiro hadn't thought of that. It made sense. So he wasn't surprised to see Quintus introducing himself to the Devan legate.

The Twentieth legion began to move across the bridge to enter the welcoming city. Clearly the citizens had heard about the switch of fortunes. Cheering townspeople were emerging from

229

their shuttered and locked houses. One or two enterprising businesses had already set up little stands along the road, with striped awnings to keep off the threatening showers, and were beckoning to the mingled ranks of the Twentieth and the Second as they made their way into the city.

Well, he thought, at least the shopkeepers and bartenders of Corinium would be happy to have two full legions to stay for a day or two. And the Londinium lads.

Chapter Twenty-nine

The new Governor's tent was comfortable, with camp seats positioned around a brazier. Bright rugs scattered over the canvas floor added warmth, and thick wall hangings kept out most of the draughts. Quintus noted how quickly the scene had been set for the first officers' briefing of the new administration.

This is an effective man with an eye for detail. A leader to keep onside with.

Aradius Rufinus was seated, dressed in a broad-stripe toga and breeches, with a thick British wool blanket draped over his knees. He welcomed them, sending his attendants out to give them privacy. Once they had all sat down—Tiro slowly and with a grimace — Rufinus began by asking Quintus about the mission, right from the initial briefing by the Castra Commander in Rome. He was interested in why Quintus had been chosen for the mission, given his career background in the East.

'I've thought about this, sir, and speaking bluntly, I was selected to fail.' Quintus worked to keep a steady face. Maybe Tiro would guess how much this admission was costing him. 'Gaius knew I was badly injured in Caledonia. I believe he also knew how shocked I was by the death of my younger brother during the same campaign. I've struggled to overcome that loss, knowing myself to have been responsible for Flavius. Frankly, I lost all ambition from that point. I took this assignment at face value, trusting my former comrade-in-arms. I didn't even question his choice of Tiro here as replacement for my injured *stator*.' He saw Tiro reddening, and carried on quickly. 'If he only knew how critical that mistake was to his own interests. Appearances can be very deceptive. In the event, Tiro was probably the best man to have by my side, and it is in no small part due to him that we succeeded.' Rufinus looked at Tiro, holding his eyes for longer than Tiro found comfortable.

Tiro looked down, missing the understanding expression on the new Governor's face when he said gently, 'Gaius made many mistakes, not least of which was his equally deluded choice of Imperial Investigator. He could not have undermined his own plans more when he requested you to carry out the investigation, Quintus Valerius. But tell me, what was it that gave him away to you?'

'White wax, sir.'

'White wax?'

'Yes, sir. On my very first day in Britannia, when I went to collect Tiro from...' Tiro flinched here, but Quintus pretended not to see '...from his previous post, I noticed that the letter from Gaius Trebonius authorising Tiro's transfer was written on a white wax tablet. I had never seen that colour wax before. My — er, Lady Julia Aureliana of the Durotriges, who has also been of great assistance in this case, told me how rare white wax documents are. Later at Vebriacum, the mines manager Tertius showed me another white wax letter, an incriminating message sent to Claudius Bulbo.'

Governor Rufinus nodded, as though this confirmed an idea he already had. Quintus saw his opening.

'May I ask a question of my own, sir?'

'Go ahead.'

'How did you know to summon the Valeria Victrix in such good time? And to undertake what must have been a difficult journey to get here in the nick of time yourself, with only the Londinium garrison? It seems so risky, sir.'

'Do you really not know, Frumentarius?' The pale man looked intently at Quintus. His hazel eyes were so light they almost merged with the pallor of his countenance. All the same, Quintus had the impression of strength in his mild face.

Quintus sighed, overcome with sadness at the waste. 'I have thought a lot about this, sir. I knew from the start that someone was sending information about events at Vebriacum. I later discovered these messages were being brought to Londinium by a young Durotriges boy, Catus, until he was murdered. A death designed to throw me off the scent by falsely suggesting a Druid revolt. It was the mines manager Tertius who had been keeping the Governor informed. Trebonius told me so himself. And his suggestion that *you,* sir, were not to be trusted blinded me to the obvious.'

'Which was, Frumentarius?'

'That Tertius, one of the bravest men I have ever met, was *your* agent.'

Rufinus stood, bracing his hands against the arms of his wooden chair, and took a few clumsy paces around the tent. He returned, seating himself carefully, and stretched his legs out. The odd bundle of his foot was on full display.

'You're correct, Quintus Valerius. Tertius was my agent. Had been since his days in Syria. It was my doing that he was freed from slavery. I promoted his appointment at Vebriacum. Gaius Trebonius used his martial reputation and his network of comrades in the British army to establish a power base to underpin his coup. Both reputation and army friendships are potent tools and have served rebelling Governors and Emperors well in the past. I have no such resources. I rely on the loyalty of different men. Such men are often unperceived for their skills, with hidden bravery and initiative. I have been very fortunate in my career to come across some of these rare men, and women, too. Tertius was one such. He is a huge loss.'

'Indeed, sir.' Suddenly Quintus knew the time was right to ask the big question, the one troubling him since he had first realised the Druid connection was a cover. 'Sir, why didn't you tell me what was in your mind when I came to your Southwark palace?'

A sad look crossed the pale face. 'After Trebonius's insinuations about my own ambitions, Quintus Valerius, would you have believed me? Would you have trusted me above your old friend?'

Quintus was silent, troubled. The sad look melted into a slight smile. 'I thought not. But now I hope and believe, matters between us are different.'

Quintus gave a heartfelt nod, and Rufinus smiled at him before dismissing them both. As they were being ushered out of the command tent Rufinus called, 'Frumentarius, when your injured arm has healed, I would be pleased if you would come to Londinium for further talks with me. I have some ideas to discuss with you. Could you be ready to travel in, say, a couple of weeks?'

'By all means, sir.'

Outside the command tent, Quintus turned to Tiro. 'Well, my excellent *stator,* how say you we find Marcellus and Antonius and visit the Corinium baths now?'

'Can't get there fast enough, sir.'

The sustained rain of the previous night was petering out when Tiro emerged from his tent into the grey light of morning. He groaned as he stood. If anything the pain in his side was worse. The wine at the baths last night, and the beer shop crawl afterwards with Marcellus and Prefect Antonius had worn off all too quickly, and he had slept little. He thought glumly of the long ride home. But where *was* home? Surely not back in Londinium? What he needed in his life now was the gentle touch of a good woman, he decided. It would be okay, perhaps, to settle down with the right person, maybe have children. Not that he had ever intended to marry, he wasn't the marrying kind. Although…and here he drifted off into the scent of lavender, until Aurelia appeared, shouting,'Tiro! Tiro! Are you here?' He said nothing, glaring at her. She was looking scruffy after several days with no change of clothes and sleeping rough in a billet. But her mood was clearly sunny, and she seemed delighted to see him. He fended off her attempts at a hug.

'Ribs!' he gasped. 'No touching.' She released him and grinned.

'I kept my promise yesterday, Tiro. I did exactly what you said — well, apart from going very quickly to warn Aunt Julia that Lucius was here. And then I got to spend the rest of the day with the Corinium Sisterhood. They're wonderful, Tiro, they know so much and all about medicines and poisons …and magic! Actual magic, Tiro, and they talk to the Gods, the old gods too, all the time. So that's what I want to be, like Aunt Julia, one day… Are you listening, Tiro?' He had closed his eyes, only for a tiny moment, mind. He opened them to see Aurelia peering curiously at him. 'Anyway, you promised me you'd say more about what you meant by "your mother and your…"'

Tiro clutched his side, and leaned back gingerly onto his

bedroll, groaning. He thought it was good acting, and anyway he truly did feel rough. But Aurelia was having none of it.

'Well, if you won't tell me, I'll tell you instead, Tiro. You meant that you would talk to my mother, my mother *Julia*, didn't you?'

Tiro wondered why the Gods had chosen to inflict such suffering on him. Hadn't he always made decent sacrifices, and carried out to the letter any promises he made in return for divine favour? And yet here he was, in this impossible position. He groaned again, for real this time. Aurelia laughed.

'It's okay, Tiro. I already guessed. I think I've known for ages. And one day last year, that wretch Lucius told me I wasn't really the heir to my father's estate. He said Claudia had told him I was the bastard mistake of my father's sister. Well, Father had only one sister, my darling Aunt Julia. And I was so happy — until I began to wonder who my father could be. She never seems to have any boyfriends, always working, only seeing people like Surgeon Anicius. And it couldn't be him!' Aurelia shuddered, which Tiro thought was unfair on the tubby little *medicus*.

'Then I met Quintus. And I heard from Britta that he and Aunt Julia knew each other many years ago.' She cast Tiro a look of importance, as if she had discovered the secret of life. Which, Tiro supposed, she had.

'Well?' he said, pretending nonchalance.

'Come on, Tiro — I've got the same grey eyes, same dark hair, nothing like my darling father Marcus. It was obvious. And then, when they started fighting every time they met—then I was sure.'

Tiro sighed. Aurelia twinkled and leaned over to kiss his rough stubbled cheek. 'You don't have to say anything. But I need you to make another promise.'

Now what?

'Err… yes?' he said cautiously.

'Now we know who my real father is, you must promise to go everywhere with him. And keep him safe.' He saw a glint of bright water in her eye. 'I can't lose a second father. And I think Julia wants him, although maybe she doesn't know it yet. And

I want *her* to be happy. So you'll get it all sorted, won't you, dearest Tiro?'

Tiro watched in astonishment as the girl pranced her way out of the tent. *So it's "Julia" now, is it?* Oh, how he regretted that night of drunken debauchery followed by prison in Londinium, all those weeks ago. Without that night he would never have crossed the path of the Governor's Man. What was he going to tell him? He gave the problem two seconds thought. Nothing. He would say absolutely nothing to Quintus. Wasn't his problem. But he would look after the *frumentarius* for Aurelia.

Once his bloody ribs had stopped hurting.

Chapter Thirty

It was the final leg of a hot journey. It was still only late April, but felt to Quintus more like June. The heat had persuaded the hedgerow flowers to bloom early. His scarred leg itched with fatigue and the dusty sweat on his clothes irked him. His chestnut horse plodded without enthusiasm along the dusty ridge road of the Poldens. They turned off to Bo Gwelt, and Quintus realised he should have planned what to say. Too late now. Cantering towards him was Milo, with Aurelia in the saddle. And, oh Gods, Drusus lying forward on his horse, galloping to catch her. His daughter saw him and shrieked, nearly tumbling off her pony with dusty hair flying awry and her worn tunic caught up.

'Sir! I knew you would come back today. I told Britta, and she said how did I know, had Tiro said something he didn't tell her, and poor Tiro nearly got in trouble till I said, no, no, I just had a feeling. And I was right!'

'Greetings, sir.' Drusus drew level. 'Is that a new *hasta*, sir?' He looked impressed at the full-size intricately-carved lance lashed to the chestnut's saddle.

'Do you live at Bo Gwelt now, Drusus?'

'Er, no, sir. Just — I just like to …er… ride out. And I've been helping Morcant and Demetrios with the workmen, y'know, supervising the rebuilding.'

Quintus smiled wryly, and the young boy looked embarrassed. 'Well done, lad. I am sure Morcant and Demetrios are grateful. I'll tell your father how useful you are here, if I see him on this trip.'

'Oh, sir, umm, please don't bother to say anything to Father. He — he rather thinks I am with my Greek tutor right now.'

'I see. Your secret is safe with me.'

They passed the new tomb of Marcus Aurelianus with its beautiful engraved reliefs. Aurelia dismounted to stroke the stone, murmuring 'Darling Father.' Next to it were two stone memorials: one carved with an image of an adolescent boy. The inscription begged the Departed to accept the spirit of Catus, "son of this estate, who was much loved and died too young". Alongside was a memorial to "Tertius, freedman and mines manager at Vebriacum, who was wise, courageous and kind".

On arrival at the house Aurelia rushed into the kitchen, refurbished and re-equipped. Enica was cooking, her glorious hair hidden in a cloth. She looked round, and dropped a curtesy when she saw Quintus.

'It's good to see you, Enica. Are you settled at Bo Gwelt?'

'Oh yes, sir. Lady Julia arranged to buy me from the widow Claudia.' Quintus was puzzled.

Aurelia burst in, 'Oh, Claudia jumped at the chance to have Julia's dresser instead. I never liked her dresser, so snooty. Neither did Julia, it turns out. So they swapped, and then Julia gave Enica her freedom. And lovely Enica, who cooks the most delicious food you will ever eat, decided to stay here with us as paid cook.'

'I'm very happy for you, Enica, and I know Tertius and Catus would have been too.' Enica turned away, hiding her face.

Aurelia impatiently steered Quintus through the house and into the courtyard, where they found Tiro. Not alone. He was leading a horse on the end of a long rein. She was a solid-looking mare with a mild eye, despite bearing perhaps the most nervous rider she had ever encountered.

Britta was leaning forward, clutching the reins, swaying at each step of the horse. Narina was dashing around the courtyard not helping the lesson proceed, until Gwenn emerged from the laundry and removed her. The little girl could be heard complaining that she didn't see why Aurelia could watch Britta fall off the horse if *she* couldn't. Britta was also complaining, muttering a stream of British oaths.

'Dearest one, you really must try harder to sit up straight,' said Tiro in a patently patient voice.

'No, I mustn't! Bring the mounting block. I've had enough of this torture.'

Tiro complied, and helped Britta dismount. Quintus managed to swallow his laughter while Britta was in the saddle. Now he openly chuckled as she said tartly to Tiro, smoothing out her ruffled *tunica*, 'It's your turn for torture. Get your books out, my man.' Tiro cast a despairing look at his boss, who shook his head.

'Off you go to your reading lesson. I'll catch up with you later.' Turning to Aurelia, he asked where Lady Julia would be.

'Oh, she's around somewhere. She got back from Aquae Sulis yesterday. She's been busy working with Anicius and the Sisterhood to train apprentices at the clinic, as she now comes to Bo Gwelt such a lot. I don't know why she worries, there are plenty of people here already to keep an eye on me. And Drusus comes a lot, too, supervising the construction workers that kind Uncle Agrippa Sorio has lent us. Come and see what a good job they're doing.'

She dragged Quintus off to inspect the new works. The main reception wing was almost rebuilt, raw amber stone and bright red tiles standing out in contrast to the remaining older parts. 'The mosaicist in Corinium brought designs to show us. They're *gorgeous,* lots of animals and gods and nymphs. Just what I wanted. But the plastering won't happen yet, they were too busy and anyway Demetrios said we should get the floors done first...' She chattered on as they walked through the quadrangle and into the garden behind. Quintus stemmed her stream of consciousness to ask her to let him to have a few quiet words with her aunt. She looked at him pertly and went away laughing, leaving him uneasy.

Julia was carrying a basket on one arm, hands gloved as she tended her bees. She wore a homespun wool dress, green-stained from gardening. Over her head was a fine veil to protect her from the bees. But they seemed to respect her intentions, and were quite content to carry on visiting the flowers along the back border. Julia turned, wiping sweat away from under her veil. She checked on seeing Quintus, and pulled the veil away.

'Ah.'

'Hello, Julia. I'm back from Londinium.' He winced, realising how foolish that sounded.

'So you are, Quintus.' Her voice was cool. It was not a promising start.

'How are you?' he tried again. 'How are things at the villa? I see a lot of work is going on.'

'Yes, Quintus, some of us do have a lot of work.' She added in a more mellow tone, 'Was your trip successful?'

'Er, yes. I came to tell you about it. But first, how is Aurelia? She looks well. How is she getting on in her lessons?'

Julia's face softened, as it always did when Aurelia was mentioned. Except, he supposed, when their impulsive daughter did something she disapproved of.

'She attends her lessons when she thinks she'll be caught truanting. Last week I had to tell her that she could not expect to run Bo Gwelt successfully when she comes of age if she doesn't concentrate on her lessons. That seemed to make some impression, and Demetrios tells me that when she applies herself, she has real ability. Speaking of Aurelia, I had a visit from Agrippa Sorio last week. A formal one.'

'Oh?' Quintus knew what was coming. He had seen the besotted look on Drusus's face several times.

'He came on behalf of Drusus, to ask for Aurelia's hand.' Julia looked strangely flustered. 'I told him she was far too young and flighty. He hadn't known that it was my decision to make, under the terms of my brother's will. I think he was surprised that a single woman was Aurelia's guardian. He mentioned —well it doesn't matter what foolishness Agrippa said.'

Her eyes flashed, and his heart sank. But he had steeled himself over the days of travel from Londinium to have this conversation, and he must not let the chance go.

'Julia, could we sit down? I have a few matters to discuss with you. Including Aurelia.'

She drew a sharp breath, but allowed him to steer her to a nearby bench. He was struck silent, unsure how to begin. She spoke first.

'You obviously have difficult things to say, Frumentarius, and I can guess what they are. Now that your business in Londinium is done, I assume you have come to collect Tiro. He has healed well, by the way, ribs mended, fever all gone. Back to his usual noisy self.' She paused, reaching for Quintus's left wrist. She gently peeled back his sleeve, a gesture at odds with her brusque tone. He let her inspect his arm.

'It's fine,' she said, looking relieved. 'I think the remaining scars will heal quickly. You've been looking after it.' Then her face seemed to drop. 'This must mean you're ready to travel again.'

Right, you have the opening. Get on with it, he thought, feeling his stomach lurch.

'Well, Governor Rufinus is confirmed in post. And he's given me permission to leave Britannia, but —'

She leapt up, standing over him with a thunderous look on her face. He stood too, reaching for her gloved hand. 'Julia, —'

Before he could move, she slapped his face hard. He reeled and nearly fell.

'It's not what you think!'

'What is it that I think, Quintus? You men, always telling us women what to think. Even your man Tiro. Although actually he's a decent man, worth any number of you.'

Now he *was* angry. The lurch in his stomach turned into a swoop and he contemplated simply walking away. Perhaps that was best. She would never let him forget Eboracum. Then he thought of Flavius, and knew he had to try again. He sat back down.

'Julia, I'm not trying to tell you what to think, I don't have that right. No-one does. I just want to explain my position, and then I'd like to suggest something to you.'

She was still glaring at him. He went on, 'Aradius Rufinus has been in touch with Rome.' She stiffened, and tried to turn her face away. He twisted the bronze owl ring off his finger and held it out to her. She grabbed the ring, jerking back to her feet. He was startled to see tears forming in her eyes.

'This is the end, isn't it, Quintus? You've come to tell me you have your orders from Rome. You're going home, leaving your daughter, leaving me. Are you even taking Tiro?'

Before he could stop her she had bolted away across the garden, her veil falling onto the lawn. It was a disaster. He could not bear it, he must go now —

'Can I offer assistance, sir?' A man he knew, a stooped older man with a long drooping nose, stood in front of him. His mind was blank. 'Demetrios, sir.'

'Yes, sorry, of course. I should have known you, Demetrios.'

'May I sit?'

The old man lowered himself slowly onto the bench. 'Sir, I have known Lady Julia since before she was Aurelia's age. To most people she seems a calm figure of authority. She will forgive me for telling you that this impression can be skin-deep. Underneath, Lady Julia is sometimes still a young girl. And if I may say so to you, sir, she is a young girl still longing for a young man she lost in Eboracum.'

Quintus stared at Demetrios in shock. Was there anyone in this house who didn't know his deepest secrets? He opened his mouth to make an angry retort, and closed it again. Anger would not help Aurelia, or Julia. He waited. The old man smiled, the corners of his eyes almost disappearing into deep wrinkles.

'Well done, sir,' he murmured. 'Now then, if you want my advice, you will try again. Once you get past the hurt of a grief-stricken girl, you will find the real Julia. It will be worth the effort, I promise you.' He stood slowly and walked away, humming to himself.

Quintus stared after him. Then he saw Aurelia approaching, dragging Julia by the hand. He groaned. He hadn't had time to marshal his thoughts, to find a different way to bridge the gulf between them. Then he realised that Aurelia *was* that bridge, the person who joined them together. He would have to make another effort, for Aurelia's sake.

His daughter smiled her wicked smile, little pointed chin raised, grey eyes gleaming. What did this mean? Perhaps she had guessed the truth. It wouldn't matter if he couldn't regain Julia's trust.

'Aurelia, thank you. Now please go away. I need to speak to Julia in private.' His daughter gave him another grin and twirled herself away.

Julia sat stiffly, not letting her back touch the bench.

'Julia, I *am* returning to Rome, but commanded by Aradius Rufinus.' She turned her eyes to his, looking puzzled. 'He wrote to the Castra Peregrina, arranging my release. He has offered me a permanent assignment, working for him here in Britannia. As a *beneficiarius consularis.*' He waited.

'What does that mean? I've never heard of that rank.' She was still listening, and he saw the base of her spine soften against the bench as she relaxed.

'It means promotion as Governor's Man, reporting only to Aradius Rufinus. I'd be a senior officer, with staff of my own. The Governor has explained he wants me to represent him in a roving role across the Province and beyond, so my base at Aquae Sulis would be notional. I will have his full authority to investigate all serious and sensitive crimes that warrant his intervention.'

'What's that got to do with Rome?'

'He wants me to go there first, to witness Trebonius's trial. And to assess how his new Governorship is being seen in Rome. The times are tricky, with such a young Emperor on the throne.'

'I see,' she said. 'Well, I must congratulate you, Beneficarius. You'll certainly be mixing with influential people. Sounds like quite a boost to your career.'

He felt irritated. Is that what she thought, that he was pushing his career? Then he remembered what Demetrios had said, and saw the apprehension on her face. Her defences were back up, he realised. He had to make her understand that Britannia was where he wanted to be now.

'Why not come with me, Julia? A holiday trip. You could meet my family. See Rome, where I grew up.'

She moved impatiently.

'How? I can't just drop everything. I have responsibilities. Aurelia. The estate. My work with Anicius ...' He studied her. Looked past the lovely grown woman to the child inside, the one who had hidden her wounds for so long. As he had too, he suddenly thought. He held his hand out again, palm flat.

'I have something else to ask you, Julia. Give me the ring again, the bronze owl ring. And let me give you a ring too. Let's go together to Rome as man and wife. We should have done this years ago. Please?' He kept his hand extended.

'If this gesture is for Aurelia, it's not needed. She's told me she knows that we are her real mother and father, and she

243

doesn't care. She doesn't need us to marry for her sake. She has high status among our people as Marcus's adopted daughter. This isn't Rome, Quintus. We do things differently here.'

He tried one last time.

'It's not just for Aurelia. She's already making her own way in the world, and always will. I'm asking you to marry me because I love you. I've always loved you, but I was too young and stupid to realise what really mattered.'

She fixed her eyes on him as if she hadn't seen him properly until now.

'I will come to Rome with you, Quintus. But I won't marry you. If I meet your Roman family, it must be as Julia Aureliana, of a British family and tribe as proud and honourable as any in the Empire.'

He had his answer, but was it enough?

He felt almost resentful, as if she had just pushed him away. He thrust down the resentment, lifting her face to kiss. She returned the kiss, pressing her lips generously against his. She felt like the Julia of old; and yet, not. Was she holding something back? And then she did pull away, looking intently at him.

'Quintus, I'm not the same girl you left in Eboracum.'

He opened his mouth to speak, but she put her finger to his lips. He waited in agony. He had offered his heart as well as his hand and name. This was his way, the honourable Roman way. But Julia clearly had different ideas.

'You might wonder why I have never married. Marriage, even back then when we were so young, never seemed to me just another stage on life's path, predictable and expected. To me, it has to be so much more. I already have my daughter, my work, my own property, and my status as a tribeswoman.'

Quintus tried to understand, but he was unsure what she was telling him. Didn't she want him? Perhaps she couldn't see how their lives could resume smoothly from the point where they had been interrupted fourteen years ago. How arrogant he had been. Thinking he could heal all that was damaged between them simply by wanting to. What a fool he was!

Then she reached for him, and kissed him again, long and

lingering. It felt like farewell. Or possibly a greeting, the first one of a new love. He pulled her tightly into his arms.

'I think I understand you now. I was naive to think we could go back to the people we were, that summer.' He felt a tear, and then another, on his fingers. The young girl was indeed gone, replaced by a mature complex woman. A stranger; one he loved and longed to learn about.

She stirred in his arms. 'Yes, I think you do understand. Those two young people are gone forever, torn apart by long years and hurt. I think we should let them go. But, maybe, the man and woman we have become could have a different, better future together?' He took her hand, and raised it to kiss.

'Lady Julia Aureliana of the Durotriges, it would be my great honour to get to know you better. And to know our daughter.'

He smiled, feeling a great relief. 'I would still love to show you the splendours of Rome, and introduce my family to you.'

'Beneficiarius Consularis Quintus Valerius, I would be delighted to come to Rome with you. Without the company of our darling daughter, this time. '

She pulled the bronze owl ring out of her pocket, and placed it on his finger. He laughed and folded her into another kiss.

All too soon Aurelia returned, demanding to know if they were ever coming in for dinner. Narina came to tell them that Enica said the evening meal was out on the table and going cold. As they entered the house, Tiro joined them, looking enquiring. Quintus sighed, wondering how much Tiro had heard. This wretched house — nothing ever stayed private.

'Sir?'

'What about it, Tiro? Fancy a trip to Rome? As my *optio*?'

Tiro looked exhilarated.

'I thought the Governor might have given you a new *stator,* sir. And packed me off, being just temporary as you know.'

Quintus smiled, and held out a small package wrapped in linen.

'There's this too. With the Governor's thanks, in recognition of your bravery on and off the field of war. He apologises for the lack of ceremony. Maybe later on our return.'

Tiro unwrapped a heavy silver disc decorated in relief with the image of Hercules.

'My *phalera*!' He looked delighted for a moment. Then he looked away, towards the servant's quarters. Quintus sighed again.

'Well, Tiro?'

'It's just ... there's Britta, you know…'

'Tell her it will give you time to save, on your higher salary.' He didn't add what to save for, but Tiro seemed struck by the notion.

'Do I get a decent sword this time, sir? And another go at that Lucius? I still owe him a shield.'

'We may well get our chance with Lucius. And you can have any damn weapon you want, Tiro. I think for once the Governor will be happy to pay the bill.'

Tiro went off, smiling and whistling. He swung into the servant's hall, where no doubt Britta was waiting to hear his news. Tiro managed to see the upside of most challenges, Quintus realised. Whatever Quintus had said to Julia about the trip to Rome being a holiday, he knew there would be challenges. Rome was always challenging.

From the dining room came the sound of laughter. Julia was thanking Aurelia for pouring out the wine without spilling, and his daughter was giving a suitably sassy riposte. Quintus lingered in the corridor. He thought fleetingly of the sad old house on the Quirinal.

Then he straightened his shoulders, and stepped over the threshold to join his family.

Place Names

Abona: river Avon, and the port at Sea Mills near Bristol

Aquae Sulis: Bath

Aust: a small ferry terminus, and the landing point on the east bank of the Severn estuary for military traffic crossing the river from   Caerleon. Now disused and under the M48 toll bridge.

Bawdrip: a villa at the west end of the Polden Hills, Somerset, home of the Sorio family

Bo Gwelt: a villa at Shapwick in the Polden Hills, home of the Aurelianus family

Bruella: river Brue, the Somerset Levels

Caledonia: northern Scotland

Calleva Atrebatum: Silchester

Camerton: hamlet on the Fosse Way, south of Aquae Sulis

Castra Deva: Chester

Chilton Polden: a small village at the east end of the Poldens

Crandon Bridge: in Roman times a port on the river Pedrida, now land-locked

Cunetio: near Mildenhall, Wiltshire

Corinium Dubonnorum: Cirencester

Durnovaria: Dorchester

Eboracum: York

Gesiacorum: Boulogne

Glevum: Gloucester

Iscalis: Cheddar, and home of the Claudius family

Isca Silurium: Caerleon, base of the 11 Legion Augusta

Lindinis: Ilchester, Somerset

Londinium: London

Pontes: Staines

Rhenus: river Rhine

Sabrina: river Severn

Salinae: Droitwich

Severn Sea: Bristol estuary

Silures, land of: roughly, south-east Wales

Soviodunum: Salisbury

The Summer Country: loosely, Somerset

Tamesis: river Thames

Vebriacum: Charterhouse-on-Mendip, a large silver/lead mine

Verlucio: Sandy Lane, Wiltshire

Verulamium: St Albans

General note:

In naming places I have used contemporary Roman placenames, except where that name is not known. In that case I have tried to use British Celtic names. E.g. Bo Gwelt may be the British forerunner to Pouelt, used in Domesday Book to denote the whole estate. The British name refers to the grazing of sheep. This estate no longer exists as such, but is thought to be the forerunner of the modern parish boundaries.

Where I haven't been able to find either a Roman or a Celtic place name, as in Crandon Bridge, I have used the modern English name.

Author's Acknowledgements

Many people have helped me with time, support and knowledge. My gratitude goes to:

The superb staff at the Somerset Heritage Centre, who showed me fascinating artefacts from their archives (sadly not on public display), and first alerted me to the existence of an archaeology report on the Shapwick dig in 1998.

The knowledgeable and enthusiastic local guides at the Cheddar Gorge.

Ilchester Community Museum — you must go on one of their Roman Heritage Days, mind-blowing.

The incomparable Sue Willetts and her colleagues at the Hellenic and Roman Library in London, who slaved through several coronavirus lockdowns to keep me supplied with research material.

My exceptional tutors at the Arvon historical fiction course in 2018, Robert Wilton and Manda (MC) Scott, who are superb teachers as well as supremely talented writers themselves.

My brother Ste Finnemore, who taught me how to cook the books Roman-style without double-entry bookkeeping, and sister-in-law and psychotherapist Ann Finnemore, who pointed me to helpful sites for PTSD research.

And Phillippa of Classic Cottages, who rescued me from a building site and found me a writing haven in a storm-tossed Cornwall January.

I was blessed with wonderful beta readers: Ian Walker, Kate Standish Hayes, Lynn Johnson, Fran Martel, Ste Finnemore, Rhodri Orders, David Orders, Debra Williams, Mark Selvester and Julie Stanbridge. My gratitude to you all, and guess what? *The Governor's Man 2* is on its way.

My independent editor Gemma Taylor was a stalwart, and great supporter.

Special thanks to Richard, Tara and all at Sharpe Books, of course.

And first and foremost, thus mentioned last: my husband and soul mate, Peter, who kept me going long after it would have been reasonable to stop. I owe this book to him.

Printed in Great Britain
by Amazon

41700230R00146